a Ross

Nothing Missing but the Samovar

and other stories

Nothing Missing but the Samovar

and other stories

Penelope Lively

HEINEMANN : LONDON

William Heinemann Ltd
15 Queen Street, Mayfair, London W1X 8BE
LONDON   MELBOURNE   TORONTO
JOHANNESBURG   AUCKLAND

First published 1978

© Penelope Lively 1978

434 42736 5

Photoset and printed
in Great Britain by
REDWOOD BURN LIMITED
Trowbridge & Esher

For Josephine

Contents

Nothing Missing but
the Samovar

It was July when he went to Morswick, early autumn when he left it; in retrospect it was to seem always summer, those heavy, static days of high summer, of dingy weather and outbursts of sunshine, of blue sky and heaped clouds. Of straw and horseflies. Blackberries; jam for tea; church on Sunday. The Landers.

Dieter Helpmann was twenty-four, a tall, fair young man, serious-looking but with a smile of great sweetness; among his contemporaries he seemed older than he was, sober, reserved, the quiet member of a group, the listener. He had come from Germany to do his post-graduate degree – a thesis on nineteenth century Anglo-Prussian relations. His father was a distinguished German journalist. Dieter intended to go into journalism himself; he was English correspondent, now, for a socio-political weekly, contributing periodic articles on aspects of contemporary Britain. His English was perfect: idiomatic, lightly accented. His manners were attractive; he held doors open for women, rose to his feet for them, was deferential to his elders. All this made him seem slightly old-fashioned, as did his worried liberalism, which looked not shrewd nor edgy enough for a journalist. His gentle, concerned pieces about education, industrial unrest, the housing problem, read more like a sympathetic academic analysis of the ills of some other time than energetic journalism.

It was 1957, and he had spent eighteen months in England. The year before – the year of Suez and Hungary – he had seen his friends send telegrams to the Prime Minister fiercely dissociating themselves from British intervention; he had agonised alongside them, outraged both with and for them; he had written an article on 'the alienation of the British intellectual' that was emotional and partisan. His father commented that he seemed deeply committed – 'The climate appears to suit you, in more ways than one'. And Dieter had written back, 'You are right – and it is its variety I think that appeals the most. It is a place that so much defies analysis – just as you think you have the measure of it, you stumble across yet another confusing way in which the different layers of British life overlap, another curious anachronism. I have to admit that I have caught Anglophilia, for better or for worse'.

He had. He loved the place. He loved the sobriety of the academic world in which he mostly moved. He loved all those derided qualities of reserve and restraint, he loved the landscape. He liked English girls, while remaining faithful to his German fiancée, Erica (also engaged on post-graduate work, but in Bonn). He liked and respected what he took to be a basic cultural stability; here was a place where things changed, but changed with dignity. To note, to understand, became his deep concern.

All that, though, took second place to the thesis. That was what mattered at the moment, the patient quarrying into a small slice of time, a small area of activity. He worked hard. Most of his waking hours were spent in the agreeable hush of great libraries, or alone in his room with his card index and his notebooks.

He had been about to start writing the first draft when it happened. 'I have had the most remarkable piece of luck,' he wrote to Erica. 'Peter Sutton – he is the friend who is working on John Stuart Mill, you remember – is married to a girl who comes from Dorset and knows a family whose forebear was ambassador in Berlin in the 1840s and apparently they still have all his papers. In trunks in the attic! They are an aristocratic family – Sir Philip Lander is the present holder of the title, a baronetcy. Anyway, Felicity Sutton has known them all her life (she is rather upperclass too, but intelligent, and married Peter at Cambridge, where they both were – this is something of a feature of the young

English intelligentsia, these inter-class marriages, Peter of course is of a working class background), and mentioned that I would be interested in the papers and they said at once apparently that I would be welcome to go down there and have a look. It certainly is a stroke of luck – Felicity says she got the impression there is a vast amount of stuff, all his personal correspondence and official papers too. I go next week, I imagine it will all be rather grand . . .'

There was no car to meet him, as promised. At least, he stood at the entrance to the small country station and the only waiting cars were a taxi and a small pick-up van with open back full of agricultural sacks. He checked Sir Philip Lander's letter: date and time were right. Apprehensively he turned to go to the telephone kiosk – and at that moment the occupant of the van, who had been reading a newspaper, looked up, opened the door and stepped out, smiling.

Or rather, unfolded himself. He was immensely tall, well over six foot. He towered above Dieter, holding out a hand, saying my dear fellow, I'm so sorry, had you been there long – I didn't realise the train was in – I say, is that all the luggage you've got, let me shove it in the back . . .

Bemused, Dieter climbed into the van beside him. It smelled of petrol and, more restrainedly, of horse.

They wound through lanes and over hills. Sir Philip boomed, above the unhealthy sound of the van's engine, of topography, of recollections of Germany before the war, of the harvest. He wore corduroy trousers laced with wisps of hay, gum-boots, a tweed jacket. He was utterly affable, totally without affecta-tion, impregnable in his confidence. Dieter, looking out of the window, saw a countryside that seemed dormant, the trees' dark drooping shapes, the cattle huddled in tranquil groups, their tails lazily twitching. The phrase of some historian about 'the long deep sleep of the English people' swam into his head; he listened to Sir Philip and talked and had the impression of travelling miles, of being swallowed up by this billowing,

3

drowsy landscape.

Once, Sir Philip stopped at a village shop and came out with a cardboard carton of groceries; the van, after this, refused to start and Dieter got out to push. As he got back in, Sir Philip said, 'Thanks so much. Very old, I'm afraid. Needs servicing, too — awful price, nowadays, a service. Oh, well . . .' They passed a pub called the Lander Arms, beetle-browed cottages, an unkempt village green, a Victorian school, turned in at iron gates that shed curls of rusting paint, and jolted up a long, weedy, rutted drive.

It could never have been a beautiful house, Morswick: early seventeenth century, satisfactory enough in its proportions, with a moderately ambitious flight of steps (now cracked and crumbling) to the front door, but without the gilding of any famous architectural hand. The immediate impression was of a combination of resilience and decay: the pock-marked stone, the window frames unpainted for many years, the pedestal-less urns with planting of woody geraniums, the weeds fringing the steps, the rusted guttering.

They went in. Dieter had a muddled impression of welcoming hands and faces, a big cool hallway, a wide oak staircase, perplexing passages and doors culminating in a room with window looking out onto a field in which a girl jumped a large horse to and fro over an obstacle made from old oil-drums. He changed his shirt, watching her.

Only later, over tea, did he sort them all out. And that took time and effort, so thunderstruck was he by the room in which it was eaten, that bizarre — preposterous — backdrop to brown bread and butter, Marmite, fish paste and gooseberry jam.

It was huge, stone-flagged, its exterior wall taken up with one great high window, as elaborate with stone tracery as that of a church transept. There were family portraits all round the room — a jumble of artistic good and bad — and above them jutted banners so airy with age as to be completely colourless. The table at which they sat must have been twelve feet long; the wood had the rock-hard feel of immense age; there was nothing in sight that was new except the electric kettle with which Lady Lander made

4

the tea. ('The kitchen is such miles away, we do as much as we can in here . . .')

He stared incredulously at the banners, the pictures, at pieces of furniture such as he had only ever seen before in museums. These, though, were scarred with use, faded by sun, their upholstery in ribbons: Empire chairs and sofas, eighteenth century cabinets, pedestal tables, writing desks, bureaux. Bemused, he smiled and thanked and spread jam on brown bread and was handed a cup of tea by his hostess.

She was French, but seemed, he thought, poles removed from any Frenchwoman he had ever known – there was nothing left but the faintest accent, the occasional misuse of a word. And then there was the mother-in-law, old Lady Lander, a small pastel figure in her special chair (so fragile-looking, how could she have perpetrated that enormous man?) and Madame Heurgon, Lady Lander's mother, and the two boys, Philip and James, and Sophie, the old French nurse, and Sally, who was sixteen (she it was who had been jumping that horse, beyond the window).

He ate his tea, and smiled and listened. Later, he wrote to his father (and forgot to post the letter): 'This is the most extra-ordinary family, I hardly know what to make of them as yet. The French mother-in-law has been here twenty years but speaks the most dreadful English, and yet she never stirs from the place, it seems – I asked her if she went back to France often and she said, "Oh, but of course not, it is so impossibly expensive to go abroad nowadays". The boys go away to boarding school, but the girl, Sally, went to some local school and is really barely educated at all, daughters are expendable, I suppose. And they are all there, all the time, for every meal, the old nurse too, and in the evenings they all sit in the drawing room, listening to the wireless – comedy shows that bewilder them all, except the children, who try to explain the jokes and references, all at once, so no one can hear a word anyway. The old ladies, and the nurse, are in there all day, knitting and sewing and looking out of the window and saying how hot it is, or how cold, and how early the fruit is, or how late, day after day, just the same, there is nothing missing but the samovar . . . Sir Philip is out most of the time, in the fields, he is nothing if not a working farmer, tomorrow I shall help him with some young bullocks they have up on the hill.

I have not yet looked at the papers.'

That first day there had been no mention of the papers at all; and he had not, he realised, as he got into bed, given them so much as a thought himself. After tea he had been shown round the place by Sally and the boys: the weedy gardens where couch grass and bindweed quenched the outline of tennis court, kitchen garden, and what had once been a formal rose garden with box hedges and a goldfish pond. From time to time they met Lady Lander, hoeing a vegetable bed or snipping the dead heads from flowers; she worked with a slow deliberation that seemed appropriate to the hopeless task of controlling that large area. To go any faster would have been pointless – the forces of nature were winning hands down in any case – to give up altogether would be craven. There was no gardener, Sally said – 'The only men are Daniels and Jim, and Jim's only half really because he's on day release at the Tech. and of course Daddy needs them on the farm all the time'.

They toured the stables (a graceful eighteenth century courtyard, more architecturally distinguished than the house) and admired the Guernsey cows grazing in a paddock nearby. Sir Philip came down the drive on a tractor, and dismounted to join them and explain the finer points of raising calves to Dieter: this was a small breeding herd. 'Of course,' he said, 'it doesn't really make sense, economic sense, one never gets enough for them, but it's something I've always enjoyed doing.'

Sally broke in, 'And they *look* so nice.'

He beamed at the cows, and his daughter. 'Of course. That's half the point.'

A car was approaching slowly, taking the ruts and bumps with caution, a new model. Sir Philip said, 'Ah, here's George Nethercott, we're going to have a chat about those top fields'. He moved away from them as the car stopped, saying, 'Good evening, George, very good of you to come up – how's your hay going, I'm afraid we're making a very poor showing this year, I'm about three hundred bales short so far. I say, that's a very

6

smart car . . .'

His voice carried in the stillness of the early evening; it seemed the only forceful element in all that peace of pigeons cooing, cows cropping the grass, hypnotically shifting trees.

Sally said, 'Mr Nethercott's land joins our farm on two sides. Daddy may be going to sell him the three hill fields because we've got to have a new tractor next year, it's a pity, you oughtn't to sell land . . .' Her voice trailed away vaguely, and then she went on with sudden enthusiasm, 'I say, do you like riding? Would you like to try Polly?'

'You will never believe it, I have been horse-riding,' he wrote to Erica. 'Not for long I hasten to say – I fell off with much humiliation, and was made a great fuss of. They are such a charming family, and have a way of drawing you into everything they do, without ever really bothering about whether it is the kind of thing you are fitted for, or would like . . . So that I find myself leading the most extraordinary – for me – life, mending fences, herding cattle, picking fruit, hay-making.

Next week I must get down to the papers.'

Sir Philip had taken him up to the attics. 'I really don't know what we shall find,' he said. 'Things get shoved away for years, you know, and one has very little idea. . . I've not been up here for ages.'

There were pieces of furniture, grey with dust, and suitcases, and heaps of mouldering curtains and blankets; a sewing-machine that looked like the prototype of all sewing-machines; gilt-framed pictures stacked against a wall; a jumble of withered saddlery that Sir Philip picked up and examined. 'I wonder if Sally mightn't be able to make use of some of this.'

Dieter, looking at an eighteenth century chest of drawers pushed away beneath a dormer window, and thinking also of the furniture with which the rest of the house was filled, said 'You have some nice antique pieces'. Sir Philip, still trying to unravel a

7

harness, said 'Oh no, Dieter, not really, it's all just things that have always been here, you know'. He put the harness down and moved away into another, inner attic room with a single small window overlooking the stable yard. 'I have a feeling the stuff we're looking for is in these boxes here.'

Later, Dieter sat at a small folding green baize card table he had found in a corner, and began to open the bundles of letters and papers. It was much as Felicity Sutton had predicted: there were family letters all mixed up with official correspondence both from and to the Sir Philip Lander of the 1840s. It was a research worker's gold-mine. He glanced through a few documents at random, and then began to try to sort things out into some kind of order, thinking that eventually, before he left, he must suggest tactfully that all this should be deposited in the Public Record Office or some other appropriate place. In the meantime it was just his own good luck . . .

Curiously, he could not feel as excited or interested as he should. He read, and made a few notes, and yawned, and beyond the fly-blown window small puffy clouds coasted in a sky of duck-egg blue, the garden trees sighed and heaved, and if he lifted himself slightly in his chair he could see down into the stable-yard where Sally was in attendance on that enormous horse of hers, circling its huge complacent rump with brush and comb. Presently Sir Philip drove the tractor into the yard, and, with one of the boys, began to unload bales of hay. Dieter put his pen down, tidied his notes into a pile, and went down to help.

He had never known time pass so slowly – and so fast. The days were thirty-six hours long, and yet fled by so quickly that suddenly he had been there for two and a half weeks. Much embarrassed, he went one morning to find Lady Lander in the kitchen and insist that he should pay for his keep.

She was making jam. The room was filled with the sweet fruity smell; flies buzzed drunkenly against the windows. Astonished, she said 'Oh, but of course not, we couldn't hear of such a thing, you are a guest'.

'But I am staying so long, originally Sir Philip suggested a few days, and with one thing and another it has got longer and longer. Please, really I should prefer . . .'

She would have none of it.

He hardly knew himself how it was that his departure was always postponed. Of course, he had done no work at all, as yet, on the papers, but he could get down to that any time. And always there was something that loomed – 'You must be sure to be here for the County Show next week,' Sir Philip would say. 'You'll find it amusing if you've not seen that kind of thing before – do you have the equivalent in Germany, I wonder?' Or Sally would remember suddenly that the first cubbing meet was in ten days time. 'You'll still be here, won't you, Dieter? Oh, you must be – honestly, if you've never seen a Meet . . .'

He protested to Lady Lander – 'Please, I would be happier . . .', but could see that there was no point in going on. 'In any case,' she said, turning back to the pink-frothing pan on the stove, 'you have been most helpful to my husband, he is always short-handed at this time of year, I am afraid only that we drive you into things you would never normally dream of doing. You must say, you know, if it bores you – we tend to forget, down here, that not everyone lives this kind of life.'

And she, he wondered, had she not once been someone quite different? On Sundays, both she and her mother appeared for church in quite unfashionable but recognizably expensive clothes – silk dresses and citified hats of pre-war style. In these incongruous outfits, they walked down the lane to the village church. The family filled the whole of the front pew; Sir Philip's confident tenor led the sparse congregation; afterwards they would all stand, every week, for the same amount of time, chatting to the Vicar. Then back to Morswick, stopping again from time to time to talk with village people.

He had thought, when he first came, that it was feudal, and had been amused. Now, his perceptions heightened, he saw otherwise. 'It is not that they are not respected', he wrote to his father. 'Far from it – people are deferential to them – a title still means something, and they have always been the big family in these

9

parts. But it is as though they are runners in a race who are being outstripped without even realising it. I think they hardly notice that their farming neighbours have new gadgets they have not – washing machines, televisions – that theirs is the shabbiest car for miles around, that the Morswick tractor is so out-of-date Nethercott (the neighbour) declined the loan of it when his broke down. And why? you will be saying, after all they have land, a house, possessions. But the land is not good, a lot of it is rough hill-grazing, I suppose that is at the root of the problem – and a mansion and a family past are not very realizable assets. I certainly can't imagine them selling the furniture. But when you come down to it – it is as though there is also some kind of perverse lack of will, as though they both didn't know, and didn't want to know.'

The children were where it most showed. Beside their contemporaries – the sons and daughters of the local farming families (many of them at private schools, their country accents fast fading), they seemed quaint, too young for their ages, innocent. Sally, talking to other adolescent girls at an agricultural show, was the only one without lipstick, a hair-do, the quick glancing self-consciousness of young womanhood. She seemed a child beside them.

At the cubbing Meet – held outside the village pub – he found it almost unbearable. Standing beside Lady Lander, he watched her. Lady Lander said, 'She's not well mounted, I'm afraid, poor darling – we've only got old Polly these days'.

It was a huge horse, with a hefty muscularity that suggested carthorse ancestry. Seated on it, Sally towered above the dapper ponies of the other children. Beaming, unconscious of the vaguely comic figure she cut, she yanked the horse's head away from a tray of glasses that was being carried around, and waved at Dieter. She wore her school mack over grubby breeches and a pair of battered hunting-boots. The other girls were crisp in pale jodhpurs, tweed jackets and little velvet caps.

Dieter was wrenched by pity, and love.

He adored her. With horror he had recognised his own feelings, which smacked, it seemed to him, of paedophilia. She was sixteen; her rounded features, her plump awkward body, were raw with childishness. He was obsessed by her. He forced himself to contemplate her ignorance, her near-illiteracy. He thought of Erica, of her sharp clever face, the long hours of serious discussion, the shared concerns, and it did no good at all.

And Sally had not the slightest inkling, nor ever would, of how he felt. She jostled him in puppyish horse-play; she worked beside him in the harvest field, her breasts straining at her aertex shirt, her brown legs as shiny with health and vigour as the rump of that incongruous horse she rode; he could hardly take his eyes off her, and was appalled at himself.

In the evenings, he played board games with the two boys, held skeins of knitting wool for old Lady Lander as she wound the balls. Sometimes, he took a book from the great high cases that lined the walls of the drawing room. They held an odd assortment: bound volumes of *Punch*, row upon row, Edwardian books about hunting and fishing, the classic Victorian novelists, books of humorous verse, Henty and Buchan and Rider Haggard. He read with perplexity novels like *The Constant Nymph*, *Precious Bane* and *Beau Geste* that seemed to fit not at all with the concept of English twentieth century literature that he had formed after two years' carefully selective leisure reading. Scanning the titles on the shelves, he had a confusing impression of being presented with a whole shadow culture of which he had been unaware. Yet again he felt his own judgements and perceptions to be hopelessly inadequate. Sir Philip, standing beside him at the book case one evening, said, 'Glad to see you're making use of the library, Dieter – I'm afraid none of us get much time for reading'. There was hardly a single recent addition, not an untattered dust-cover to be seen.

On a day of sullen rain clouds, when the whole landscape seemed sunk in apathy, the old tractor broke down with more than usual finality. For hour after hour, Sir Philip and Daniels crawled around it, oiling and adjusting; Dieter, on edge with vicarious anxiety (it was needed for several urgent jobs), watched in frustration, cursing his lack of mechanical know-how. The worry on Sir Philip's face distressed him greatly; he longed to help. Eventually, the tractor sputtered into fitful life, and everybody stood back smiling. Sir Philip said, 'Well, Daniels, we shan't have any of these crises next year, when we've got the new one, I hope'. And Daniels said, 'That's right, sir, we'll be in clover then', and added, looking down the drive, 'here's Mr Nethercott now'.

Nethercott had come, though, to talk not about fields but to look at the bull Sir Philip proposed selling. It was a young bull, whose performance was proving unreliable. Daniels was in favour of going over to artificial insemination. Sir Philip had reluctantly concurred, as they stood side by side at the gate, a few days before, watching the bull at work among the cows in a steeply sloping field opposite. Sir Philip said, 'You're right, Daniels, I'm not too happy about him either'.

'Silly bugger don't realise he got to do it downhill.'

Sir Philip turned away. 'Oh well, there's nothing to be done – he'll have to go. Now, George Nethercott's wanting a bull, I know – I'll give him a ring tonight.'

And now Nethercott too stood at the field-gate, studying the bull. Other matters were talked of for a while, then he said 'How much were you thinking of asking for him?'

Sir Philip named a price.

Nethercott nodded. There was a brief silence and then he said with a trace of embarrassment, 'He might well work out more satisfactory than he looks just now – but the fact is, what I'm looking for's going to cost a fair bit more than that. Thanks for letting me have a look at him, though'.

A week or so later, they heard through the postman that Nethercott had paid five hundred pounds for a bull at the Royal Show. Sir Philip said, 'Well, good heavens! Lucky fellow'. He was standing with Dieter in the front drive, the two or three brown envelopes that the postman had brought in his hand. 'I really don't know how people manage it, these days. He's a good chap, Nethercott – they're a nice family. His grandfather used to work here, you know, for mine – stable-lad he was, I think. Well, I suppose we might get on with that fencing today, eh?'

Up in the attic, the sun striking through the window had

browned Dieter's single page of notes; there was a faint paler stripe where the pencil lay.

At the beginning of September, the boys went back to boarding school. The corn was down, the blackberries ripening, the green of the trees spiced here and there with the first touch of autumn colour. Since he had come here, Dieter realised, the landscape had changed, working through its cycle so unobtrusively that only with an effort did one remember the brimming cornfields of July, the hedgerows still bright with wild flowers, the long light evenings. Now, the fields were bleached and shaven, the hedges lined with the skeletal heads of dried cow-parsley and docks, the grass white with dew in the mornings. It came as a faint shock to realise that the place was not static at all, that that impression of deep slumber was quite false, that change was continuous, that nothing stood still. That he could not stay here for ever.

There was a dance, in the local market town, in connection with some equestrian activity, to which he went with Sally and her parents. It was the first time, he realised, that he had ever been anywhere with them when the whole family had not come, grandmothers and all. Sally wore an old dress of her mother's that had been cut down for her; it did not fit and was unbecoming, but she shone with excitement and anticipation. In the hotel where the dance took place, the other young girls were waiting about in the foyer in sharp-eyed groups and he was stricken again at Sally's frumpish looks in contrast to their fashionable dresses, their knowingness. But she was quite happy – laughing, greeting acquaintances.

He danced with her once at the beginning, and then left her with a group of her contemporaries. But later, the evening under way, whenever he saw her she was dancing with friends of her parents, or sitting alone on one of a row of gilt chairs at the edge of the room, holding a glass of lemonade, but still radiant, tapping her foot in time to the music. After a while he went over and sat beside her.

'Are you having a good time, Sally?'

'Marvellous!'

'Let's dance, shall we?'

She was clumsy; he had to steer her round the room. She said, 'Sorry, I'm hopeless. We did have dancing lessons at school but it's quite different when it's a real man, and anyway I always had to take man because of being tall, so I'm no good at being the woman. I say, Mummy says perhaps I can go to the Hunt Ball this year – will you still be here?'

He said, 'I'm afraid not. I have to go back before the term begins in October'.

'Oh, what a pity.' They danced in silence for a minute or two and then she said suddenly, 'What are you going to do after you've finished your – your what's-it, the thing you're writing?'

'I shall go back to Germany and get a job. I expect I shall get married,' he added after a fractional pause. He had never spoken of Erica at Morswick.

'Will you?' she looked amazed. 'Gosh – how exciting. Do write and tell us, won't you, so that we can send a present.'

She beamed up at him; she smelled of toothpaste and, very faintly, of a cheap scent that she must have acquired in secrecy and tentatively used. He had seen, once, into her room; there had been a balding toy dog on the pillow, photographs of horses pinned to the walls, glass animals on the windowsill. She said, 'Do you know, they want me to go to a sort of finishing school place in Grenoble next year'.

'I should think you would like that.'

She said, 'Oh no, I couldn't possibly go. I couldn't bear to leave Morswick. No, I can't possibly'.

Dieter said 'Sally, I think you should, I really do'.

She shook her head.

Later, back at Morswick, he sat with Sir Philip in the drawing room; Sally and her mother had gone to bed. Sir Philip had taken a bottle of whisky from the cupboard and poured them both a glass: it was almost the first time Dieter had ever seen alcohol produced at Morswick, except for the glass of sherry offered to their rare visitors. Sir Philip said, 'Quite a successful evening, I thought. Of course, you get rather a different kind of person at this sort of do now – it's not really like before the war. I daresay my father would be a bit taken aback if he was still alive'.

He began to talk about his war-time experiences in Italy and France: he had been with the Sicily landings, and then in Normandy shortly after D-day, advancing through France and into Germany. Remembering suddenly the delicacy of the subject, he looked across at Dieter and said, 'I hope you don't . . . of course, one realised at the time how many people like yourself, like your father . . . What a wretched business it all was, so much worse in many ways for you than for us'.

Dieter said, 'I think you would be interested to see Germany now. I wish you would come to visit us – my father would be so delighted to make arrangements, if all of you could come, or perhaps at least the boys and Sally'.

'How awfully kind. We really must try to – you know, I can't think when we last had a holiday of any sort. Yes, we really must.' He swilled the whisky in his glass, peering down into it. 'Yes. Of course, one is so awfully tied up here, being pretty short-handed nowadays. I daresay things will pick up in time, though. I must admit, it is getting a bit hard to manage just at the moment – still, we keep our heads above water. Anyway, I really mustn't burden you with our problems. By the way, I hope you didn't mean what you said earlier about leaving us next week – I'd imagined we'd have you with us for some time to come. There's the Harvest Festival on Sunday week – I'm sure Jeanne was intending to rope you in for one thing and another.'

'I have to get back – the term begins soon, you see. My supervisor – well, they must wonder what on earth has become of me. And in any case, you've been far too kind already, too hospitable. I don't know how to thank you enough.'

'I'm afraid what with one thing and another you've not had all that much time to put in on those papers. They've been of some interest, I hope?'

Dieter said, 'Oh yes, extremely interesting'.

The day before he was to leave he went to the attic to clear up the green baize table. His note-pad, with its single page of notes, was curled at the edges now, and dusty. Insects had died on the opened bundles of letters. Beyond the window, the landscape had slipped a notch further into autumn: there was a mist smoking up from the fields, and long curtains of old man's beard hanging down the wall beside the stable yard. He tied up the letters again and put them away in the trunk, folded the card table, gathered up his own things. He opened the window for a moment, with some vague notion of airing the place, and heard, faintly, Sally whistling as she did something out of sight in one of the loose boxes.

His departure for the station was delayed for a few minutes by the arrival of Nethercott. Sir Philip stood with him at the field gate nodding and listening. When at last he finished, and Nethercott, apologising for turning up at what was obviously an inappropriate moment, had driven away, the whole family was gathered on the steps to say good-bye to Dieter. He had shaken hands with them all, several times; everyone was smiling and interrupting. Sir Philip came across the drive to them and said, 'Sorry about that – had to have a word or two since he'd taken the trouble to come up'.

Lady Lander said, 'What was it about?'

'Oh, just the fields – you know, the hill fields. He'd like to make an offer for them but I'd got things a bit wrong, I'm afraid – they're worth rather less than I'd imagined, on the current market. Rather a lot less, I'm afraid. George was awfully apologetic – you'd have thought it was his fault. He's a good chap.'

'Oh dear, does that mean no new tractor?'

'I suppose it does. I don't know how I'm going to break that to poor Daniels. Well, anyway,' he went on cheerfully, 'we'll be able to send the old one for a thorough overhaul, we'll have to make do with that. Now, Dieter, we'd better be on our way, hadn't we, where's your case . . .'

He saw them like that, in his mind's eye, for long after – the women – standing on the front steps waving and smiling. 'It's au revoir, anyway' Lady Lander had said, 'because we shall see you again, next time you're in our part of the world, shan't we?' And her mother-in-law, that frail old lady in her pale floppy clothes and regimental brooches, had piped up 'Oh yes, we're always here, you know, you'll always find us here', and Sally was calling out not to forget to let them know about the wedding. She had given him a hug and a kiss; the feel of her arms, her warm soft face, the smell of her, stayed with him all the way to the station, and beyond. And the sight of them, and of the house behind, frozen in the furry yellow light of the September morning, like an old photograph – the figures grouped around the steps, the house with its backdrop of fields and hills and trees.

At the station, Sir Philip shook him by the hand. 'We've enjoyed having you, Dieter. You must get down to us again sometime. You'll find everything goes on much as ever at Morswick. And the best of luck with your doctorate.'

In the train, Dieter began a letter to Erica, and then sat staring out of the window at that placid landscape (the landscape of Constable, he told himself, of Richard Wilson, of the English novelists) and saw only the irresistible manifestations of change: the mottled trees, the tangle of spent growth in the hedgerows.

The Voice of God
in Adelaide Terrace

Miss Avril Pemberton, in her fifty-seventh year, suffered from insomnia. She did not consider this an insupportable affliction; she would lie with her eyes open in the protective darkness of her bedroom, think her thoughts, and listen to the nocturnal London sounds. These were not many, for Adelaide Terrace was a quiet and respectable neighbourhood, its inhabitants given to early nights and not inclined to car ownership.

It was on such a night, in that static tract of time between three and five in the morning so familiar to insomniacs, that Avril first heard the voice.

She was a devout woman and a regular churchgoer. Even so, she did not regard herself as blameless; merely as a reasonably proficient Christian, given to occasional error rather than deliberate transgression. She had certainly never expected to be singled out in this way.

The voice said, 'Avril?'

She sat up, and stared into the dusky cavern beside the wardrobe from which it seemed to come; later, she recalled its curious sexlessness, the voice of neither man nor woman.

'Avril,' it said, 'are you listening carefully? There is something I want you to do.'

Avril, wide awake, more interested than awed, said 'What would You like me to do?'

'I shall explain,' said the voice. 'Pay attention. I wish you to make a start with the attic room . . .'

Avril listened, with mounting astonishment.

It should be explained at this point that Avril Pemberton let rooms. She let rooms because her mother had done so before, ever since, indeed, Mr Pemberton had died in 1951, because the house was too large for her own needs and because the money came in very handy. Without it, she would have found it difficult to manage on her salary from the part-time secretarial work for a local firm of accountants. She let the first floor front and back (single, with washbasins) and the large attic room (own bathroom). Cooking facilities for the tenants were provided in the small scullery on the first floor. Avril herself occupied the ground floor, using the second floor front as her bedroom. The two small back rooms on the second floor remained empty, in use as boxrooms. Her mother had not liked the house to become overcrowded.

Mrs Pemberton had died four years before, irascible in extreme old age. To the bitter end, she had exercised her powers of discrimination over would-be tenants, vetting them, finally, from her bed. Avril had found it all extremely embarrassing; so, presumably, had the tenants. Two of the present three, Mr Harris, the bank clerk in the first floor front, and the nursing sister in the attic had been her mother's choices. Sandra Lee, the student from the teacher training college round the corner, Avril had admitted a year or so ago, irritably aware that the pasty girl, with her total absence of personality, opinion or discernible tastes, was exactly the kind of person of whom her mother would have approved as a tenant.

There had never been any shortage of people wanting rooms. Adelaide Terrace was conveniently near bus routes and a tube station, not too far from central London, but quiet. The area was something of a buffer state; to the east, middle-class 'reclamation' had sent prices rocketing and let loose a tide of primrose and terra cotta front doors, bay trees in tubs and petunia-crammed window-boxes; to the west, quite other things had been going on. There, Indian take-aways alternated with Chinese, the market stalls were piled high with garish and glittery stuffs, peculiar vegetables and cut-price carpets and pop records. The streets ran with black school children and the pubs blared forth unfamiliar music. The inhabitants of Adelaide Terrace kept their eyes turned resolutely to the east, and hoped for the best.

And, where possible, played a part. Many of the tall terrace houses, like the Pembertons', belonged to elderly people and diminished families who let out rooms; others were divided, rather inefficiently, into flats. The long-term inhabitants, such as Mrs Pemberton and her immediate neighbour, Mrs Fletcher, knew one another well and were resolute as to certain matters, though divided about methods of exercising that resolution.

Mrs Fletcher sported, for many years, a small notice stuck to the inside of a glass panel in the front door. It said 'No coloureds' and had been nicely lettered, with stencils, by her niece who had done a year at art college.

Mrs Pemberton thought this silly and unnecessary. It was a simple matter, she said, to make one's position perfectly clear without that. Occasional small unpleasantnesses might arise, but could be quickly dealt with: front doors open, but they also close again. It was with a certain satisfaction that she had pointed out to Mrs Fletcher, in 1965, that the notice would have to be removed.

'Who's to make me?' said Mrs Fletcher, bristling.

'Well, dear' said Mrs Pemberton, 'you'll have to do as you think best, but I wouldn't like to see you get had up, and personally I've never found the need in the first place.'

Mrs Fletcher went on at some length about individual liberty and diabolical interferences therein and how you couldn't pass laws to make people think differently to what they always had done. Mrs Pemberton pointed out, smoothly, that all this was true enough but what was clear as day was that you could pass laws until you were blue in the face but there would still be ways and means.

Mrs Fletcher removed the notice and took instructions from Mrs Pemberton as to ways and means. There were seldom, if ever, misunderstandings or unpleasantnesses, and Adelaide Terrace remained much as it had been before. At the far end, where

Mrs Pemberton's influence was weakest, there was a certain falling-off. An Indian family took one of the flats and were to be seen, on Sundays, immaculately dressed, pushing a pram in Adelaide Gardens. Their eldest son, in grey flannel trousers, navy blazer, spotless white shirt and puce turban, cycled down the street to school every day. Avril, watching once from the window, was misguided enough to say that they seemed quite nice people; her mother was unmanageable for a week.

And now, lying there in the dark, she listened to the voice – a little hectoring in tone – as it went on and on. Instructing. Lecturing. 'Remember the Bishop?' it said. 'Now supposing *he* had come to the door . . .'

'I know,' said Avril. 'I said as much to mother at the time.'

The Bishop of somewhere in Africa, he had been, but you couldn't tell that at once from the name. He had come as visiting preacher to St Bartholomew's, one autumn Sunday. They had been invited to the Vicar's after the service, for coffee, because Mrs Pemberton was treasurer, then, of the Mother's Union. And he had been as black as your hat. Big and black and beaming. Avril had thought, at first, seeing him climb into the pulpit, that her mother wouldn't go to the vicarage. But she had. She had gone, and sat there, and drunk coffee and eaten biscuits. And afterwards she had said that she wouldn't have Mrs Brinton's job, not for the world. Mrs Brinton was the Vicar's wife. And Avril had said what she had said and there had been unpleasantness between them. And now here was the voice, harking back.

'I spoke my mind,' said Avril sulkily.

She had never taken up arms against her mother lightly: the cost was too high. As the years went by, she did so less and less, the instinctive resistance of her youth snuffed out by her mother's more implacable temperament. She ceased to counter Mrs Pemberton's vaunted opinions and preferences, ceased to say, from time to time, 'There are two sides to everything, mother,' and 'Well, personally I do think . . .' She took to silence.

By and large, she conceded Adelaide Terrace as Mrs Pemberton's territory and guarded jealously the privacy of her life beyond it, what little there was – the voluntary evenings at the Scout and Guide hut, her Red Cross afternoon, and her job at Hackle and Starbuck.

Never, for instance, would she have told Mrs Pemberton about Gloria.

Gloria came to the office as a temp when the senior, and permanent, secretary, had to have several weeks' sick leave after an operation. She was seventeen, fresh from school, an indifferent typist, as noisy as a puppy, and West Indian. Her abundant, frizzy hair was worn in two huge puffs elaborately teased out at either side of her head; she had wide, flat features with large brown eyes, big lips delicately painted; there was a bloom to her skin that entranced Avril. Surreptitiously she kept glancing at Gloria; bewildered, she realised that she found the girl beautiful.

Gloria bounced and giggled her way through the days and played merry hell with the filing system. The office was torn between amusement and irritation; Mr Hackle, who had been as startled as Avril when Gloria appeared from the agency, grumbled at the mangled letters with which Gloria presented him, and enjoyed, like Avril, the throaty laughter that brightened office hours. Gloria teased the office boy, charmed clients, bungled every telephone message, and spent much time in the washroom attending to her appearance. At the typewriter, she moaned and whimpered and, every now and then, leaned back to indulge in a huge luxuriant stretch that made it seem as though her plump rubbery young body might spring apart entirely, like an over-ripe pea-pod.

One day, looking across at Avril, she said, 'Hey, that's nice'.

'What?' said Avril.

'That sweater you got on. It suits you – it's your colour, blue. You look really good today.'

Avril had flushed and muttered something and gone back to the letter she was typing. Later, tidying her hair before she left the office, she stared at herself in the mirror, turning this way and that, adjusting the collar of her jacket.

She had been sorry when Gloria left, and Maureen Davidson returned, with her migraines and her proficiency and her faint odour of Lifebuoy soap.

Guiltily, she dismissed recollections of Gloria and returned to here and now, and to the voice, which seemed to be concluding its homily.

'. . . as quickly as you can, with the normal period of notice to the present tenants.'

As she listened, the corners of Avril's mouth turned up in an incredulous smile.

'*All* black?' she said.

'Every one of them,' said the voice sternly.

There was not a great deal of difficulty with Mr Harris, Sandra Lee and the nursing sister. Since she gave formal notice to all three at once, it was simply assumed that she wished to reclaim the house for her own occupation. Mr Harris, who had been there for nine years, was clearly a little put out, but gave her a large box of chocolates as a parting present and made over to her the tradescantia in the scullery, which he thought might not take kindly to a move. The nursing sister asked if she wasn't going to rattle around rather, all on her own. Sandra Lee vanished, wordless, into the obscurity from which she had come.

The process, allowing for the correct periods of notice, took nearly four months. Not until the last tenant had departed did Avril place her advertisement in the *Gazette*; she had decided to deal with the attic room first, and retained her usual wording, except that she added 'Married couples not objected to'.

There was a flood of responses. Avril, turning away, with her mother's murmured formula of regret — 'So sorry . . . already taken . . . person who called last night' — first a young Irish couple, and then a Scottish nurse and another girl of indeterminate extraction, realised that covertly exercised discrimination is indeed extremely easy.

The Singhs presented themselves at the door on a Tuesday morning. By Friday they were installed in the attic.

On Saturday morning, returning from the shops, Avril was halted, key in the lock, by Mrs Fletcher, springing from her own door at the sound as though released by an elastic. 'I been wanting to have a word with you, dear' she said. 'I must say I couldn't hardly believe my eyes, seeing them pull up in the taxi like that, with all their stuff. I said to myself what old Mrs P. would say I don't even like to think . . .'

Avril stood there, her foot inside her own door, half-listening, and it came to her with sudden welcome clarity that, in nearly thirty years of enforced congress, she had never really liked Mrs Fletcher. It was as though you might discover that tea, bread, or some other unconsidered object of routine was not really to your taste. She stared at her opening and closing mouth, the tuft of hairs that crowned a surface irregularity on her chin, the cameo brooch that puckered the neck of her blouse, and thought: silly old bag.

'. . . seen some perfectly nice people come to the door, Sunday and Monday, after you put your ad. in,' concluded Mrs Fletcher, 'so I don't know what to think, I simply don't.' She stared at Avril. 'And who are they, one would like to know?'

'They're my new tenants,' said Avril coolly (she liked that: *my* new tenants). 'They've taken the attic room.'

There was a silence. In Mrs Fletcher's face, whole volumes of analysis, speculation, and adjustment to circumstances were written, revised, re-written; granite assumptions crumbled to dust, and were reconstituted in other forms. When she spoke again, it was from twenty miles away, and ten years on. She said, 'That girl's expecting. I daresay you'll not have noticed that'.

Avril, who had not, flushed a little, and went into the house.

The Singhs were quiet tenants; they pattered up and down the stairs like well-behaved children, talking to each other in low tones if at all. Occasionally, radio music, turned low, seeped from beneath their door, and with it, culinary smells.

With complete detachment, Avril considered the smells. She had once taken a meal in an Indian restaurant with two girls from the office and had not, in fact, much cared for it. The smells, at first, raised a whisker of alarm. And then, considering over a day or two, she decided that they were no more, indeed rather less, disagreeable than the bacon (cut-price, she had always suspected) Mr Harris used to do himself for breakfast every day. In fact, they grew on you.

Over the next three weeks she filled the first floor front and back.

The front went within three days to a bescarved and bespectacled student from Nigeria. The back was less straightforward; there was a tussle of wills with a forceful woman who refused to believe that the room had already been taken within an hour of the advertisement (the 'occasional small unpleasantness' that old Mrs Pemberton had grown accustomed to) but Avril held her own, then and for a further day and a half until the arrival of an immensely fat black dental nurse called Brenda.

In the silence and darkness of her room she said, 'All right?' There being no reply, she assumed that her arrangements had met with approval.

The house was no longer so quiet. The Nigerian student turned out to have many friends, some of whom, Avril suspected, were not entirely transitory visitors. Having always respected the privacy of her tenants (unlike her mother, who kept duplicate keys and made forays into their rooms in their absence) she made no comment. He and Brenda struck up a friendship, conducted for the most part rather noisily on the stairs. Both, though, were unfailingly genial; the Nigerian cleared a blocked sink in the kitchen and Brenda, when Avril took to her bed with a throat infection, plied her with hot drinks laced with suspect but delicious substances. She would stand at Avril's bedroom door, entirely filling it, brandishing a thermos and shouting encouragingly, as though to a slightly deaf child; she was a maturer and more strident version of Gloria.

Avril felt a greater affinity with the Singhs, their deprecating smiles and self-effacing comings and goings. Mrs Singh — Kamala, as she whispered once, in a rare moment of intimacy — was indeed swelling week by week, as Avril had now to observe and admit. Nothing was said, until one day Brenda, in raucous progress up the stairs, said casually, 'That Kamala, she goin' to have it any day now', which alarmed Avril but left her better prepared for contingencies. When, a week or so later, she heard Mr Singh come down the stairs with more than usual haste, and

26

then his soft voice on the telephone, asking for the doctor, she was calm and indeed quite excited. Being familiar with the processes of childbirth from her reading of novels (though the kind of novel, admittedly, in which the narrative tended to shift, at the crucial moment, to the rôle of non-participant characters such as husbands and sisters) she amassed all the kettles and saucepans she could find and set them to boil. Only as they began to hum, did it occur to her that she really did not know for what all this boiling water was required: the novels never went into that. And when she came out into the hall to find Kamala, smiling weakly, coming down the stairs on her husband's arm, suitcase in hand, she was distinctly disappointed. The birth was to take place in hospital, apparently. She went rather glumly back into her room, and forgot the saucepans, which were boiling briskly ten minutes later, when Brenda returned, filling the house with steam and prompting much noisy comment and enquiry. Avril, who suspected that she might have been rumbled, gave some sheepish explanations about sterilising jamjars.

Kamala returned, after what Avril thought a surprisingly short period, with a tiny, fragile baby (a boy, apparently) cocooned in yards of shocking pink blanketing. The Nigerian produced a couple of bottles of wine for the household to drink the baby's health: everybody gathered in the kitchen, the Singhs silent but beaming, Brenda and the Nigerian loudly talkative, Avril, who had seldom in her life touched alcohol, feeling increasingly unstable, but stimulated. It was all rather enjoyable; afterwards, she watched television, a little restlessly, and tried not to pay attention to the curious sounds from the Nigerian's room, where he and Brenda were completing the evening on their own.

Mrs Fletcher, tight-lipped, had complained a number of times about the pitch of Brenda's transistor radio. She spoke seldom to Avril, but was frequently to be seen in the street, in eloquent discourse with one or other of the neighbours. They are talking about me, Avril would think, and found that she did not care at all.

It was curious: she was a person who had always been deeply sensitive to the opinions of others.

27

At night, in the privacy of her room, she checked with the voice for approval and encouragement, and received it. Her life, in every other respect, continued much as it always had done: she went to the office, on Monday and Tuesday mornings and Thursday and Friday afternoons, to the Scout and Guide Hut on Monday evenings, the Red Cross on Thursdays, St Bartholomew's on Sunday for communion and again for evensong. She was not entirely surprised when the Vicar called one day. He was a man easily swayed by others (an opinion she seemed always to have had, though only now did it express itself – tacitly – with ease and conviction) and she heard in his voice the conspiratorial tones of Mrs Fletcher. He sat uneasily on the edge of a chair and asked Avril if she had been keeping well lately; afterwards, the two indentations of his behind remained for some while on the upholstery, prolonging the tension of the visit. When Avril replied, shortly, that she had, he hummed and hawed, reflected on the weather, the new block of flats springing up alongside the churchyard, and his summer holiday plans, before hoping that if she, er, ever felt at all, er, in need of a chat she must remember that she had many good friends in the neighbourhood, many good friends. There was a silence, at the end of which the Vicar made the proposition that some people find living alone a bit of a strain, especially after the sad loss of a dear relative, that sometimes possibly, er, a chat with a sympathetic friend . . .

Avril said that she did not live alone.

The Vicar, with some eagerness, said that yes, quite, and since she'd mentioned it he wondered if . . .

Avril asked what he wondered. And the Vicar's voice had trailed off, and with it the Vicar, till all that was left of him were those two dents in the chair seat.

Avril wondered if the voice had ever addressed the Vicar, in the darkness of *his* nights.

The Singh baby prospered. Mr Harris's tradescantia in the scullery died; the Nigerian presented Avril with a rather violent oil-painting attributed to his brother which she felt obliged to hang on the stairs. She did not like it and indeed had asked the voice for guidance over the matter, and the voice had suggested the darkish corner on the first floor landing. She frequently asked the voice for guidance, these days, and was frequently given it.

When Brenda, coming in from work one evening, heard her in one of the boxrooms, she peered inquisitively through the door.

'My, you got a lot of stuff in there, Miss Pemberton. You havin' a tidy-up, then?'

'The room's going to be used,' said Avril. 'I have to clear it out.'

'You expectin' a visitor, then?'

Avril, distracted by the problem of a broken table-lamp, replied that she was making room for a further lodger. Brenda did not receive this news with the enthusiasm Avril had expected: she said it was enough hassle getting that Pius to hurry up with the bathroom in the mornings and the shelves in the scullery were cram full as it was. She implied a fit of profiteering on Avril's part. Avril ignored this, with dignity.

She got rid of the first two applicants for the room, who were unsuitable; the third threw her into a quandary. He stood before her on the doorstep, small, slight, brown, and almond-eyed. Avril had little idea from which part of the world he hailed, but knew on which side of the dividing-line her mother would have placed him. She hesitated, showed him the room, and succumbed.

In the night she was woken by the voice (she had been sleeping much better of late). It was displeased.

Avril said defensively, 'Well, mother wouldn't ever have taken him'.

The voice continued, didactic in its assertions as to what was what. Avril, lying there in the dark, felt a twinge of resentment: there was a note, a distinct note, of Mrs Pemberton's hectoring dogmatism. She pointed out, sulkily, that it was too late to do anything about it now, and Mr Lee had looked a good dark brown to her. She did not say that in any case she had rather taken to him, a nice-spoken boy who had stood aside to let her come down the stairs first.

29

The voice, unmollified, issued further instructions.

'*Both* the boxrooms?' said Avril. And then, thoughtfully, 'Very well, then'.

The Health Visitor sat at the kitchen table and said that she had just thought she would pop in, since she was in the house anyway to see Mrs Singh. She said the baby was coming along nicely. Avril agreed. She said you must miss your mother a lot, I gather it's three or four years since she died. Avril agreed, wondered from whom the gathering had been done, saw Mrs Fletcher pass the window, bundled against the spring wind, and shoot a quick glance sideways. Looking after yourself all right, are you? said the Health Visitor. Avril said she was, and observed the Health Visitor's quick, surreptitious professional examination of the room.

The Health Visitor believed that Avril was thinking of letting another room. Avril neither confirmed nor denied this: with a spurt of indignation she thought, nosey thing. The Health Visitor made some enquiries about toilets, and washbasins, which Avril answered with restraint. The Health Visitor left. Through the window, Avril watched Mrs Fletcher's interception of her, in Adelaide Terrace.

Mr Lee had been installed for a week when she put her second advertisement in the *Gazette*. She had cleared out and prepared the second boxroom during the daytime, in the absence of all the other tenants except Mrs Singh and the baby, who kept themselves to themselves on the top floor. Consequently, the first they knew of her new arrangements was the arrival of the new tenant.

There were comments, amounting to open hostility. The Singhs said nothing, but pattered with a little more assertion in their journeys up and down stairs. The Nigerian grumbled, outside Avril's kitchen door, about the additional strain on the resources of the scullery: he had quite a nasty temper, Avril realised. Brenda said, 'She *stayin'* here, that Chinese girl? You running some kind of United Nations in this house, Miss Pemberton?' A sour expression replaced her normal grin.

The voice, too, had its say.

'I will choose my own tenants,' said Avril, in the darkness of her bedroom. 'I will use my own discrimination.' She lay there, these nights, with the house silent around her, and contemplated the filling of it, and the nature of the filling of it, and her part therein, and experienced the most satisfactory feeling of having created. The house was a kaleidoscope, but the jugglings of its occupancy were no longer random: they had form. She ceased to pay much attention to the voice, which nagged on irritatingly from beside the wardrobe.

The atmosphere of the house was no longer harmonious, but Avril did not notice; she was preoccupied with her own plans.

She transferred her possessions from the second floor to her ground floor sitting room by degrees, those that she could handle on her own. The bed, which presented too great a problem, she left where it was, and ordered a new one for herself from the furniture shop in the High Street. It was its delivery that alerted Brenda; she stood, hands on massive hips, at the turn in the stairs and said, 'You not letting *another* room, Miss Pemberton? This house getting too full by half, you know, that lavatory up here's only working half-cock again, you're going to have the health people after you, you not careful'. Avril went into her room and closed the door, intent upon the phrasing of the advertisement for the *Gazette*.

After she had installed Mr Achimota in what had been her bedroom, she locked herself into her sitting room, whenever she was in the house. She did not really feel like talking to people, and was dimly aware of unrest around her. People whispered on the stairs, and sometimes did not whisper: on one occasion she heard Brenda's raised voice saying, 'She barmy, I'm telling you, she not right in her head any more'.

The Health Visitor hammered on the door, once. She said, 'I'd like to have a chat with you, dear, just for a few minutes'. Avril ignored her.

At night, she held dialogues with the voice, but nowadays it was she who did much of the talking: the voice had grown feebler and feebler and as it whined on, asserting and instructing, its tones had become more and more like those of Mrs Pemberton, but diminished, and susceptible to counter-arguments in a way that Mrs Pemberton never had been. 'Nobody's right all the time,' said Avril, 'not even You. Not on every subject. Now in my opinion . . .'

Mrs Fletcher had avoided her for months, crossing the street when they happened to coincide in Adelaide Terrace. Now, Avril noticed, other neighbours did the same, or observed her furtively, in shops or from adjacent pews in St Bartholomew's. Hurt, though not greatly so, Avril maintained a lonely dignity. She missed, more, the convivial atmosphere that had prevailed in the house during the early months of its re-organisation. Nowadays, there were arguments on the stairs about the bathroom and the scullery, complaints about the lavatory and the telephone, noise and contention. Moreover, it seemed to her that her tenants did not like her, which distressed her more than anything: they were, after all, her chosen people, each and every one of them. Thus isolated, she was prepared even to relinquish the upper hand and mention this to the voice, to seek, maybe, its advice and guidance as in the old days: the voice, disconcertingly, was silent. She lay alone in her bedroom and brooded on what had come about.

And so, when next she heard the Health Visitor in the hall she opened her door.

The Health Visitor did not mince her words. She said there were too many people in the house, too few lavatories, and a smell of drains from out the back somewhere that must be investigated forthwith. She was brisk, but not unpleasant. Avril, less disposed to hostility than on the previous occasion, promised to summon a plumber. The Health Visitor, studying her intently across the table, said 'And another thing, dear, it's neither here nor there but you do seem to go in for coloured people as tenants, don't you? You've got some of your neighbours properly upset, I can tell you, though as I say that's neither here nor there.'

And so it came about that Avril, because she never had anyone to talk to these days, and because the Health Visitor seemed really quite a nice little body after all, began to tell her about the voice. And as she talked, the Health Visitor, who had been gathering her belongings and indeed had got up from the chair to go, sat down again, and let her bag slither to the floor, and listened with an expression that grew more and more alert and more and more unfathomable. She said, 'Yes?' and 'I see, dear' and nodded and smiled her nice professional smile; it was quite impossible to know what she thought. 'So you see,' Avril concluded, 'It wasn't altogether my choice, though I'm not saying I wasn't perfectly willing to go along with it, more than willing.' And the Health Visitor said yes, she quite understood that, and then she patted Avril on the hand and said she'd look in again, quite soon, in a few days' time maybe.

The conversation, Avril found, had been a release. She'd been keeping herself to herself too much, she realised, no wonder people had been behaving as though she were a bit peculiar or something. And, thinking things over, and remembering the Health Visitor's sympathetic, encouraging interest, it came to her that her experience had been a singular one and, as such, should be shared, not kept from others. And the one person, she reflected (though with slight regret, for she had never really cared much for the man) with whom it should be shared, whose professional concern, after all, it was, was the Vicar. She telephoned the vicarage, and made an appointment to call that evening.

Later, she mulled over her disappointment in the privacy of her room. She had not, before her visit, speculated much if at all about what kind of response she would get: she had expected professional interest, that was all there was to it. And what she had met with had been something quite different.

It could most nearly be described, she thought with anger, as embarrassment. He had sat there, that rather colourless man (even her mother, she now recalled, used to describe him as wishy-washy), and avoided her eye and leapt with alacrity to the phone when it rang and eventually, it seemed to her, cut short the visit and bundled her from the house. There had been a look on his face of alarm, no less. He had said not one thing that had been in any way appropriate. And, Avril thought with bitterness, which, if any, of his parishioners can ever before have come to him and told him, in cold blood and in all humility, what I told

33

him?

She went about her affairs, but in a state of some cynicism. The voice remained silent, though she made tentative overtures, in the privacy of her nights.

The Health Visitor returned, bringing with her another woman, described as Mrs Hamilton who would like a little chat with you, dear. Mrs Hamilton had the same quality of attentive, sympathetic and yet non-committal interest as the Health Visitor. She wondered if Avril would like to tell her about this voice she sometimes heard and Avril, with the bitter taste of the Vicar's inadequacy still in her mouth, was glad to do so. Mrs Hamilton asked if she still had conversations with the voice and Avril explained that a coolness had arisen, but she hoped in time to put that right. She might possibly, she realised now, have been a bit assertive with it, a bit forceful; she would make amends for that. I like, Avril said, talking to it, even if it was, to begin with, on the bullying side, inclined to order people around, if you see what I mean. I don't mind telling you, she went on confidingly, it remined me of my mother, there was quite a resemblance there.

Mrs Hamilton listened and nodded and smiled. She asked Avril some questions, questions that were maybe a bit personal, Avril thought, and that did not have anything to do with what they had been talking about, or not in any way that she could see. But she seemed a nice enough person, and Avril did not really mind; nor did she mind, though she was surprised, when Mrs Hamilton asked if she would come and have a chat (everybody seemed to want a chat . . .) with a colleague of hers, a Doctor someone, at a place where Mrs Hamilton worked, called the Clinic.

It was nice to have people taking so much interest in you.

And at the Clinic they took even more interest. They nodded and listened and from time to time jotted down a few words on a little white notepad. They seemed to have nothing to do but listen, these people. Avril began, at their suggestion, to pay regular visits to the Clinic; the visits became part of the cycle of her week, like the Red Cross, and the Scout and Guide Hut, and evensong. And as the visits went on the voice was heard once more, in the solitude of the nights. And Avril, pleased to have something more substantial and up-to-date for her new friends, reported everything it said, though what it had to say was sometimes embarrassing. For it evidently distrusted these people. Don't, it said. Don't go there. Don't talk to them. Don't talk to them about me.

They won't understand, it said. It spoke sulkily. It knew what it was talking about, it said. It had come across all this before. If you knew what I know, it said darkly, if you'd seen what I've seen. They're what we're up against, it said, people like that.

Avril answered conciliatingly. She placated. She tried to conceal her visits to the Clinic.

The voice, of course, knew.

She thought the voice a little uncompromising; the people at the Clinic after all, displayed no such unswerving prejudice, where the voice was concerned. They were interested, not hostile.

The situation in the house deteriorated; the drains flooded again, Brenda and the Chinese girl, at loggerheads, had a scrap on the stairs in which blood was shed.

At the Clinic, they wondered, in their quiet friendly voices, if Avril would like to come in for a few weeks. For a rest, they said, for treatment. They used the expression in-patient, which startled Avril. She had not realised how things were, until it was put like that, and now it seemed too late to turn back.

But it's not that I . . . she wanted to say, there's no question of . . . But there, now, were the little white note-books, and the filing cabinets and her name on a pink form, and it seemed so much easier to go along with them, be obliging, and in any case it was not all that disagreeable a place, the Clinic, and the problems of the house, its drains and its plumbing and its tenantry, hung round her neck like so many albatrosses.

She did not tell the voice. She packed her small case that very afternoon and left. Neither did she tell the tenants. With sudden detachment, she thought, well, they will have to sort things out for themselves, I have played my part, I have arranged the house, as I was told, now they must take care of themselves. I have myself to think of.

And in a different bed, that night, she waited for the voice. And presently, in the populated gloom of the ward, it manifested itself. Now look where you have got us, it complained, now look where you have landed us.

Listen, it said, craftily, listen and do as I tell you. Tell them that this is what I said to you . . . Tell them that this is what I told you to do . . .

It lectured on, with renewed confidence, so loudly that she thought it impossible that she alone could hear.

Interpreting the Past

The town of Houghcester (pronounced Hosta) was much given over, in the summer of 1977, to its antecedents; indeed, you could have called the past a growth industry. And Houghcester had, of course, plenty of it, ranging from prehistoric – not much to show of that, bar some quite nice flints, axe-heads and reconstituted burial urns in the City Museum – on through the more conveniently demonstrable layers of Roman, Saxon, medieval and so forth. It was a well-endowed place, and never had its endowments been more skilfully exploited; it had taken to tourism with magnificent effect. Since towns cannot do their book-keeping as precisely as other commercial concerns, it would not be possible to estimate even roughly how many dollars, yen, francs etc. Houghcester had earned, but if it were, the place would have been justified in claiming a Queen's Award to Industry.

All this, though, makes the town sound insensitively profit-minded. In fact, Houghcester was decently proud of its history, and concerned to make the most of it in every sense.

The excavation of the Priory was being carried out by the Houghcester City Archaeological Unit, financed by public money (with a few private contributions), and supervised by the Chief Archaeological Officer. The diggers, rank and file, were a mixture of professional archaeologists and volunteer helpers.

The volunteers ranged in age from sixteen to thirty-one and had various reasons for being there. Three were students of archaeology, one had been sent by her parents, one wished to impress her history teacher at school, with whom she was emotionally obsessed, another was unemployed and wanted to get away from home, and three liked outdoor life and were at a loose end.

Susan Price was there because she had been crossed in love.

She was nineteen and the experience was new to her; she found its effect devastating. She had never been profoundly unhappy before, but being a sensible and stoical girl she had decided to treat her condition like a debilitating illness, battle with it alone, look to the future, and seek some useful occupation. She saw the dig advertised in *The Times*, and applied.

The objectives of the dig were briefly stated: to establish, as far as possible, the ground-plan of the Saxon church which pre-dated the medieval Priory church (itself almost literally in the shadow of Houghcester's famous cathedral) of which little now remained except the walls, and investigate the Priory burial ground which lay above the foundations of the early church. The skeletons, after removal and examination for demographic and medical purposes, were to be reinterred with Christian rites (most of them were thirteenth and fourteenth century, with a few from the Saxon Christian period), and the site tidied up and planted out as a municipal garden, preserving the ruined walls.

The diggers crouched as though in worship above their allotted squares of ground, each with paraphernalia of plastic bucket, trowel, brush, shovel and paintbrush for meticulous clearance work. It was a good summer, and they wore, for the most part, jeans or tattered shorts, T-shirts or (for the men) nav-vies' vests. Some of them had straw hats. The site, at this stage of its clearance, looked like the dusty section of a bee-hive – many shallow dirt pits, some with the delicate tracery of a person laid bare, dome of skull, rib-cage, hand splayed out like a fan, others with leg-bones sticking out from the dry wall of soil, or a huddle of tibia, fibula, crania and so forth that must be carefully exposed and photographed before being removed.

Maggie Spink, the director of the dig, moved all day long around the site, checking, measuring, photographing, removing finds (the detritus of sherds, fragments of china, buttons, gnarled twigs of metal, bits of clay pipe and lumps of aged glass that had accumulated at every layer) and chivvying those who knocked off periodically for a smoke in the sun. Since the site lay at the very heart of Houghcester, and on the route from the multi-storey car park to the cathedral, she had to deal also with the mild curiosity of the public, who were fenced off with wattle hurdles. When obliged to answer their questions, she was patient, but a little aloof; she would explain – briefly – the objectives and achievements of the dig, while – tacitly – making it clear that a more complex account would be above their heads. Those professionally concerned with the past, she seemed to suggest, are indeed accountable for what they are doing, but only up to a point; we are all technicians, now, and our ancestors are best approached with a proper expertise.

She was a dumpy woman in her late thirties, with short straw-coloured hair, a large bottom and brusque manner. She dressed with what seemed an aggressive disregard for femininity. Susan Price was much alarmed by her, during her first few days on the dig, and deplored particularly the ankle-socks worn with open sandals.

'You're reading what at Bristol?' she had said to Susan, and when Susan had replied, English, she had said 'Why?'

To which Susan could find no reply at all.

The other professional archaeologists treated her with respect: she was, they informed the volunteers, first-class at the job, she had a growing reputation, had dug at this place and that, been associated with a string of impressive names. The volunteers approached her with circumspection; they had all, on arrival, been a little surprised to find their presence accepted not with gratitude, but rather as though the benefit were the other way round. They were privileged, Maggie seemed to suggest, on her introductory tour of instruction and explanation, to be apprenticed in this way. It was as though they were permitted to be acolytes at the religious ceremony of some sect from which they were bound, by their nature, to be excluded. For some, this was tantalising; they picked up the technical jargon of the archaeologists and brandished it around. For a few it was irritating; one young schoolteacher left after two days, complaining that he had been patronised. For most, it was neither here nor there; they had come to pass the time, not to have opinions.

Susan Price, at the beginning, was only partly there in any case.

She squatted over Burial No. 38, brushing crumbs of soil from a battered rib-cage, and addressed someone quite different: I expect you will be in France by now, she said, you and Jane. I can see you – I only wish I couldn't – sitting by the road, waiting for the next lift. Jane is all brown by now, I daresay, looking very nice. I am brown, too, as it happens, for what that's worth which is not much since I never look at myself in a mirror, these days, there doesn't seem a lot of point.

When, exactly did you start to go off me? I have to put it bluntly, because I suspect that only through bluntness am I going to get over this (do people?). I think, examining things, it must have been around that time we went to Bath for the day; I didn't realise it then, but looking back, I can detect a whiff of indifference. And then, there was that time you didn't turn up when we'd arranged to meet after my lecture and now I realise you must have . . .

The dig packed up, each day, at five thirty. The plastic bags of finds were removed to the disused Victorian school nearby which had been made over to the Unit for the summer; there, Maggie Spink would begin her evening's work of sorting and classification, while the rest filled in their 'skelly charts' – the surviving bits of person coloured in on a blue-print of what there ought to be, a heap of eccentric skeleton portraits with one red leg, six ribs, half a cranium, or pelvis and right foot only. They then dispersed to their homes or to the old police station scheduled for demolition in the autumn – allotted to the rest as a billet. There, they heated baked beans on primuses, talked, read, or wandered off into the city.

Susan, for whom the process of self-distraction was a primary concern, bought guide-books and did the job properly. She studied the place as though she might be required to answer examination questions on it. She wandered in the cathedral for hours on end.

The cathedral prospered all summer long; tourists flowed through it from early morning till sunset — American, French, German, Dutch, English — a quick canter, a leisurely stroll, a protracted tour of inspection according to age, temperament and degree of interest. Not since the era of pilgrimages could the place have done such good business. Admittedly, the poor and the uncharitable slid quickly past the prominent Appeal Box at the entrance, but almost everyone bought postcards, tea-towels, leather book-marks tooled in gold with a brass-rubbing of Sir Toby and Lady Falconer (c. 1428), pottery mugs picturing the west front, transparencies of the stained glass. The chapter house, converted into a tea-room and snack bar, was also enjoying a boom. Outside, in the cloisters and on the green, itinerant young of all nationalities sprawled in the sunshine. The cathedral officials presided with benevolence and tact, discreetly hovering behind pillars and at entrances, ready with information should it be required, not intruding unless invited. Not everyone wants Perpendicular windows, late Saxon wall-paintings or fifteenth century misericords thrust upon them, after all, they may be there for quite other reasons — to placate their relatives, for a cup of tea, a break from driving, a snooze or a cuddle on the grass. The past has no right to impose itself on people; it is there to be taken or left, as we see fit, as it suits us. It is our turn now.

Susan, her guide-books in hand, diligently sorted out styles and periods. She noted the surviving medieval street plan of the city — surviving in name and spirit only for most of the early buildings had been torn down in the post-war zest for reconstruction. She agreed with Professor Pevsner that not all — indeed not much — of the reconstruction was successful. The shopping precinct, the Public Library, the new council offices, all had an aggressive immaturity, at odds with their background. They had not yet settled down, were in uneasy conflict with the old almshouses, the one remaining medieval gateway; in Sheep Street, which suggested quite other things, Boots and Mothercare confronted one another with a blaze of plate glass.

The cathedral was mature, all right. It had been quietly

maturing away there since its foundation in the early eleventh century, to such effect that the west tower was now in need of a massive underpinning job, the roof would have to be completely stripped and re-leaded, and the external carvings were in a sorry state. The appeal target had been pushed up perforce from £750,000 to a round million. The Friends (of the cathedral, that is) were working flat out.

Susan, who had never before paid much attention to architecture, found herself not only distracted from her mourning but curiously soothed by the cathedral. There was something reassuring about this juxtaposition of period and mood, in which, eventually, what has been and what is now are reconciled and live together.

Her fellow diggers were less concerned with the place. The professional archaeologists spent much of the evenings, when they were not helping Maggie Spink in the school, discussing their career prospects; the rest – the amateurs – regretted the lack of a television and amused themselves as best they could. If they could afford cinema or pub, they went out; if not, they lounged on their camp-beds, ate, drank tea and gossiped. In the intimacy of their closed society a sense of being cronies had soon been established, a defensive solidarity as the unskilled labouring mass. The student teacher and the girl from Nottingham had begun a flirtation that looked like developing into something more; the Welsh boy taught everyone to play poker and kept intense noisy games going till late at night. They talked about themselves, about each other, about Maggie Spink.

'Hey . . .' said Gwyn, dealing the cards one evening. 'I found something out today. She's not a Miss at all, our Maggie, she's a Mrs. There's been a mister, but there ain't no more. He skipped out on her.'

Someone said, 'Wouldn't you?' There were giggles.

Maggie Spink appeared, on the dig's official documents, as Dr Spink. And yet, it was true, a married state was inconceivable, for less easily definable reasons than her ringless hands, her stridently self-sufficient manner. The girl from Nottingham said, 'How do you know?'

42

'John Hacker told me' – John Hacker was one of the career archaeologists – 'It was all years ago and she's dropped her married name and gone back to what she was called before and she gets hopping mad if anyone ever mentions it.'

'Lots of people don't use married names now – women –specially if they've been working before, had careers.'

'Get Ms Women's Lib there!'

'Oh, shut up,' said the girl from Nottingham. 'I was only saying. Here – it's your deal.'

Susan Price was vaguely moved by this exchange; she felt a creak of compassion for Maggie, a person who had not, hitherto, seemed in any way approachable. Even so, the feeling did not go very deep; she was still bound up in her own day to day survival, was only superficially present. Her internal monologues, though, she was surprised to note, were taking on a slightly different tone.

What about you? she said to Burial No. 47. Did you ever have to endure this kind of thing? Sexual jealousy, it's called, and it's just about the nastiest feeling I've ever come across. Actually, since you were probably a nun I daresay it didn't arise – I hope not, for your sake. You didn't live all that long, of course – female, aged thirty to forty, level 306, right arm, pelvis and ribcage, lower jaw-bone, left femur and metatarsus. You had a lot of trouble with your teeth, and what was probably arthritis, according to John Hacker, and there is evidence of malnutrition.

I'm not a lot better, not yet. Curiously, the thought of her – Jane – is the worst; that's the one I have to squash firmest. With him it's different; since I've got to think of him all the time, can't help it, then I might as well accept it. Re-run things, as it were, like an old film. It hurts; the funny thing is that each time it looks ever so slightly different.

That weekend at his parents' he was a bit off-hand with his mother; I didn't notice at the time. It's as though, then, I saw him head-on, in one way only (is that's what meant by love being blinkered?); now I remember things I didn't really register then. That conversation we had once about abstract pictures, in that art gallery, I remember every word (what I have to avoid is the feel of his arm round me, when we were having it . . .) but I find I'm

43

not agreeing with him quite so much. Oh, but . . . I'd want to say, if we were having it again, and, no I think you're wrong about that what I think is . . .

July became August; the cathedral clocked up its first hundred thousand of the Appeal, and celebrated by staging *son et lumière* for the next four weeks; the diggers, scratching their way down through levels 273–401, became a small, enclosed sect, in much the same way as the priory whose detectable past they were so efficiently interpreting. There was a hierarchy, alliances and enmities, in-jokes and tribal jargon. One or two departed, a couple more came and were absorbed. The weather held. In the school the burials were stacked in heaps of plastic bags, awaiting collection; the skelly charts filled two walls; trestle tables were covered with trays of finds. Unexpected dramas or reverses punctuated the routine of the days: a conjectured drain turned out to be the entrance to an eighteenth century charnel house, heavily populated, which was re-sealed after hasty investigation; the interesting depressions running parallel to the nave of the Saxon church proved to be Victorian celery beds, also an irrelevant intrusion. The past is a disorderly and unreliable affair; you cannot trust it very far.

Susan, all one long, hot day, scraped with paintbrush and trowel around the fragile, bird-like bones of a baby (level 372, male, probably still-born, date uncertain, and what was *that* doing in a nunnery?). You'll have got to the Mediterranean by now, she said, if you've been lucky with lifts, or maybe you're in Spain, like you said you might, when we had that last talk, that awful one, when I cried (which makes me hot with shame to think of, I never cry). I slept rather well last night, you might be interested to hear, first time for ages.

I have been going over everything we ever said to each other; sometimes, quite frankly, you seem to me a bit opinionated. Not that that means I *feel* any different, now; it is just rather interesting.

The thing is, am I changing you, or is that how you were? How will I ever know?

Either the heat, or the Victorian celery beds, had put Maggie

44

Spink into an irritable state. She chivvied everybody, extended the working day by half an hour, and kept going on about how the excavation was behind schedule. 'That is the trouble about a dig with a predominantly amateur element – you simply cannot get the right sense of urgency into people.' Susan, tracing the tiny bleached splinters of the baby's foot, felt a shadow across her back and looked up into Maggie's sun-reddened face. She was agitated, on the edge of an outburst. After some discussion of the burial, and examination of a small heap of sherds, she said suddenly, 'I've had to separate those two. I really cannot stand all that whispering and pawing on the site. Tim can go and number finds in the school'.

The affair between the student teacher and the girl from Nottingham had prospered.

Susan smiled. 'Oh dear,' she said, 'I'm sure they don't really mean . . .'

Maggie said violently, 'If they want to fuck that's entirely up to them, but not on my dig, thank you very much'. Her outrage seemed quite out of proportion to the offence; Susan, embarrassed, turned back to the baby. Lately, she had found herself for some reason the object of the older woman's gruff favour; she was considered apparently more serious and responsible than the rest. Once, Maggie had said 'It's a pity you didn't think of reading archaeology. You might have done quite well'. Susan had repeated this to one of the younger career archaeologists, who had laughed – 'Oh, Maggie doesn't recognise other branches of study. You should have told her English literature is quite well-regarded too'.

Now, Maggie had walked off along the narrow earth balk that served as a cat-walk among the burial pits, Susan, sitting back for a moment to wipe her face – the heat was exhausting – saw her ankle-socks, her stocky legs, her large loose bottom, and felt a rush of pity; there was something schoolgirlish about the woman, as though she carried an albatross adolescence with her, some fatal undevelopment of the heart.

The separation of the lovers caused general merriment. Maggie was determined to run a clean site, it was suggested, in every sense. Or maybe she wished to preserve the moral spirit of the priory.

Susan had taken to wandering around the cathedral and its precincts for half an hour or so most evenings, before it grew dark and the place was given over to the portentous booming of the *son et lumière*. It was there, a few days later, that she met Maggie, who came striding through the cloister where Susan was sitting on a low inner wall, enjoying the effects of evening sunlight on the fan-vaulting. Seeing her, Maggie stopped.

'Oh, hello, what on earth are you doing here?'

'Nothing, particularly. Just that it's specially nice at this time of day.'

'Is it? I wouldn't know. I had to see the cathedral people about this Open Day idea — endless talk, wasting half my evening. I haven't even started on the finds yet, or mapping these new walls.' She had begun to move on again, saying 'Are you going back?' Susan, who had intended to sit for longer, found herself drawn alongside. She said, 'Open Day?'

'They want us to have an Open Day on the site,' said Maggie irritably, 'to coincide with their junketings. It's the thousandth anniversary of the reconsecration or something. Anyway, they want us to do conducted tours of the site, with explanatory talks and stuff, and a display of the finds and whatnot.'

Susan said, 'Isn't that rather a nice idea?'

'Why?'

'Well, get people interested. And they are, they're always asking us things . . .' Catching Maggie's expression she added, 'Of course, I'm afraid we're not all that good at explaining, but we do what we can'.

Maggie said, 'Oh, I suppose so. But it means losing a whole day'.

They had reached the west door of the cathedral. Susan, arrested as always by the delicacy of the carvings, the tier upon tier of saints, the lavish complexity of leaves, of beasts, of fact and fantasy, of the pious and the secular, was silent. Maggie, walking quickly through, said 'We can do a short cut through the building, can't we? Oh, I suppose I'll have to go along with them — I did point out that it was mucking up our schedule, but I doubt if that sank in far. There was one bloke who had what I suppose was quite a valid point about attracting possible funds. You never know who may show up – local big-wigs and so forth. We need at least another season on this dig and if the Ministry grant is the same next year it quite frankly won't do'.

It was almost eight; the tourists had ebbed, leaving the cathedral in a sombre peace, except for occasional quackings over the loud-speakers outside, getting themselves into good voice for the night's event. The Gift Shop had closed, and the Chapter House Refreshment Bar. Evensong (shifted forward by an hour to accommodate the *son et lumière*) was over. It was chill, much cooler than outside, and there was that curious unanalysable ecclesiastical smell of stone, brass polish and something that could not in an Anglican cathedral be incense, and yet was oddly reminiscent. It was as though the place generated its own climate, regardless of contemporary conditions. Sunlight poured through the clerestory windows, defining quatrefoils and shafts, losing its intensity as it fell down the heights of the building to become a rainbow reflection on the hefty piers of the nave. Elsewhere, at ground level, dusk had muted all the conflicts and confusions of daylight – the material variety of marble, stone, wood, brass, iron; the shufflings of time and style; the polyglot babble of visitors. It had, for once, a unity.

Susan said, with diffidence 'I always think it's odd you can have this part so Norman, and then all the rest later, and somehow it works. I've never really looked properly at a cathedral before'.

'Mmn' said Maggie. 'Of course there's a lot of nonsense talked about the original plan – the official guide-book's quite wrong, Battersby did it and he's notoriously unsound.' They had reached the main entrance. Standing in a flood of multi-coloured light from the rose window, her face bathed in it, suddenly beautified, as though by some divine intervention – the miraculous staunching of a wound, the non-putrefaction of a corpse – she went on grudgingly, 'Oh well, I suppose I'll have to lay it on, this bally Open Day. You could help John and Steve with the chat bits, I won't be able to do it all and you've picked up quite a lot really'. She moved, and her face turned from rose to gold. 'By the way, why did you come on the dig? One wonders vaguely sometimes – you know, what brings people.'

It was the first time Susan had ever heard her express curiosity about another person, she realised; Maggie seemed usually quite set apart from ordinary probings and exchanges, like someone with a heavy cold, or the impediment of a language difficulty.

Susan had never told anyone on the dig of her private preoccupation. Now, she said 'Oh, I just thought I'd like to do something different for part of the summer, learn about something new'.

Saying it, she felt shabby in the untruth, as though she had in some curious way misused the place: the beauty of the cathedral, those inaccessible people whose bones she handled every day.

But Maggie had already lost interest. She said, with a glance at her watch, 'Oh God – nearly half past eight, I'll be in the school till all hours. See you tomorrow', and strode away over the precinct; at the far side, people were assembling on the scaffolding from which the *son et lumière* could be best appreciated; behind, the cathedral awaited its nightly bashing by searchlight and sepulchral voices.

The preparations for the Open Day drove Maggie into a frenzy of exasperated activity ('. . . though I don't know what the hell I'm thinking of, letting the schedule be set back by at least two or three days just so we can stand around answering a lot of no doubt irrelevant questions, still, I suppose public relations *do* matter . . .'): the school was cleared, insofar as possible, and a display of finds arranged on trestle tables. A large, explanatory plan of the site was drawn by Gwyn and the girl from Nottingham, the chronology clarified by the use of different coloured tempo pens. Maggie and the other professionals divided up the site between them, each to guard and explain his or her own territory. The volunteers were detailed off onto stewarding duties. Susan was in charge of the school, and had the job of explaining the finds.

They were all surprised by the success of the occasion. Admittedly, the weather helped, but even a warm sunny day could not entirely account for the file of people who shuffled through the site, tiptoeing along the cat-walks, keeping a respectful distance from Maggie's NO VISITORS BEYOND THIS POINT signs, listening, asking questions. In the school, Susan was hemmed in. She felt like an overtaxed shop-assistant or barmaid, explaining her wares for hour after hour – the Roman pottery, the fragments of painted tile from the Priory, the coins and buttons and broken combs, the medieval shoe, the fourteenth century slipware dish (almost complete), the pins and nails and pipe-bowls, the bones of the stillborn baby arranged on cottonwool in a shoebox (the rest of the burials were stacked away in their plastic bags in the school washroom).

It had been intended that they should close down at five o'clock. However, this was presumably not made clear in the publicity put out by the cathedral authorities, for at five fifteen the queue waiting for admission still reached the length of the outer wattle barrier. There was a hasty consultation. Maggie wanted to make a firm announcement and have any further comers turned away; she was prevailed on to continue till six, and grudgingly agreed. By a quarter to six she had left her own section of the site and was patrolling, looking at her watch and frowning, as though she would stem the flow by sheer force of will. She seemed in an odd state of combined irritation and elation. All day, her voice had been high-pitched in its rattle of explanation and instruction; she had been impatient with questioners.

Coming into the school, where a couple of dozen people were still filing past the trestle tables, she lifted her wrist, tapped her watch, mouthed at Susan 'Time's up'. She edged past the visitors, and said sharply to a small child whose fingers had crept towards the shoebox containing the baby's bones, 'Don't touch, please'.

The baby had roused interest, all day. Everybody had wanted to speculate about how old, and why, and when. A midwife had offered technical explanations, gleaned from something about the shape of the skull. This particular child had been staring, fascinated, for several minutes. Now, he said suddenly to Susan, 'Am I like that inside?'

She said 'Yes'. His parents, over by the door, were signalling to him to come. Slowly, he spread out his hand, staring at the fingers. Looking up at her again, he said 'Will I be like that when I'm deaded?'

She hesitated, glancing for a moment at the parents, still signalling, at Maggie's expression of fretful endurance. She said, 'Yes. And me'.

The child nodded gravely; he shot out his thin arm and stared at it. Then he turned and went after his parents. Maggie sighed and said 'Well, I suppose we must count ourselves lucky if nothing's been damaged or nicked. I hope nothing *has* been damaged or nicked?'

Susan said, 'I don't think so'. The last visitors were leaving now. Maggie said 'Well, that's it'. She drew her hand across her forehead, and Susan saw that it was shaking. From outside, the other volunteers were waving with glass-raising gestures: they were off to the pub. She said to Maggie, 'I'm going now. I'll come back later and help straighten up in here, if you like'. She felt another of those small rushes of sympathy: that shaking hand – why, in what way, had the day been such a strain?

It was a couple of hours before she returned to the school, and was surprised to find Maggie alone: she had imagined that John Hacker and the others would have been there. Maggie said 'Oh, I told them to push off, I can get on quicker on my own', adding – not very graciously – 'I'd forgotten you said you'd come – actually you could give me a hand with these sherds, they seem to have got somewhat muddled up'.

Her voice was slightly slurred. She reached under the table and brought out a half empty bottle of wine, 'Here, d'you want a drink? There's another glass on the windowsill, I think.'

She had done little about clearing up; the display of finds was much as it had been earlier. Instead, she seemed to have been fiddling with some bits of glazed pottery, the pieces of the slipware dish which, it was thought, could probably be reconstructed for the City Museum.

Susan said, 'It's just like stuff in trendy shops now, isn't it, that glaze?'

'Is it? I s'pose so.' Maggie began to talk about the day. '. . . Pretty well impossible to get across to people what this sort of thing is really about' – she squinted at a glazed fragment, 'That's later – how's that got in with this lot? Yes, it's from Pit 18 – I knew people would start messing things about. And all those endless irrelevant questions – like that kid you were talking to. There were kids all over the place – I was going spare at some moments, thinking they'd crash down into a burial or something.'

Susan said, 'I didn't think he *was* irrelevant – that little boy'.

'What?' Maggie slopped some more wine into her glass, waved the bottle at Susan – who saw now with a twitch of alarm that there was another bottle, empty, under the table.

Maggie talked. About past digs; about her doctorate; about the write-up of the current dig which, if things worked out right, should do her reputation '. . . no harm at all, in fact rather a lot of good – I think I may put out an interim thing even before next season'. And then, suddenly, she was talking about more personal things '. . . You didn't know I was married once, did you?' She chuckled, waving the bottle again. 'More? Come on, we might as well finish it.'

Susan, embarrassed, said 'Well, actually, someone did once say . . .'

'That's something that simply isn't relevant either, my marriage. What's happened is over and done with. You just don't give it another thought, if you've got any sense – you move on. It's the only way to live, if you ask me.' She paused, shoving the sherds around on the table in front of her like pieces of a jigsaw puzzle. 'When Derek walked out on me I thought, right, that's that. Finished. Kaput. Take a deep breath and forget it. He wasn't an archaeologist, by the way – that was one thing that was wrong from the start. And, frankly now, it's as though he never was. Do you know, I can't really remember what he looked like.' She squinted up at Susan, her expression distinctly triumphant. 'He absolutely no longer exists.'

There was a silence. Maggie took a swig at her drink. Susan said awkwardly, 'Actually, I think – I don't know – if it was me,

I think I'd want to try to work out why – try to see what it was that had happened to me, after all it's all going to be part of the person you end up being and in that case . . .'

'You're wrong,' said Maggie flatly. 'You go nuts that way, mulling things over. Take my word for it. Wipe the slate clean – wham!' She swept her arm across the table in a decisive gesture; sherds and other bits and pieces went flying; she was quite drunk now. She slumped with her head cupped in her hands, elbows on the table, as Susan scrambled on the floor, picking things up. 'Wham! Bam! Finish!'

A large piece of floor tile from the early church was shattered into several smaller pieces; the base of a glass bottle was broken, too; the shoebox had upended, scattering the baby's bones all over the place. Carefully, Susan gathered everything up. Some bones, she saw anxiously, had slipped down between two worm-eaten floorboards and would have to be retrieved tomorrow, somehow, with pincers or something, or at the worst one would have to take the boards up.

She said to Maggie, gently 'Wouldn't you like to go back to your digs now? You look awfully tired'.

'I'm never tired. And I'll tell you another thing – celibacy's a damn sight more comfortable than people make out. Don't you be fooled.' She scowled at the sherds in front of her, roughly assembled in the form of a dish, and shunted them into confusion again with a savage gesture, spilling more onto the floor. Susan said, 'Oh please – come on, Maggie, let's go now'.

Maggie shoved her chair back from the table. She stared vacantly at the window, at the night sky, at the lurid glimmer of the cathedral, 'You take my advice, Susan, I'm a lot older than you and I know how it goes. I know the score. Don't you ever let yourself be lumbered with what's over and done with. Travel light, that's what.' Her face was red and shiny; she looked older than she was and also, in some elusive way, younger: her features had, still, the chubbiness, the expectancy, of a girl's face. She groaned suddenly. 'Oh God, what a day! I *hate* having people all around me like that, on and on . . .'

Susan took her arm. 'I'll walk back with you.'

They went out together. Maggie, staggering a little, would have left the place open; Susan found the key hanging behind the door and locked up. Walking through the empty streets, Maggie said blearily, 'Well, thanks for helping, anyway. You know, as I say, it's a pity you never thought of doing archaeology'. She tapped Susan's arm, peering sideways at her in the darkness. 'It's not half a bad career – I mean, yes, it's badly paid and all that, but there's more important things than that, aren't there? I'll tell you one thing – I've never been bored, not for fifteen years, and you can't say that in every job, can you?'

Susan walked slowly back to the police station. It was quite late; she had not been back since that morning; the others were playing poker. Someone said, 'Hey – there's a letter for you.'

She sat on the edge of her camp-bed, reading it. 'I got back a few days ago' he wrote. 'Actually, Jane and I parted company around Rouen. It wasn't really working out all that well. I rang your mother and she said you were on this dig thing (that threw me a bit, I must say! Whatever put that idea into your head!) but probably going to finish at the end of the week. So what I've been wondering, Sue, is should I come down there and fetch you? I think I could get hold of my dad's car and maybe we could go off and have a few days somewhere . . .'

She sat there for a while, holding the letter, seeing, beyond the windows, the flare of the cathedral, hearing, behind the slam of the poker players' cards, the muffled and distorted boom of the loudspeakers, ending their nightly re-enactment of Houghcester's long and complex history. Then she got out her pad and began to write a reply: 'Actually,' she wrote, 'I think I'll stay on here a bit longer, maybe till the beginning of next term, more or less – some of the others are off soon, and I'd like to help out the woman who is in charge, I've come to feel a bit sorry for her. I suppose she's not all that nice but she means well. It has been in-teresting – seeing what people do who are professionally involved with history, as it were, I feel I've learned things, though I suppose nothing that's likely to be useful . . .'

Servants talk about People:
Gentlefolk discuss Things

'I think I knew his father', said my uncle. 'Was he in India during the war?'

I said, 'I've really no idea. I don't know Mark all that well. I only mentioned him because I . . .'

'That'll be him,' said my uncle, with furrowed brow. 'He was in Calcutta in '43. Man with a limp. Played the trombone. Waiter! Could we have the menu?'

The menu, size of a wall-poster, was propped up before us by, in fact, a waitress. Even in the expensive murk of the restaurant it was difficult not to sense barely restrained passion of some kind; she stared over my uncle's head at the swing door leading to, presumably, the kitchens. My uncle, poring over the tortuously hand-written placard, said 'I hope this place'll be all right. Neighbour of ours recommended it. They seem to go in for veal in a big way. Would you like a starter?'

The room was small – not more than half a dozen tables, only four of which were occupied – decorated in dark reds and browns with vaguely Edwardian connotations. The cuisine, from the menu, was an uncommitted mixture of continental and Sunday newspaper. My uncle said to the waitress, 'Three sherries, please, we'll order when my wife comes back'. He had to repeat himself, the girl being apparently locked in her communion of hatred with the kitchen door. 'Lucy's taking her time,' said my uncle, with irritation, looking towards the stairs.

They had arrived late and my aunt sped at once in the direction of the Ladies. She returned now with an expression of relief, freshly combed and made-up, and dabbed each cheek in turn against mine before she sat down. 'Lovely to see you, Tim. Do you know, there was a woman in there *exactly* like Aunt Christie. Do you remember Aunt Christie?'

'Not really, I was only about two when she died.'

'This woman had longer hair. Otherwise she was the spitting image. Fortyish.'

My uncle handed her the menu. 'Christie was fifty when she died. Tummy cancer. I've ordered you a sherry, Lucy. Forty-five pence, I may say – disgraceful.'

'It's a rip-off' said my aunt, who took pride in modernity of speech. She fished her glasses out of her handbag and studied the menu. 'I'll have veal with marsala sauce, and avocado to start. Now, we want to hear all your news, Tim.'

'Well,' I began. 'I suppose the main thing is that . . .'

My uncle interrupted, 'Does Mark Sadler live in Tunbridge Wells? That's where his father hailed from, I remember'.

'Honestly,' I said, 'I hardly know him – it was just that I went to a party of his once, when I was at college, in this street, so I knew where the restaurant was when you suggested meeting here.'

'Sadler?' said my aunt, putting her glasses away. 'Did I know him?' She was as spry as ever, her appearance nicely adjusted to the times; the glasses, at first sight grannyish, were up-to-the-minute fashion. Her calf and ankle, sticking out from under the dark brown linen tablecloth, were elegant. My uncle, as always, had the extremely clean, slightly over-fed look of a certain kind of upper-class Englishman. He was looking round now, with some impatience, for the waitress. 'Where's the fellow gone, we want to order?'

In fact, the sound of raised voices had been clearly audible, for the last five minutes or so, from beyond the swing door. As my uncle spoke, a longish male monologue, rising to a crescendo, was answered by something that resembled the hiss of escaping steam, followed instantly by a noise of breakage. I said, 'It was a girl, actually. There seems to be . . .' At the same moment the door opened and the waitress bounded through, her face contorted. She came to rest at my uncle's elbow, sniffing loudly.

My uncle said, 'Ah. Now we want a veal marsala, a cannelloni, and I'll have the duck. And an avocado and two pickled herrings to start with. And the wine-list, please. You wouldn't have known Sadler' he went on, to my aunt. 'It was in the war. But he'd been at school with Jimmy Phillips.'

'I never liked Jimmy Phillips all that much. I hope they hurry up, I'm starving.'

The waitress had returned to the kitchen, and re-emerged now with two main courses for the table next to ours, at which a pair of young and spruce executives were engaged in competitive discourse. In the confidential light of the red-shaded wall lamps, tears could be seen trickling down her face. My aunt said, 'That girl's got a filthy cold – I hope she doesn't give it to us'.

'Well' – my uncle raised his glass – 'Cheers. By the way, thanks very much for that thing you sent us, the er . . .'

'Article' I said.

'That's right. I read it. Very interesting.'

'I'm going to work it up into a book eventually' I said, 'I hope. That was just some preliminary work on sixteenth century land tenure – what I want to do is develop it into something rather more general on pre-enclosure peasant status and the regional differences in that and in land-holding generally – there's not been a lot done on that and I think the variations, particularly between north and south, are greater than people have thought.'

'Quite,' said my uncle, 'I hadn't come across that periodical before, the er . . .'

'*English Historical Review*.'

'That's right. Who runs it?'

'I think it's someone called Henderson, at York.'

My uncle looked thoughtful, but made no comment.

My aunt said, 'I always thought it was philosophy you did – I could have sworn. Oh, we met someone from your college the other day – at least he used to be there. Peter Samuels'.

Peter Samuels was given due attention. We had been waiting

for ten minutes or so, with no sign of sustenance. There had been further outbreaks of contention from beyond the swing door, but now a sinister silence. My aunt, fidgeting, said 'I want my avocado'. A moment later, a small dark man wearing a blood-stained apron shot from the kitchens, a tray on his arm, dealt avocado and pickled herrings to our table and two lemon sorbets to the neighbouring one, and retreated once more. The door, swinging open, released a brief spasm of sobbing and the noise of a saucepan boiling over.

My uncle, dismembering his herring, said 'How's that girl? Sarah Axbridge'.

I had hoped not to talk about Sarah. I said, 'Well, actually we don't see each other any more'. My aunt said 'Pity. She was very pretty, I thought. I loved that dress she was wearing when we met – I don't suppose you know where she got it?' She scoured the shell of her avocado, dabbed at her lips with her napkin and went on, 'Well, anyway, it's a good thing you didn't get married, it would have been much worse breaking up then'.

There was a loud thump against the kitchen door and the waitress came bursting through, using a brown suitcase as a battering ram. She had taken off her apron and wore a coat over jeans and a T-shirt. In the other hand she carried a fistful of paper carrier bags, which banged against the tables as she stumbled through the restaurant and out of the street door. My aunt, lifting her eyes as far as the perambulant carrier bags said, 'That reminds me, I must pop into Selfridges this afternoon. We saw Dottie last week, Tim – she sent you her love'.

We worked our way through various members of the family – their physical appearance and personal quirks; at least, my aunt and uncle did. There was, by now, a considerable restiveness apparent at the other tables; my uncle, infected, said, 'I must say this place is very slow'.

I said, 'I think there's some kind of trouble in the kitchen'.

My uncle drummed his fingers on the table irritably. In the ensuing pause I said, 'I've been getting involved in politics since I last saw you – real grass-roots politics. I'm standing for the local council, going round knocking on doors and all that.

What's interesting is that local issues aren't always . . .'

'Goodness,' said my aunt. 'How frightfully energetic of you, Tim. Rupert, do yell for that waitress again.'

My uncle, thumping peremptorily on the table, said 'Bob Chambers should never have recommended this place. I shall mention it next time I see him'.

'Bob Chambers has the most enormous wife,' said my aunt. 'She is quite the largest woman I have ever seen. Colossal.'

My uncle said with mild reproof, 'Tim hasn't actually met Bob Chambers, Lucy'.

'Oh, goodness,' said my aunt. 'Tim knows perfectly well I'm absolutely fascinated by people. I can't help that, can I?' She stared across the table at my uncle with girlish defiance.

'All right, darling' said my uncle amiably. 'Keep your hair on. I must say if we don't get something to eat soon . . .'

There was an inrush of culinary smells, pitched to a somewhat worrying state not far short of burning, as the door swung open again and the – presumably – chef, darted through. He looked round the tables, then at the series of dishes teetering on the tray he balanced along one arm, and gave a kind of moan. Then, shooting over to our table, he said in one gasp, 'Oneduckcannellonivealmarsala?'

'What?' said my uncle. 'Oh yes, that's right. And some vegetables, I hope. Oh – and we asked for a carafe of red wine. Some time ago' he added, severely.

The man, whose face, one now saw, was incandescent with sweat, was muttering to himself in an indecipherable language as he tipped the lid of another dish, peered into it, and glanced wildly round the room. At the neighbouring table, the executives were in a state of loud complaint.

'I daresay he's foreign' said my aunt, inspecting her veal. 'This looks nice. Try again, Rupert – we want the wine now, not later.'

My uncle, busy at his duck, repeated the request; it was met with a *tour de force* display of suffering, resignation, despair, incredulity and exasperation. My uncle said 'Oh, and some butter, please'. The swing doors spun twice more; the executives departed acrimoniously; somewhere out of sight a telephone rang and rang; the wine, apparently self-propelled, arrived on the table. My uncle, pouring it, said 'Now, Tim, you're not telling us a thing about yourself – what are you doing these days?'

'Well, in fact what I was going to tell you is that I've got a job.'

'Oh, super' said my aunt. 'What doing?'

'It's nothing very grand, but I'm very pleased about it. It's a lectureship in history at Liverpool.'

'University?' said my aunt.

My uncle, throwing her a severe glance, said 'Liverpool. Now isn't that the place Melton is vice-chancellor of?'

'Yes.'

'You knew him, I suppose?'

'Actually, no. In any case an appointment to a junior lectureship wouldn't be . . .'

'You should have told me you were after a job at Liverpool,' said my uncle reprovingly. 'One of my co-directors is a close friend of Melton's, I happen to know.'

'Is that John Peterson?' said my aunt. 'Or Duggie?'

'Duggie.'

'Duggie's not looking well these days. Let me see now – Liverpool? I don't believe I know a soul in Liverpool. Do you think you'll like it there?'

'I really don't know. But they're going to let me do the lecturing course I'd prefer and there are some people in the department interested in the same kind of thing as I am, and I hope . . .'

My aunt put her knife and fork down and said in triumph 'No, I'm wrong, there's those people we met years ago on holiday in Tossa – Harker, that's right – Paul and Maisie. He was something in shipping, they lived just outside, I think . . .'

The theme was developed, with occasional assistance from my uncle, until we had all finished our main course and indeed had sat in front of our empty plates for a considerable time. My uncle, looking at his watch, exclaimed 'Good lord, going on for two. What about a pudding?'

We were alone in the restaurant now, except for two women

deep in confidences and coffee on a shadowy banquette at the far side. For at least the last ten minutes or so there had been such a silence from the kitchens that it seemed possible that we had been abandoned altogether. I said, 'Perhaps we'd better just help ourselves'.

'Not a bad idea,' said my uncle. At the same moment the street door opened and the waitress came in, still coated, carrying the same suitcase and paper bags. She was no longer weeping but wore an expression of proud endurance – the bearing of the wronged heroine of Greek drama, immeasurably experienced in suffering. She swept through the room; I found myself shifting my chair to ease her passage, with deference.

My aunt stared at her. 'I should think she's a bit late to get a meal, that girl. They'll be closing soon.'

I said, 'Actually, she's the waitress'.

'No,' said my uncle. 'She's just come in from the street, I saw. The waitress was a chap with a dirty apron, I always remember faces.'

'No, you don't,' my aunt interjected. 'Helen Simmonds said you walked straight past her in the street the other day.'

'Oh, come' said my uncle, 'I doubt that very much. In fact, I distinctly recall . . .'

Further dissension was forestalled by staccato sounds from the kitchen into which the waitress had vanished, leaving her suitcase in front of the serving-table.

'They are foreigners.' My aunt cocked an ear. 'Italian, I'd say. What a racket. Sounds as if someone's being killed.'

One of the women from the banquette, in search of a bill, opened the serving door; through it, and over her shoulder, I glimpsed a scene of enthusiastic reconciliation – steamy, in every sense. The woman who had opened the door coughed and retreated. I said 'No, I don't think that's what they're doing, at least not now'.

My aunt obtained a menu from the neighbouring table. 'I fancy raspberry mousse. What about you, Tim?'

'Cheese for me,' said my uncle. I said I'd have the same. My uncle looked towards the kitchen, rapped on the table, and called

'Waiter!'

Nothing happened. My aunt began to say 'Really, this is . . .'
The waitress, her coat shed and an apron inadequately arranged
on top of her jeans and T-shirt, came tripping through the door,
radiant with promise of various kinds. Snatching up a menu, she
thrust it between us, at the same time making recommendations
of main course dishes, and perhaps the pâté maison for a starter.

'We've had that bit,' said my aunt crossly. 'We want a pudding.' The waitress stared at us with evident disbelief, and reluctantly accepted my uncle's order. The two women on the
banquette achieved their bill, though not without also being re-
offered the menu. As she returned to the kitchen I glimpsed, for
an instant, the chef, arms akimbo, in beaming expectancy. My
aunt said, 'Why do you keep looking through that door, Tim?'

Our puddings arrived. The waitress, now, exuded an aggressive satisfaction, clearly not related to the food, which bore
signs of neglect. My aunt, mercifully, was too preoccupied with
recollections of a man she had met who had once known my
former girlfriend to notice. In mid-discourse, she interrupted
herself for a moment to say 'Just one thing, Tim, and you mustn't
think I'm getting at you but you're not going to get too boring
and wrapped up in your work, I hope' – she laid two fingers on
my arm and smiled sweetly, to sugar the pill – 'I mean, I know it's
marvellous doing a think-job like that, but you mustn't forget
about people, in the end it's people that are interesting. There!
That's my lecture said'.

'Don't you know the saying, Lucy?' said my uncle. 'History is
about chaps; geography is about maps. Chaps are Tim's business.'
He repeated the tag, with satisfaction.

'*Real* people,' said my aunt loftily. 'Well, I suppose we'd better
be going.'

My uncle called for the bill, and paid; there was some confusion, the waitress having apparently no record of our orders. My
uncle said, 'I don't think all that much of this place – a bit run-of-
the-mill. Well, Tim, it's been good to hear what you're up to.
Give my regards to Melton when you get to Liverpool – we
haven't actually met but he'll know my name well through

62

Duggie Hiscocks'.

Outside, my aunt kissed me warmly. 'And don't you go shutting yourself up in an ivory tower, Tim – keep in touch with the real world. 'Bye, now.'

After they had gone, I remembered that I had left some books in the restaurant. The waitress greeted me with fervour and non-recognition, offering the menu and a table at the window; it was only with difficulty that I rescued the books and escaped.

Help

Henry said, 'You'll have to get some help'. He said it in the quiet, level tone that meant there was to be no discussion, the matter was decided now. But nonetheless Jenny said, 'What?' She said it not because she had not heard, but, like a child, because she did not want to hear.

'You'll have to get some help. I'm tired of this mess.'

Guiltily, Jenny followed his glance across the smeared table (teak, from Heals, Aunt Mary's wedding present), the children's coats tumbled behind the sofa, the clutter of toys and newspapers in the corner; on the other side of the wall she saw, as though through a glass screen, the ravaged kitchen.

'Oh dear,' she said. 'I suppose . . .' and then, hopefully 'I don't think we could really afford it.'

'Why ever not? You make it sound as though we were on the bread-line. We're not short of money just now.'

'You have to pay about seventy pence an hour, I think.'

'Rubbish. The cleaners at the office get sixty.'

'I would feel frightfully awkward having someone polishing my floors and things, Henry, I honestly would.' That was a real objection, but he brushed it aside with a snort.

The main objection, of course, could not be stated. It was the thought of a daily – or three-mornings-a-week or whatever it was to be – witness to her household disasters. To her failures with the children, to her panics, to her frantic sorties at inappropriate times of day because there was no milk for the baby, no bread, nothing for dinner again. To the fact that she was never quite certain how to work the washing machine, that she was capable of leaving Emma alone in the kitchen with a pan of water boiling on the stove (and had twice done so), that she dithered and forgot and neglected. That, from time to time, that old sinister feeling of fear and desolation came over her and she sat weeping for an hour or so at a time, with the children as mute, uncomprehending spectators. Henry did not know that she occasionally had these brief recurrences of the old trouble; by the time he came home she had pulled herself together, cleaned up her face, and the children (so far . . .) were too young to tell.

Henry said, more kindly, 'She could do the worst chores. Give you time for the rest.'

And perhaps that was true. Perhaps if there were someone to wash and hoover and do nappies and all that, perhaps then she would be able to keep the shiny things polished as Henry liked, make nicer food, empty ashtrays and plump up cushions before he came home, have clean and ironed shirts ready and available. She said, 'What do I do?'

He put the paper down and said in the slow and careful voice that meant: listen because I am not going to repeat this, 'You write out a card saying that you want a domestic help, and you put on it your name, address and telephone number, and you take it along to the tobacconist on the corner and ask them to put it in the window. Or, alternatively, you telephone or visit the local newspaper offices and put an advertisement in the paper. But that might be technically beyond you – I should settle for the tobacconist's window'.

She studied the phrasing of the postcards: Woman Wanted 2–3 hrs. Mons. or Weds.; Domestic Help 2 mornings weekly, times to suit, fares paid. She copied some of them down and, at home, composed a version of her own with which she felt quite pleased, and took it to the shop. The newsagent pinned it up on the board, and she walked back down the street feeling bold and resolute, pushing the pram with one hand and trying to stop

Emma dashing into the road with the other. A confidence grew; tomorrow, or the next day, the house would be swept and dusted, the meals pre-arranged and successful, Henry pleased. Henry cared a great deal about such things. It was, he had once explained, in a clipped voice, a simple matter of efficiency. Other women seemed to manage, he had said. And indeed they did – Jenny was all admiration. Henry's sister, with her four children . . . . Fiona Talbot next door . . . And how could Henry have known, in their courting days, that she would turn out like this? He had had a bit of a raw deal, she could see that, and except for the occasional sharp remark, he was very patient. Sometimes he polished things himself, or cleaned a sink or bath, and she was filled with a sense of guilt and inadequacy. Mercifully, the worst crises took place during the day, when he was at the office. Poor Henry, how could he have known . . ? But, a small voice cried out occasionally, how could I have known either?

She waited for a response to her advertisement, vacillating between confidence and anxiety. When the front-door bell rang, and simultaneously Emma fell down the stairs, while she was in the middle of bathing the baby, she imagined another calm, efficient presence sorting things out, and the future seemed rosy indeed. But when, half an hour before the dreaded hour of Henry's return, Emma deposited a garden trug of dirt on the hall carpet and Jenny, in her haste to clear it up, stumbled against the kitchen table and knocked over the only bottle of milk, she was glad to be alone with her panic. She could always lie, and say Emma spilled the milk. But nothing happened all day; there was no response to the advertisement.

The next day there was a phone call. It was about the job, the caller said. Were there, she enquired, any children? Jenny said yes, there were, uncertain if this was desirable or not. The caller said, regretfully, that she didn't care for a place with children, not that she had anything against them, but you never saw a job finished, did you, if there were small children around to mess the place up? They parted, with mutual apologies, and Jenny felt an unmistakeable lift of relief. Later, she said to Henry, 'I'm afraid there's no luck with the help. There aren't many answers'.

He said, 'Give it a bit longer'. It was a bad evening: the dinner undercooked, and he had found all the children's toys under the sofa where she had pushed them in her efforts to tidy the room before he came home. In silence, he removed them and took them through to the playroom; she could hear the staccato sounds of his irritated sorting of bricks, beads, pieces of Lego and small wheeled objects. Later, he went next door to have a drink with the Talbots. There wouldn't be toys under Fiona's sofa.

By the next day she was again waiting hopefully for the telephone. It rang twice; the first caller decided the bus routes were not convenient. The second said she was Mrs Porch, and she would like to call this afternoon.

Mrs Porch arrived precisely at the time she had suggested. Jenny watched her from the sitting room window, shutting the garden gate carefully behind her and walking up the path, pausing only to take an appreciative sniff at one of Henry's roses. Jenny felt a mixture of relief and apprehension. At least she was not old – one of her fears had been the embarrassment of someone middle-aged, old even, slaving away to do the work that she, Jenny, should be capable of doing herself. But this woman, though older than herself, was only in her later thirties or early forties. On the other hand, she looked disconcertingly brisk and competent, potentially critical.

Jenny opened the door. Mrs Porch said, 'Mrs Taylor? I'm Mrs Porch – about the job'.

Jenny, confused, found herself blushing and talking incoherently. She had rehearsed this moment: now, it was Mrs Porch who led the way into the sitting room, looked round for somewhere to put her coat, sat down after a moment and said, 'They're nice, these houses, aren't they? Have you been here long, Mrs Taylor?'

They talked. She was a pleasant woman, easy. Jenny began to relax. She said, with diffidence, 'It does seem a bit silly, needing help when the house really isn't very big. But the children are so – well, they do need such a lot of looking after, you know – and my husband does like things to be nice when he gets back in the evening'.

Mrs Porch said, 'Well, they do, don't they? It stands to reason – they've had a hard day, they want things ready for them, like. It's only natural'. She didn't sound critical in any way, and leaned down to the baby, crawling around her feet, to say 'I don't think you ought to have that in your mouth, now, my love, ought you?' She removed the button that the baby had been sucking (Henry's, the lost one from his office suit, so that was where . . .) and put it on the table, diverting the baby with a pencil from her handbag. Emma sidled through the door and Mrs Porch said, 'Hello, dear. What's your name, then? How old is she, Mrs Taylor – threeish?'

'Three next month.'

'It's a difficult age. You can't take your eyes off them for long. And the baby's into everything, I don't doubt. You've got your hands full.'

'Oh, yes,' said Jenny gratefully. 'Honestly, some days I get so tired. I know it's silly, lots of other people seem to manage so much better, but . . .'

'Oh, my goodness, you're not the only one. You can feel at the end of your tether, one way and another. When mine were this age there were times when I'd have willingly upped and walked out of the house.' It didn't seem likely, but Jenny was glad to hear her say so. She was just going to suggest showing Mrs Porch round when Emma lurched into the low coffee table and knocked over the vase of roses.

'Oh, Emma . . .' said Jenny. 'Oh, dear . . .' She began desperately stuffing the roses back, dabbing at the spilled water with a wad of Kleenex from her pocket.

'Let me,' said Mrs Porch. 'You want to be careful with those polished surfaces, they spot so easily with a drop of water. Where's the kitchen? You come along and show me, dear.' She took Emma by the hand and left the room, returning a moment later with basin and cloth. 'There we are – a wipe over with a duster and he'll never know. You pick up the flowers, now, Emma – mind the prickles, though. That's a nice table, Mrs Taylor.'

'It was a wedding present from my husband's aunt. I think it's antique. My husband's awfully fond of it.'

'I don't wonder. It's a lovely piece.' Mrs Porch wrung the cloth out with strong, freckled hands. 'There, now you run and find me the polish and a duster, Emma, there's a good girl. You've not been married all that long, then, I daresay?'

Jenny found herself telling Mrs Porch about one thing and another. About the wedding and about how frightened she'd been of doing something silly and making Henry cross, because she'd been ill on and off before (she didn't explain what kind of illness, but Mrs Porch nodded sympathetically) and about how nervous Henry's mother made her, being such a different sort of person, so busy and competent, running that enormous house and all those committees and things. Mrs Porch made reassuring remarks about everyone having their weak spots, and no one being perfect, and so forth. She seemed quite interested in Henry's parents, and indeed it turned out she'd been to the house once, one of the days the garden was open to the public. 'Must cost a lot to run, that place. I daresay they've got some lovely things there. Your husband the only son, is he?'

'Yes,' said Jenny vaguely. Mrs Porch was busy admiring the silver tea-set that had been Henry's mother's wedding-present. It badly needed polishing, Jenny saw with guilt. But all she could think of now was the need to make a favourable impression on Mrs Porch.

They toured the house. In the kitchen, Mrs Porch hung the cloth up to dry, put away the basin. At the same time she rinsed out a couple of dirty milk bottles and emptied the sink basket. Jenny said 'Oh, please . . . You mustn't bother'. And Mrs Porch, popping the milk bottles outside the back door, said that she believed in doing things as you went along, and then you didn't have everything piling up on you, did you? Upstairs, Jenny felt her eye on the rimmed bath, Emma's unmade bed, the clouded windows, and grew confused again, hastily picking things up, trying to put clothes in piles. 'You can't expect them to clear up, can you, at that age?' said Mrs Porch. 'Bless them. And your husband's just as bad, I daresay – I've never known a man hang his own trousers up. My husband's the same – I say to Bob, if I had a pound note for every time I've folded a pair of trousers of yours, I'd be in clover by now. Here, shall I do that . . . ' She put Henry's tweed jacket in the cupboard, and stood for a moment, looking. 'I can see he likes things nice, Mr Taylor.'

When she left they had arranged that she should start on Monday. Jenny could hardly believe her luck: she wandered around for a while in a daze of contented anticipation and then remembered that the delicate subject of money had not been raised. At least, Mrs Porch had said at one point, 'The usual rate will do all right, Mrs Taylor', but Jenny, too preoccupied by her relief that all was well and she had been accepted, had not followed this up by asking what the usual rate was. She would have to go next door and ask Fiona Talbot, who would be certain to know: Fiona knew about everything.

The very fact that she was able to decide to call on Fiona, and then do so without hesitation, was an indication of her mood. It wasn't that Fiona was not welcoming: far from it, she was never put out, too busy, caught in a dressing-gown, or in the bath, or washing her hair. She was always crisply dressed – jeans clean and pressed, shirts and smocks fresh and new – her hair tidy, her house spruce but comfortable-looking, her children playing happily in airy, swept rooms with good quality educational toys. They had startlingly large vocabularies for such young children, though Fiona insisted that of course she and Tim didn't believe in pushing them, they must go at their own pace. They never had runny noses, either, and did not seem to whine like Emma . . .

Jenny thought of all this as she went down her own garden path, and up Fiona's. No, it wasn't that Fiona was unwelcoming. It was just that she didn't seem to need company very much; or perhaps that she didn't much care for other women. She was polite, welcoming, and bored. She got on very well with Henry. When she and Tim came over – or when Henry and Jenny went to the Talbots – Fiona would talk a lot and make everyone laugh, or else get involved in long, serious arguments while Jenny sat silent. She had a degree and had had some rather important job in journalism before she got married. Jenny once asked her, timidly, if she did not get bored just being a housewife – she had had a

71

couple of glasses of wine or she would never had dared.

Fiona had said, 'Good gracious, a degree isn't just a vocational training, is it? It furnishes the mind, and all that. Of course I'm not bored. I've got more time to myself than I've had for years'. Jenny had felt crushed.

She rang the bell. When Fiona came to the door, Jenny said 'I'm awfully sorry to bother you – I hope you weren't in the middle of something – it's just that I wondered if by any chance you knew how much one ought to pay for help nowadays'.

Fiona said, 'Psychiatric, or some other kind?' Jenny was unpleasantly taken aback for a moment until she remembered that actually Fiona couldn't possibly know . . . It was a joke, obviously – one of Fiona's queer, dead-pan jokes that one didn't always follow – so Jenny laughed and said, 'Oh, domestic, I meant'.

'Never having used any I couldn't be quite certain,' said Fiona. 'But I believe the going rate is about sixty-five an hour. Scandalous, but that's the way it is.'

Jenny wasn't quite sure who it was scandalous for, but since the Talbots were said by Henry to be rather left-wing, she decided it must be for the helps.

Fiona said come in and have a cup of coffee, so she did. Emma and the baby, as usual, fell happily on the educational toys. Jenny and Fiona sat in Fiona's gay sitting room and drank coffee made quickly and without fuss by Fiona at the same time as she smoked, talked, and sorted out the occasional squabble among the children with a quick re-distribution of toys.

'What do you want help for?'

'I – well – I know it seems silly but things do get in such a mess and Henry does hate it so. It was his idea, but she seems awfully nice.'

'Why shouldn't she be?' said Fiona. 'Sorry, I didn't mean to sound sharp. Have some more coffee?' Her glance drifted to the open book on the table beside her: Jenny had the feeling that she was bored already. Presumably she had been reading the book. It was impossible to read the title upside-down, but the pages were all long chunks of text without conversation so it did not look like a novel. Most of the Talbots' books were rather new paper-backs, on politics and things like that: Henry often borrowed them.

Jenny's mood of confidence had begun to evaporate. She could not think of anything more to say to Fiona. She would have liked to comment on the very attractive shirt she was wearing, or the new curtains, but felt that it would probably be wiser not to, as she had once heard Fiona be very amusing, but scathing, about women who discussed clothes and furnishings all the time. Emma, passionately acquisitive over one of the Talbot children's brightly-coloured, unbroken toys, snatched it away and hit the other child over the head with it. Jenny smacked Emma and met Fiona's coolly disapproving gaze across the weeping children. Fiona, she remembered too late, thought that there were really no situations with children that justified physical violence: one could always deal with things rationally and calmly. Fiona went into the kitchen to fetch biscuits with which to soothe everyone's ruffled feelings and Jenny sat uncomfortably. The trouble was that Fiona always reminded her of various particularly awful crises: the Christmas she forgot half the shopping and had to trail backwards and forwards to Fiona for three days to borrow bread, tea, sugar, potatoes. The time both the children had chicken-pox together and she was reduced to such a weeping, trembly state of nervous exhaustion that Fiona came over and coped till Henry came home. She'd heard them talking in the hall, later, Henry apologising, Fiona saying, 'Good heavens, Henry, think nothing of it – some people just find it harder to manage than others, that's all there is to it'. Jenny hadn't known then that both Fiona's children had been ill at the time. Henry liked Fiona very much: he had a special tone of voice when he was talking to her, that didn't seem to crop up with anyone else.

It wasn't until she was back in her own house that Jenny remembered Mrs Porch again, and cheered up.

Mrs Porch's first weeks were positively exciting. She trans-formed the house within three days. Pockets of dirt that Jenny had assumed to be ineradicable vanished; the bath and basins ceased to be slimy; mounds of dirty clothes disappeared and were found later in the airing-cupboard, washed and ironed. Jenny hadn't realised that the oven was meant to be that nice grey-blue colour inside, or that you could get all those marks off the floor around the stove. Henry was delighted, and Jenny found herself getting undeserved credit. There were other advantages, too. The children loved Mrs Porch; when she was around they played more and cried less. She brought Jenny the occasional home-made pie or cake.

'Oh, Mrs Porch, you mustn't . . .'

'If you're making one you might as well make two, mightn't you?'

On these occasions Jenny left extra money out, and hoped she was doing the right thing. The business of payment had filled her with embarrassment: it seemed so awful to hand over notes, just like that, so she had taken to putting the money discreetly in an envelope which she left on the kitchen table on the appropriate days, from whence it duly disappeared, leaving their relationship untarnished.

It was such a nice relationship. There had never been any need to tell Mrs Porch what to do. She just knew — far better than Jenny had, anyway. She thought of everything. She reminded Jenny of household shortages, prompted her to have the baby's second vaccination done, told her how to get the broken window repaired and noticed, in time, that Jenny had left Henry's good secateurs (birthday present from his mother . . .) out in the rain. She answered the telephone if Jenny was in the garden, posted the letters that Jenny had forgotten, turned out the larder. When the milkman rang the door bell during the baby's bath, as he invariably did, Mrs Porch called up the stairs, 'Don't you bother coming down, dear. I'll settle up with him for you, shall I?'

'Oh, you are an angel, Mrs Porch. My purse is in the top drawer of the dresser.'

And at eleven they drank coffee together in the kitchen and Mrs Porch talked endlessly about her family, which was large, diffuse and unpredictable. It was like being plunged into a serial story: Jenny found herself looking forward to the daily episode.

'What happened about your sister-in-law in the end, Mrs

Porch?'

'Well, she told Fred she wasn't having any more of that, and he knew what he could do, and she upped and off to her auntie's round the corner. And then, the next thing I knew, there was my mum come tanking over on her bike to say . . .'

Henry's mother, on her next visit, did not fail to observe the altered state of the house. She said she gathered Jenny had this awfully good women now, and she'd better hang onto her. The tone in which she said it made Jenny faintly defensive: it sounded as thought she doubted Jenny's capacity to do so, and Jenny found this annoying, because she was such friends with Mrs Porch, really friends she felt, and actually Henry's mother wasn't all that nice to her helps, she ordered them about and checked up on what they had been doing.

Several weeks after Mrs Porch's arrival she met Fiona. Fiona had called to ask if Henry would like to come over on Saturday evening and meet this friend of theirs from Cambridge – she thought he'd be interested. She added hastily, 'And you, of course'. Jenny, knowing that Mrs Porch would be making the coffee, was able with confidence to ask her in for a cup. Mrs Porch, appearing from the kitchen, said 'I'll bring the coffee for you and your friend into the sitting room, Mrs Taylor', but Fiona said quickly 'Oh heavens, no, if you usually have it in the kitchen don't start being posh for me'. So they all three sat in the kitchen. Fiona and Mrs Porch got on at once. It turned out that Fiona's eldest child was just starting at the primary school where Mrs Porch's had been, and they talked with animation about the new maths teaching, and different kinds of reading primer, and what the teachers were like. Fiona stayed for ages, and then said good heavens, she'd no idea it was that late, she really must rush. On the doorstep she said to Jenny, 'What a nice woman – awfully bright. Lucky you, Jenny – I suppose she's what used to be called a treasure, in the bad old days'.

Jenny repeated this remark to Henry, and after that he sometimes referred to Mrs Porch as the treasure, with an indulgent grin.

Henry himself did not meet Mrs Porch for some time, and

when he did it was not under the most auspicious circumstances. He got 'flu, badly, and was in bed for over a week. Mrs Porch came in every day, because, as she said, Jenny couldn't cope with him up there needing trays and all that, and the children underfoot. Consequently the illness went off with great smoothness. Jenny was able to make enticing little meals which Mrs Porch laid on a tray covered with a starched cloth and a crisply folded napkin. Henry loved it. He became very affectionate and teasing with Jenny, like he used to be before they were married, when he had seemed to find her failings more endearing than irritating. During the convalescence, before he went back to the office, he met Mrs Porch properly: they had long conversations and once or twice Jenny had the feeling that they had talked about her. There was a faintly odd look in Mrs Porch's eye, and Jenny hadn't been able to help hearing Henry's voice through the door, on one occasion, saying something about being so grateful, made such a difference, my wife finding it hard to cope, rather prone to nerves, bit of a breakdown when she was younger, luckily quite cleared up now . . . Jenny went quickly past and into the kitchen where she sat quite still for a minute until that awful, reminiscent, shaky feeling went away.

The months passed. Everything was so much better that it became hard to remember the dark days before Mrs Porch came: life without her was unimagineable. The days when she didn't come still had their dangers and crises, but fewer of them because there was always salvation around the corner, the next day, after the weekend . . . And if catastrophe threatened when she was there she could always avert it with some deft action, a few reassuring words. Jenny was hardly ever gripped by that sense of bleak hopelessness now, as though the house, the children, Henry, were some kind of trap waiting to be sprung. Mrs Porch, even in absence, propelled her through the days, gave her reserves of strength. Nor was she ever patronising or critical; she seemed to take the line that far too much had been expected of Jenny all along.

The only snag was that for some reason it was working out much more expensive than Jenny had anticipated. Naturally

Henry had given her extra house-keeping money to cover Mrs Porch's wages, but even so there always seemed to be less money than there should be. Twice she took out her purse in shops and found she had less – quite a bit less – than she'd thought. She had to ask Henry to give her more money.

'I'm awfully sorry. It's just I never seem to have enough.'

'Well, never mind – no need to look so guilty, Jen. You don't have to go short – we can afford a bit more nowadays.'

She said to Mrs Porch that everything seemed to be terribly expensive. 'Oh, don't I know it! Shocking, that's what it is. Every time you're in the supermarket there's another penny on this and twopence on that. You can't keep track of where it goes, not like you used to.'

And then one day Jenny found that there was a pound note missing from her purse – at least she felt almost certain there was. She'd been to the corner shop for something and they'd given her change for five pounds: four notes and some silver. Now there were only three, and the loose change. She was puzzled and slightly worried.

'Emma, just come here a moment, darling. Listen, you haven't taken anything from Mummy's purse, have you? No, don't cry, just tell me. You didn't? No, I'm not cross, darling, I just wanted you to tell me . . .'

She hunted in the places where Emma often hid things, and found nothing. She began to have doubts: had they perhaps only given her three pounds in the shop by mistake? And yet she had felt so sure. Oh well, never mind . . .

A week later, it happened again. This time, she felt a little thud of shock in her stomach. She'd been trying to be more careful about money, budgeting, working out what she had spent, noting prices . . . She'd been quite sure she had fifteen pounds in her purse, and now there were thirteen. At least she *thought* she'd been quite sure . . .

In the evening, she said to Henry, slipping it in casually while she was washing up the dinner, 'You didn't by any chance borrow some money from my purse this morning, did you?'

'No, why?'

'Oh, nothing. It's just I seem to have less than I thought.'

'Well, how much did you have?'

'Fifteen pounds, I think.'

'What do you mean — you think? Either you had fifteen pounds or you didn't.'

'Well, I suppose it mightn't have been. I did count, I feel sure — perhaps I didn't.'

Henry said, 'Do you mean you don't always know how much money you've got?'

She said unhappily, 'No, I'm afraid not. I do try to'.

'You really must be more careful, Jen.'

She flushed. He didn't know some of the awful things she'd done with money, in fact. Leaving her purse in shops, or stuck on the top of her basket where anyone could take it, or dropping it in buses. Only the other day she'd left it on the wall outside the garden gate when Emma had fallen on the pavement, but mercifully Mrs Porch had spotted it and brought it in. He was right: she must be more careful.

The next morning she went out early, even before Mrs Porch came and bought a little notebook from the corner shop. With a glow of determination, she wrote down the exact sum in her purse on the first page. Then, later, she would enter any expenditures on the other side and check notebook against purse at the end of the day. That way, there wouldn't be these silly muddles, and she would be able to keep an eye on how, and where, the housekeeping money was going. She put the notebook away in satisfaction and went to open the door to Mrs Porch.

At the end of the day there was a pound less in her purse than there should have been. Shakily, she counted and re-counted the notes out onto the kitchen table, added and re-added the five items of expenditure. There wasn't any doubt, absolutely no doubt at all. She sat down, still clutching the notebook and purse, overcome by a strange feeling of unreality, as though this were a dream — or a nightmare. Or, said a sinister little voice in her head, was the *other* unreal — *did* you count properly this morning, write down exactly what you spent? You make mistakes, don't you — dither, get things wrong . . ?

There had been no one in the house all day except herself and Mrs Porch. And the children. She searched again in Emma's hiding-places, under cushions, beds, chairs, carpets. Nothing.

It just isn't possible. I counted wrong, I must have done.

Forget it. Ignore it. Pretend it didn't happen. Start the notebook again – something went wrong that time. Give it another try.

For five days the opposing pages of the notebook tallied exactly. Seventeen pounds forty-nine there should be, and seventeen pounds forty-nine there were; fifteen twelve and fifteen twelve . . . It was a small private triumph – just a matter of persevering, and there was nothing to worry about after all.

On the seventh day two pounds were missing. It was a Friday, one of Mrs Porch's days.

Jenny lay awake much of the night. She tossed and turned, experiencing in manifold versions the conversation she would not, could not, have with Henry.

'Henry, I'm afraid Mrs Porch has been taking money from my purse. Quite a lot, over quite a long time.'

'What the hell do you mean, Jenny? That's a very serious accusation to make against anyone, you know. Are you sure?'

'Yes, quite sure, really sure, Henry. I've counted and counted. I . . . either it's that or I . . .'

'Or what?'

'Or I'm imagining it all, I'm going mad . . .'

And Henry stared at her in silent assessment, joined, from time to time in that tormented night, by his mother, whose serious but resigned expression said that she had known all along, been prepared for a recurrence, that kind of problem never really . . . When at last Jenny slept it was to plunge into a frenetic dreamscape where pound notes floated like beach leaves, elusive and uncountable.

She felt rather ill and shaky the next day. She tried to avoid Mrs Porch, but she seemed to be everywhere, talking loudly and cheerfully. Once or twice she looked at Jenny with an odd sharpness. 'You feeling all right, dear? You don't look all that good – sure you're not going down with something. There's a tummy

79

bug about.'

'I'm quite all right,' Jenny said.

Halfway through the morning the bell rang. Mrs Porch, coming into the playroom, where Jenny was giving the baby a belated breakfast (it had been a wretched morning, everything going wrong, just like the old days. . . .) said, 'It's the bread man – I'll just pay him, shall I? I can't seem to lay hands on your purse, though, Mrs Taylor – it's not in the usual place'.

Jenny said in a strangled voice, 'It's all right, Mrs Porch, I'll do it'. She got up hastily, spilling the baby's milk as she did so.

'Don't you bother,' said Mrs Porch. 'Ah, there it is'. She reached forward to take the purse from the table beside Jenny, adding 'I'll bring a cloth for that milk when I've seen to him. Coming, Mr Binns . . .'

'No!' said Jenny shrilly. 'Please leave it, Mrs Porch. I'll pay him myself.' The baby was crying now, and the bread man ringing the bell again. She left the room hastily.

When she came back Mrs Porch was soothing the baby. Jenny, her heart thumping horribly, sat down again and said, 'I'll take him now – thanks'.

Mrs Porch was looking at her intently. She said, 'I don't think you're quite yourself this morning, Mrs Taylor, I don't really'. Jenny, still holding the purse, put it on the floor beside her, self-consciously, and Mrs Porch went on, 'I'll put that back in the dresser for you, shall I, before young mischief here gets hold of it'.

Jenny said 'No, it's all right, I'll see to it'.

There was a silence. When Jenny looked up from the baby's bowl of half-eaten cereal Mrs Porch was still standing there; her expression was hard to analyse – she might have been angry, or concerned. She reminded Jenny of firm-faced sisters in hospital wards. Jenny found herself shaking again, though she was trying to hold herself rigid. Her eyes met Mrs Porch's, and she looked away again at once.

Mrs Porch said slowly, 'Is there something wrong with the purse, Mrs Taylor? Something bothering you?'

'No,' said Jenny wildly. 'At least I don't want – I couldn't bear . . . There's some sort of mistake, I'm sure, it's just I felt certain . . .'

'I see,' said Mrs Porch. She sounded, for a moment, subdued, sad almost, but when she spoke again it was with her old briskness. 'If it was anyone else I'd be very angry, Mrs Taylor, but I've got fond of you, I really have, I like working here, we get on, I thought. And I'll tell you what I think, I think you're having a spot of that old trouble of yours, that's what I think. So I'm not going to say anything more about it, nor mention it to your husband, not that I don't feel perhaps I ought to, but it would be a worry to him, poor man. So we'll keep it between us two, Mrs Taylor, and pretend it never happened, and that's all there is to it.'

There was a pause. Jenny could not look at her. 'All right, Mrs Taylor?'

Jenny said, 'There's really nothing wrong with me. It was all ages ago, that, and ever since I've been . . .'

'Unless, of course' said Mrs Porch, 'you'd rather I didn't come any more?'

After a moment Jenny said 'No, honestly, I . . . I'm sorry, I expect there's been a mistake'.

'Then we'll forget about it. Right?' Mrs Porch gathered up the dirty crockery from the table. As she was leaving the room she turned and said, 'And I'd put the purse back in the dresser, if I were you, Mrs Taylor, it'll be a nuisance if I can't find it, next time the milkman's wanting his money, when you're not about, won't it?'

Jenny said 'Yes. Yes, all right, Mrs Porch'. She sat in the empty playroom – Mrs Porch had borne the baby away with her, to wash and change him – staring at the door. She felt exhausted: there was a ringing noise in her ears. I don't know, she thought, I don't know, I don't know, I don't know . . .

That evening she said to Henry, 'I'm afraid I need more housekeeping money again'.

'Good grief, Jen, again! It's only a few weeks since last time.'

'I'm sorry.'

Henry sighed. 'All right, then. How much?'

She said dully, 'I think about another couple of pounds a week will do. For the moment, anyway'.

Miss Carlton and the
Pop Concert

It was Miss Carlton's custom to walk in Hyde Park most after-noons from three till four: up the Broad Walk, round the Pond, a short excursion to the hinterland beyond, and then home. She preferred the park in winter; then, the misty shapes of the trees receding into undefined distances gave it a spaciousness and a mystery which it quite lost in summer. Now, in late June, it was at its worst, the dusty growth of trees and bushes only a pale reflection of the real summer going on elsewhere, the poor grass worn quite down to the roots by the tramp of feet. Even the sun-light had a tawdry quality. In the country, Miss Carlton thought, it would not be like this. But her regret was perfunctory: Miss Carlton was a townswoman at heart, and she knew well that a country field, however delectable, could never provide her with the spectacle, the interest, the endless variety of the park.

She studied her fellow walkers with avid attention. Each visit provided some new entertainment, some small incident. She delighted in novelty: eccentricities of dress, perplexing snatches of conversation. She moved up and down the wide paths, across the grass, between the neat flower beds, alert and expectant – an inquisitive ghost foraging among the walkers. Few people spare a second glance for trim, elderly ladies.

Today the park was more than usually crowded. Miss Carlton, crossing the Broad Walk and heading for the Round Pond, had a busy time absorbing the many people who surrounded her.

Indeed, it was some while before she became aware of a uniformity only in their persons, but in their movement. They were all young, all were bizarrely dressed, and all were drifting, in an unhurried but purposeful manner, towards the centre of the park, somewhere east of the pond. Miss Carlton, deeply interested, began to drift with them.

There were men and girls; somewhat similarly clad in garments that were often long and flowing in a way that pleased Miss Carlton. She liked the style, the colours. Nearly all had long hair; many of the men were bearded and whiskered. There was an overwhelming impression of profusion, of abundance. Some of the girls wore trailing skirts, many were barefooted. There were trousered girls, and men wearing feminine shirts of lace or velvet; everything seemed interchangeable. Miss Carlton was not especially surprised: one frequently saw people thus dressed nowadays. These were the Young, and she secretly enjoyed their variety, and admired their self-absorption. When her friends complained about them and deplored their dress, their manners and their attitudes, she was silent; she was of a gentle disposition and did not relish dispute. Moreover, she suspected that we often attack that which we envy. The old have always criticised the young; sometimes the criticisms may be just, but the violence with which they are made betrays a deeper resentment. Miss Carlton, having herself come to terms with age, felt none of this. She was an observer, detached and uninvolved.

This strange crowd became thicker and thicker. Miss Carlton, moving over the grass with them, found herself touched by the hem of a skirt, brushed by a bare arm, forced to change direction for a motionless or slow-moving group. And now she saw that they did, in fact, have an objective. In the distance was a large, raised platform, and before and all around this was a vast crowd, sitting, squatting and lying on the grass. As the drifters reached the edge of this crowd they too would sink down on the grass so that the dense mass expanded gently all the time, amoeba-like, spreading over the park and engulfing trees and bushes. On the platform, figures moved about, and from time to time a loudspeaker crackled, blaring a short burst of music or

84

garbled language.

Miss Carlton increased her pace a little to draw level with a couple of girls just ahead of her.

'Excuse me,' she said, 'I wonder if you could tell me what is going on?'

They turned to look at her, still walking. They both wore brightly-patterned trailing clothes, and bands around their hair that gave them a faintly oriental appearance, though their round, pink and white faces were unmistakably anglo-saxon. Miss Carlton thought they looked very nice: she had always liked the eastern influence. Many of her own clothes came from Liberty's.

One of the girls said, 'It's a pop concert. The Applejacks and a whole lot of other groups'.

'Oh, dear,' said Miss Carlton. 'I have no ticket.' She looked at them in dismay: suddenly she wanted very much to remain with these young people.

'It's free,' said the girl. They both stared at her for a moment, and then turned away.

How very pleasant, thought Miss Carlton, like a brass band. Full of anticipation, she approached the crowd. Already people around her were beginning to sit down on the grass and the mass ahead was so dense that it was becoming difficult to move but she felt a strong desire to achieve the very centre of this event and struggled along, murmuring 'I'm sorry . . . please excuse me . . . thank you so much'.

The crowd of young people was like a gently waving sea-anemone. Their hair lifted in the wind, their clothes made a kaleidoscopic pattern of colour so that the whole mass, shifting, rippling, ebbing and flowing at the edges, was like some primitive sea-creature and Miss Carlton, advancing, felt herself, like a shrimp, most pleasantly digested. She continued until at last she reached a point where the crowd was so closely packed that further advance would be anti-social. People were sitting and lying all around, except for isolated figures who stood swaying in a trance-like way. Miss Carlton took her small folding stool from her bag, sat on it, and looked around her with interest.

The platform was some way away, but she could see it more

clearly now, and from the considerable activity going on there guessed that the concert must be about to begin. Musical instruments were being assembled. She began to study her immediate neighbours. Next to her was a young man with the bearded, long and tragic face of a Renaissance Christ. Miss Carlton observed him, fascinated. He wore a flowered shirt, gaping open to the waist to reveal a thin, hairless chest. Below that were very tight trousers, faded in patches that had a curious symmetry, and bare feet. He looked every inch the religious ascetic. In front of Miss Carlton, and facing her, was a girl. Indeed, they were so close that Miss Carlton could feel the stuff of her dress shiver delicately under the girl's breath. She was very young, with a pale face and long thick wavy hair, hanging over either shoulder almost to her waist. She too had associations with some other age; she was, Miss Carlton thought, the very image of a Rossetti painting. Her clothes, too, suited the part – thin and floaty, in the muted colours of which Miss Carlton herself was fond: plum, russet and heavy greens. As Miss Carlton watched her she leaned forward suddenly and touched the ropes of beads around Miss Carlton's neck.

'Hey,' she said, 'that's nice.'

Miss Carlton looked down. She was wearing her amber necklace, as she usually did, and her mother's pearls – the long rope that came nearly to her waist – and several strings of jet.

'Fantastic,' said the girl, in an appreciative tone. Miss Carlton realised that she, too, wore several strings of beads, and indeed, looking around, she saw that most of the girls and some of the men were decked out with necklaces much like her own. There was, she now saw, a conformity about their dress, and her own appearance matched it in many ways. The style, the colours, and the materials they favoured were much like the things she wore herself. Miss Carlton, who knew that she stood somewhat apart in taste from many of her own generation, felt for the first time in her life a member of a group. Only her age distinguished her from her companions.

The girl had turned aside to talk to a friend, and Miss Carlton looked around her again. What she saw filled her more and more

86

with a strange nostalgia. These people, she knew – had known for some time – were ghosts from her own past. They were the students she had watched go in and out of the art school her father would never allow her to attend; in their brave, flamboyant clothes, their huge-brimmed hats, their beards, they were the people of *Trilby*, of William Morris, of the pre-Raphaelites, of all that culture she had secretly admired in her own youth. They were the bohemians against whom her father had railed – the disrupters of society, the profligates, the fiddling grasshoppers. How she had admired and envied them! Not that she had borne her father any ill will, but by the time he died she had been over forty – far too old to do any of those things for which she had yearned so deeply. She had always kept up her interest in art, of course, visiting the Summer Academy every year, and after her father's death she had allowed herself certain indulgences of dress and behaviour that would never have been permissible in his lifetime. What would he have thought of these young people? Miss Carlton gave a sudden little laugh.

The girl who had admired her necklaces stared at Miss Carlton, a faint look of enquiry on her rather impassive face. She was a nice girl; Miss Carlton had seen that at once, before she spoke. She reminded her slightly of her great-niece in Dorset, though she was prettier.

'I was thinking of my father,' said Miss Carlton apologetically. 'He so disliked that they called aesthetes in his day, you know. Very intolerant, I'm afraid. My brother too – he used to tell me how he and his friends would go round de-bagging them when he was up at Oxford. I must say I always found the story distasteful.'

'What?' said the girl.

'Taking their trousers off,' said Miss Carlton, 'to indicate disapproval.'

'I think that's disgusting,' said the girl. 'Hey, did you hear that?' She leaned over and nudged the Christ-like young man, who shrugged.

'I quite agree,' said Miss Carlton with enthusiasm. 'It was barbaric. Anti-aestheticism was something of a cult, of course. I always felt *Patience* was responsible for a lot of it.' Seeing that the girl again looked bewildered, she added, 'Gilbert and Sullivan, you know. There was that song — "A greenery-yallery, Grosvenor Gallery, foot-in-the-grave young man".'

The man and the girl gazed at her and after a moment the girl said, 'I never heard of that'.

The conversation flagged and indeed it was becoming difficult to talk above the increasing noise from the platform. The loudspeaker crackled almost non-stop now; people, in their appearance much like the members of the crowd who stared up expectantly, scurried on and off with microphones and coils of wire. And then, suddenly, four young men came onto the platform and the crowd began to scream and yell; even the Rossetti-girl opened her mouth and shrieked, but any sound she made was quite lost in the noise all around. Miss Carlton shrank a little, assaulted by the din.

The music, when it began, was no better. To begin with, it was far too loud: the very ground seemed to throb with it. Miss Carlton decided that something must be wrong with the microphones, but then, looking at the unconcerned faces around her, changed her mind. However, she soon discovered that by the simple expedient of turning down her deaf-aid she could reduce the sound to a distant murmur, in no way offensive. Thus insulated, she was able to appreciate the spectacle and the company without any aural discomfort.

She gave herself up to enjoyment. Just to sit among these people was to experience a sense of release. Here she was, at last — too late, but at last — surrounded by people who were as she had longed, once, to be. Young people free to follow the direction of their own creative urges, unfettered by social conventions, released from the restraints of conformity. They were the heirs, half a century later, of those little pioneer groups, the brave and the fortunate, who had escaped the Edwardian world to feed in the lush pastures of Art and Literature. And there were so many of them. They reached as far as the eye could see: it was amazing. Miss Carlton, aged seventy-five, had a sudden dizzying sensation that the society in which she lived was totally alien to her, that she knew nothing of it. There she was, passing quietly from one day to another in the Campden Hill house left her by her father, and there outside, all around but unknown to her, was this great new England, vibrant with sensitivity and awareness. Of course, she had always tried to keep abreast of the times. She read the newspapers, listened to the wireless, was a member of an art appreciation group, an amateur dramatic society, and a book club. But she had thought herself one of a minority – few of her friends, even, shared her tastes. Now, she realised, with a surge of excitement, things had changed beyond all possible belief. The world was simply not as it had been; here, in Hyde Park on a Saturday afternoon, was the stuff of which it was made now, the new generation. It was a heady moment; just to look at her companions, to project herself into what their lives must be, gave her a thrill. She studied their faces, tried to penetrate for herself the wide-ranging thoughts in their heads, longed to eavesdrop their conversations. She noted girls with the delicate features of Botticelli angels and madonnas, appropriately clad in dresses that floated and swam around their thin bodies. She slanted cautious stares (sideways, not to be too obvious) at young men plumed like tropical birds, hung about with velvet and satin, their faces whiskered and bearded, the faces of artists, poets and playwrights. It was as though she had strayed, all accidentally, into the cultural nub of England, the very nerve-centre of the nation, and she felt appropriately awed. She did not want to participate, but she wanted most desperately to absorb all that there was to be absorbed. That, at least, she was owed by the grudging Fate that had cheated her of experience. These fortunate people, born into a more generous age, could allow her at least a vicarious taste of their more expansive lives.

The song finished and the performers left the platform. It seemed that there was to be a short interval. Miss Carlton edged herself closer to the pair of young men behind her, velvet-jacketed youths with the faces of desperate Chekhov heroes, all side-boards and silky whiskers, and listened unashamedly to their conversation.

'You get fantastic suspension, on a BMW.'

'Yeah.'

'Great acceleration, too.'

'What about the m.p.g.?'

'Thirty or so. 'Course, you got to remember there's a higher premium on a sports job.'

'Yeah.'

Miss Carlton was disappointed. It was inevitable, though, that the conversation of people closely attuned to one another's patterns of thought should have an allusive, excluding quality. She abandoned the young men and turned her attention to the group of girls on either side, exquisite creatures, all long hair and pale, oval faces, like Primaveras dumped down on the dry London grass. Their exchanges were equally baffling.

'Thirty-eight fifty, with lunch vouchers. And no Saturdays.'

'That's fantastic. Commission?'

'Ten per cent.'

'Great.'

Frustrated, Miss Carlton decided that there was nothing for it but a direct approach. She would resume contact with the young man and the girl in front of her. She had been thinking about them in particular during the song, and was filled with a deep curiosity. The young man, for instance: what did he do when he was not listening to music in Hyde Park? It was hard to envisage him in other, more mundane, situations, but presumably he had to support himself in some way, unless, of course, he had private means.

She leaned towards him and tapped his knee. 'Please forgive me – I hope you won't think me impertinent – but I should so very much like to know more about you. Do you have a job – or are you some kind of student?' She hoped she had not offended him by her curiosity.

He turned his saint-like face towards her and contemplated her. 'I'm with the Thames Gas Board' he said.

Miss Carlton was thunderstruck. For a moment she thought it was a joke, and was about to laugh, and then she caught sight of the dead-pan face of the girl, dead-pan not in collusion but acquiescence, and choked back the laugh.

'He's a fitter,' said the girl. 'When your cooker busts it's him comes along to fix it. Eh, Len?' She nudged her companion and he said, 'Yeah. That's about it'.

Shaken, Miss Carlton looked again at the man's thin, ascetic face. It was a face she knew well: it looked at you, almond-eyed, tilted at unnatural angles, from Russian icons; it stared through encrustations of brown varnish from the walls of the National Gallery; gilt-haloed, it watched you from triptychs in Italian churches.

And there was, after all, no reason why it should not also be the face of a young man who repaired gas cookers. Miss Carlton decided to probe further. Her first question had been met not with resentment, but indifference.

She said, 'Are you enjoying the music?'

'It's all right.'

'Are the performers especially talented, or merely average?'

'They're all right.'

The lack of commitment was disturbing. Miss Carlton, studying the faces of the young couple, had to admit to herself that they had a quality of flatness. The features were beautiful, but flat. There was no animation. Miss Carlton had always believed that feelings showed. Inner qualities were displayed in a face. This belief had brought her much pleasure – in buses, on trains, in shops. She turned to the girl. 'And what do you do, my dear?'

'I'm still at school, aren't I?' said the girl. 'Roll on July, that's what I say.'

Miss Carlton was surprised: she had not realised the child was so young. 'And what are your plans after that?' she asked hopefully. She had – a few minutes ago – had an interesting future mapped out for her: art school, the Royal College of Music, a university.

'I dunno,' said the girl. 'I'm not bothered. I may go on the Gift Counter at Boots. My sister's there.'

Miss Carlton was silent. After a moment she said, 'You hadn't thought of any – well, further training?'

'Training for what?'

Miss Carlton plunged. 'I was thinking,' she said, 'that with

91

your – well, with your nice taste in clothes, that dress is really quite charming – that perhaps you might be artistic. Are you at all interested in painting?'

She had their attention. The young man, in the act of lighting a cigarette, lowered his hand and turned brown eyes upon her. Surprise and self-consciousness lent a new depth to the girl's features; she smoothed down her dress, patted a strand of hair.

'They had one of my drawings up in the art room at school.'

'Hey!' said the young man. 'What's all this, then?'

Miss Carlton beamed encouragement.

'My friend Eileen,' said the girl, 'she got a job as a window-dresser with the Co-op.'

'That the one with the frizzy hair?' said the young man.

'Yeah. Anyway,' the girl went on decidedly, 'I'm not staying on at school, am I? I'm leaving, July.'

The conversation withered. Miss Carlton was beginning to feel dispirited. Her folding chair was uncomfortable, the place was hot and dusty. The music had started up again and battered the whole city, it seemed, for the duration of the next song. Miss Carlton's deaf-aid had revealed some fundamental deficiency and no longer filtered the sound as it had before. She was obliged to listen to the singer, a manic creature who sang of love in tones of strangled loathing. It was a relief to see him subside, at last, in a Laocoon tangle of wires and microphones. Miss Carlton took out her handkerchief and wiped her forehead. She was perspiring most unpleasantly, and would have liked a cup of tea. The young man was slumped with his head in his hands, apparently dozing, and the girl was studying her own hair with minute attention. She prodded her companion and said, 'Eh, you! I've got split ends'. He made no reply.

Fragmented talk reached Miss Carlton. A man and a girl picked their way through the crowd, brushing past without apology, and their conversation floated down to her: they had loud, educated voices and spoke of car racing. 'Fantastic!' they said. 'Really great!' The young men she had listened to before were discussing the money earned by the singer who had just been heard. 'A thousand quid a week, easily, and he'll dodge the tax somehow.' 'The Dead Beats get five for a concert.' The girl, abandoning the investigation of her hair, said, 'My mum's going into hospital, Monday'. The young man lifted his head for a moment and said, 'Do you mind? Who wants to hear about Monday on a Saturday afternoon?' And she said 'Sorry, Len'. Somewhere a baby cried; two girls were dancing together; skeins of midges hung in the sunlight; on the platform instruments were being assembled for the next song. Miss Carlton got to her feet with difficulty. She folded the stool and stowed it away in her bag. She looked down at the young man and the girl and said, 'Good-bye. It was so nice to talk to you', and they nodded. There was a momentary distortion of the girl's features that was not a smile but might have been some kind of acknowledgement.

Miss Carlton extracted herself from the crowd. It took some time; bodies protruded wherever she tried to put her feet. She saw things she would have preferred not to see. Nobody looked at her or responded to her apologies, though she felt as alien and conspicuous now as a clothed person among sunbathers. A faint smell lifted from the crowd, of sweat, hair and cheap scent. There were flies and discarded cigarette packets and little piles of dog mess. Miss Carlton battled on, and reached the point at last where the crowd began to diminish, like a nebula disintegrating at the rim. She was able to walk without interruption; behind her, the music crashed again, but with reduced volume. And behind her, also, sat and sprawled the young people in their floating dresses, their silks and velvets, their wide-brimmed hats and their strange, misleading faces.

Miss Carlton walked to the Round Pond. She sat down on a bench and saw small, white-winged yachts skim to and fro. Gulls rode above her head on translucent wings. The water was delicately pleated by the wind; squadrons of ducks moved to and fro. Under the water, Miss Carlton knew, was a disagreeable deposit of old Coke bottles and rusty tins, but it was pointless to dwell on that. All around the edge of the pond were small children, skipping, playing with balls, doing things with boats. Miss Carlton had never much cared for children, but she found herself looking at them intently, noticing, for the first time, it seemed, their small unformed features across which emotion and involvement flitted like the shadows of the birds on the water.

Revenant as Typewriter

Muriel Rackham, reaching the penultimate page of her talk, spoke with one eye upon the public library clock. The paper ('Ghosts: an analysis of their fictional and historic function') lasted precisely fifty-one minutes, as she well knew, but the stamina of the Ilmington Literary and Philosophical Society was problematic; an elderly man in the back row had been asleep since page seven, and there was a certain amount of shuffle and fidget in the middle reaches of the thirty odd seats occupied by the society's membership. Muriel skipped two paragraphs and moved into the concluding phase; it had perhaps been rash (not to say wasteful) to use on this occasion a paper that had had a considerable success at the English Studies Conference and with her colleagues at the College Senior Seminar, but she had nothing much else written up at the moment and had felt disinclined to produce a piece especially for the occasion. She paused (nothing like silence to induce attention) and went on 'So, leaving aside for the moment its literary role as vehicle for authorial comment in characters as diverse as Hamlet's father and Peter Quint, let us in conclusion try to summarize the historic function of the ghost — define as far as we can its social purpose, try to see why people needed ghosts and what they used them for. We've already paid tribute to that great source book for the student of the folkloric ghost — Dr Katherine Briggs' *Dictionary of British Folk-Tales* — of which I think it was Bernard Levin who remarked in a review that a glance down its list of Tale-Types and Motifs disposes once and for all of the notion that the British are a phlegmatic and unfanciful people.' (She paused at this point for the ripple of appreciative amusement that should run through the audience, but the Ilmington Lit. and Phil. sat unmoved; there were two sleepers now in the back row.) '... We've looked already at the repetitious nature of Motifs – Ghost follows its own corpse, reading the funeral service silently; Ghost laid when treasure is unearthed; Revenant as hare; Revenant in human form; Wraith appears to person in bedroom; Ghost haunts scene of former crime; Ghost exercises power through possessions of its lifetime – and so on and so forth. The subject-matter of ghostly folklore, in fact, perfectly supports the thesis of Keith Thomas in his book *Religion and the Decline of Magic* that the historic ghost is no random or frivolous character but fulfils a particular social need – in a society where the arm of the law is short it serves to draw attention to the unpunished crime, to seek the rectification of wrongs, to act as a reminder of the past, to . . .'

She read on, the text familiar enough for the thoughts to wander: Bill Freeman, the chairman, had introduced her appallingly, neglecting to mention her publications and reducing her Senior Lectureship at Ilmington College of Education to a Lectureship – she felt again a flush of irritation, and wondered if it had been deliberate or merely obtuse. They were an undistinguished lot, the audience; surely that woman at the end of the third row was an assistant in W. H. Smith's? Muriel observed them with distaste, as she turned over to the last page; schoolteachers and librarians, for the most part, one was talking right above their heads, in all probability. A somewhat wasted evening – which could have usefully been spent doing things about the house, or going through students' essays, or looking at that article Paul had given her, in order to have some well thought-out comments for the morning.

She concluded, and sat, with a wintry smile towards Bill Freeman, at her side, who, as one might have expected, rose to thank her with a sequence of remarks as inept as his introduction. '... our appreciation to Dr Rackham for her fascinating talk and throw the meeting open to discussion.'

Discussion could not have been said to flow. There was a man who had been to a production of *Macbeth* in which you actually saw Banquo and did the speaker think that was right or was it better if you just kind of guessed he was there . . . and a woman who thought *The Turn of the Screw* wasn't awfully good when they made it into an opera, and another who had been interested in the bit about people in historical times believing in ghosts and had the speaker ever visited Hampton Court because if you go there the guide tells you that . . .

Muriel dealt politely but briefly with the questioners. She glanced again at the clock, and then at Bill Freeman, who would do well to wind things up. There was a pause. Bill Freeman scanned the audience and said, 'Well, if no one has anything more to ask Dr Rackham I think perhaps . . .'

The small dark woman at the end of the front row leaned forward, looking at Muriel. 'I thought what you said was quite interesting and I'd like to tell you about this thing that happened to a friend of mine. She was staying in this house, you see, where apparently . . .'

It went on for several minutes. It was very tedious, a long rigmarole about inexplicable creakings in the night, objects appearing and disappearing, ghostly footsteps and sounds and so on and so forth, all classifiable according to Tale-Type and Motif if one felt so inclined and hadn't in fact lost interest in the whole subject some time ago, now that one was doing this work on the metaphysical poets with Paul . . . Muriel sat back and sighed. She eyed the woman with distaste; the face was vaguely familiar, someone local, presumably. An absurd little person with black, straight, short hair (dyed by the look of it) fringing her face, those now unfashionable spectacles upswept at the corners and tinted a disagreeable mauve, long ear-rings of some cheap shiny stone. Ear-rings, Muriel noted, more suitable for a younger woman; this creature was her own age, at least. Her skirt was too short, also, and her shirt patterned with what looked like lotus flowers in a discordant pink.

'. . . and my friend felt that it had come back to see about

97

something, the ghost, something that had annoyed it. I just wondered what the speaker had to say about that, if she'd ever had any experiences of that kind.' The woman stared at Muriel, almost aggressively.

Muriel gathered herself. 'Well,' she said briskly, 'of course we've really been concerned this evening with the fictional and historical persona of the ghost, haven't we? As far as I'm concerned I would subscribe to what has been called the intellectual impossibility of ghosts – and of course experiences such as your friend's, if one stops to think about it, are open to all kinds of explanation, aren't they?' – she flashed a quick, placating smile – 'And now, I feel perhaps that . . .' – she half-turned towards the chairman – 'if there are no more questions . . .'

Going home (after coffee and sandwiches in someone's house; the black-haired person, mercifully, had not been there) she shook off the dispiriting atmosphere of the evening with relief: the dingy room, the unresponsive audience. The paper had been far too academic for them, of course. She felt glad that Paul had not come. He had offered to, but she had insisted that he shouldn't. Turning the mini out of the High Street and past the corner of his road, she allowed herself a glance at the lighted window of his house. The curtains were drawn; Sheila would be watching television, of course, Paul reading (the new Joyce book, probably, or maybe this week's TLS). Poor Paul. Poor, dear Paul. It was tragic, such a marriage. That dull, insensitive woman.

'Your friendship is of the greatest value to me, Muriel' he had said, one week ago exactly. He had said it looking out of the window, rather than at her – and she had understood at once. Understood the depth of his feeling, the necessity for understatement, for the avoidance of emotional display. Their position was of extreme delicacy – Paul's position. Head of Department, Vice-Principal of the College. She had nodded and murmured something, and they had gone on to discuss a student, some problems about the syllabus . . .

At night, she had lain awake, thinking with complacency of their relationship, of its restraint and depth, in such contrast to the stridency of the times. Muriel considered herself – knew herself to be – a tolerant woman, but occasionally she observed her students with disgust; their behaviour was coarse and vulgar, not to put too fine a point upon it. They brandished what should be kept private.

Occasionally, lying there, she was visited by other feelings, which she recognised and suppressed; a mature, balanced person is able to exercise self-control. The satisfaction of love takes more than one form.

She put the car in the garage and let herself into the house, experiencing the usual pleasure. It was delightful; white walls, bare boards sanded and polished, her choice and tasteful possessions – rugs, pictures, the few antique pieces, the comfortable sofa and armchairs, the William Morris curtains. It was so unlike, now, the dirty, cluttered, scruffy place she had bought five months ago as to be almost unrecognisable. Only its early Victorian exterior remembered – and that too was now bright and trim under new paint, with a front door carefully reconstructed in keeping, to replace the appalling twenties porch some previous occupant had built on. The clearing-out process had been gruelling – Muriel blenched even now at the thought of it: cupboards stacked with junk and rubbish that nobody had bothered to remove (there had been an executors' sale, the elderly owner having died some months before), the whole place filthy and in a state of horrid disrepair. She had done the bulk of the work herself, with the help of a local decorator and carpenter for the jobs she felt were beyond her. But alone she had emptied all those cavernous cupboards, carting the stuff down to a skip hired from a local firm. It had been a disagreeable job – not just because of the dirt and physical effort, but because of the nature of the junk, which hinted at an alien and unpleasing way of life. She felt that she wanted to scour the house of its past, make it truly hers, as she heaved bundle after bundle of musty rubbish down the stairs. There had been boxes of old clothes – too old and sour to interest either the salerooms or Oxfam – brash vulgar female clothes, shrill of colour and pattern, in materials like sateen, chenille and rayon, the feel of which made Muriel shudder. They slithered

99

from her hands, smelling of mould and mouse droppings, their touch so repellent that she took to wearing rubber gloves. And then there were shelves of old magazines and books — not the engrossing treasure-trove that such a hoard ought to be (second-hand bookshops, after all, were an addiction of hers) but dreary and dispiriting in what they suggested of whoever had owned them: pulp romantic fiction, stacks of the cheaper, shriller women's magazines (all sex and crime, not even that limited but wholesome stuff about cooking, children and health), some tattered booklets with pictures that made Muriel flush — she shovelled the beastly things into a supermarket carton and dumped the lot into the skip. This house had seen little or no literature that could even be called decent during its recent past, that was clear enough; with pleasure she had arranged her own books on the newly-painted shelves at either side of the fireplace. They seemed to clinch her conquest of the place.

There had been other things, too. A dressmaker's dummy that she had found prone at the back of a cupboard (its murky shape had given her a hideous shock); she had scrubbed and kept it, occasionally she made herself a dress or skirt and it might conceivably be useful, though its torso was dumpier than her own. A tangle of hairnets and curlers in a drawer of the kitchen dresser, horribly scented of violets. Bits and pieces of broken and garish jewellery — all fake — that kept appearing from under floorboards or down crevices. Even now she came across things; it was as though the house would never have done with spewing out its tawdry memories. And of course the redecorating had been a major job — stripping away those fearful wallpapers that plastered every room, every conceivable misrepresentation of nature, loud and unnatural roses, poppies and less identifiable flowers that crawled and clustered up and down the walls. Sometimes two or three different ones had fought for survival in the same room; grimly, Muriel, aided by the decorator, tore and soaked and peeled. At last, every wall was crisply white, a background to her prints and lithographs, her Georgian mirror, the Khelim rug.

Now, she felt at last that she had taken possession. There were one or two small things still that jarred – a cupboard in her bedroom from which, scrub as she might, she could not eradicate the sickly smell of some cheap perfume, a hideous art nouveau window (she gathered such things were once again in fashion – chacun à son goût) in the hall which she would eventually get around to replacing. Otherwise, all was hers; her quiet but distinctive taste in harmony with the house's original architectural grace.

It was just past nine; time for a look at that article before bed. Muriel went to her desk (which, by day, had a view of the small garden prettily framed in William Morris's 'Honeysuckle') and sat reading and taking notes for an hour or so. She remembered that Paul would be away all day tomorrow, at a meeting in London, and she would not be able to see him, so when she had finished reading she pulled her typewriter in front of her and made a résumé of her reflections on the article, to leave in his pigeon-hole. She read them through, satisfied with what she felt to be some neatly put points. Then she got up, locked the back and front doors, checked the windows, and went to bed.

In the night, she woke; the room felt appallingly stuffy – she could even, from her bed, smell that disagreeable cupboard – and she assumed that she must have forgotten to open the window. Getting up to do so, she found the sash raised a couple of inches as usual. She returned to bed, and was visited by unwelcome yearnings which she drove out by a stern concentration on her second year Shakespeare option.

She had left her page of notes on the article in the typewriter, and almost forgot it in the morning, remembering at the last moment as she was about to leave the house, and going back to twitch it hastily out and put it in her handbag. The day was busy with classes and a lecture, so that it was not until the afternoon that she had time to write a short note for Paul ('I entirely agree with you about the weaknesses in his argument; however there are one or two points we might discuss, some thoughts on which I enclose. I do hope London was not too exhausting – MCR'), and glance again at the page of typescript.

It was not as satisfactory as Muriel remembered; in fact it was not satisfactory at all. She must have been a great deal more tired than she had realised last night – only in a stupor (and not even, one would have hoped, then) could she have written such muddled sentences, such hideous syntax, such illiteracies of style and spelling. 'What I think is that he developped what he said about the character of Tess all wrong so what you ended up feeling was that . . .' she read in horror '. . . if Hardy's descriptive passages are not always relivant then personally what I don't see is why . . .' And what was this note at the bottom – apparently added in haste? 'What about meeting for a natter tomorrow – I was thinking about you all last night – ssh! you aren't supposed to know that!' I must have been half-asleep, she thought, how could I write such things?

Hot with discomfort (and relief – heavens! she might not have looked again at the thing), she scrumpled the paper and threw it into the wastepaper basket. She wrote a second note to Paul saying that she had read the article but unfortunately had not the time now to say more, and hoped to discuss it with him at some point; she then cancelled her late afternoon class and went home early. I have been overdoing things, she thought – my work, the house – I need rest, a quiet evening.

She settled down to read, but could not concentrate; for almost the first time, she found herself wishing for the anodyne distraction of a television. She polished and dusted the sitting room (finding, in the process, a disgusting matted hank of hairnets and ribbon that had got, quite inexplicably, into her Worcester teapot) and cleaned the windows. Then she did some washing, which led to an inspection of her wardrobe; it seemed sparse. A new dress, perhaps, would lift her spirits. On Saturday, she would buy one, and in the meantime, there was that nice length of tweed her sister had given her and which had lain untouched for months. Perhaps with the aid of the dressmaker's dummy it could be made into a useful skirt. She fetched the dummy and spent an hour or two with scissors and pins – a soothing activity, though the results were not quite as satisfactory as she could have wished. Eventually she left the roughly-fashioned skirt pinned to the dummy and put it away in the spare room cupboard before going to bed.

A few days later, to her pleasure, Paul accepted an invitation to call in at the house on his way home to pick up a book and have a drink. He had hesitated before accepting, and she understood his difficulties at once; such meetings were rare for them, and the reasons clear enough to her: the pressures of his busy life, Sheila . . . 'Well, yes, how kind, Muriel' he had said. 'Yes, fine, then. I'll give Sheila a ring and tell her I'll be a little late.'

Poor Paul; the strains of such a marriage did not bear contemplation. Of course, they always appeared harmonious enough in public, a further tribute to his wonderful patience and restraint. Nor did he ever hint or complain; one had to be perceptive to realise the tensions that must arise – a man of his intellectual stature fettered to someone without, so far as Muriel understood, so much as an A-level. His tolerance was amazing; Muriel had even heard him, once, join with well-simulated enthusiasm in a discussion of some trashy television series prompted by Sheila at a Staff Club party.

She was delayed at the College and only managed to arrive back at the house a few minutes before he arrived. Pouring the sherry, she heard him say, 'What's this, then, Muriel – making a study of popular culture?', and turned round to see him smiling and holding up one of those scabrous women's magazines that – she thought – she had committed to the skip. Disconcerted, she found herself flushing, embarking on a defensive explanation of the rubbish that had been in the house . . . (But she had cleared all that stuff out, every bit, how could that thing have been, apparently, lying on the little Victorian sewing table, from which Paul had taken it?)

The incident unnerved her, spoiled what should have been an idyllic hour.

Muriel woke the next day – Saturday – discontented and twitchy. She had slept badly, disturbed by the muffled sound of a woman's shrill laugh, coming presumably from the next house in the terrace; she had not realised before that noise could penetrate the walls.

Remembering her resolution of a few days before, she went

shopping for a new dress. The facilities of Ilmington were hardly metropolitan, but adequate for a woman of her restrained tastes; she found, after some searching, a pleasant enough garment innocent of any of the nastier excesses of modern fashion, in a wholesome colour and fabric, and took it home in a rather calmer frame of mind.

In the evening, there was the Principal's sherry party (Paul would be there; with any luck there would be the opportunity for a few quiet words). She went to take the dress from the wardrobe and indeed was about to put it on before the feel of it in her hands brought her up short; surely there was something wrong? She took it to the window, staring – this was never the dress she had chosen so carefully this morning? The remembered eau-de-nil was now, looked at again, in the light from the street, a harsh and unflattering apple-green; the coarse linen, so pleasant to the touch, a slimy artificial stuff. She had made the most disastrous mistake; tears of frustration and annoyance pricked her eyes. She threw the thing back in the cupboard and put on her old Jaegar print.

Sunday was a day that, normally, she enjoyed. This one got off to a bad start with the discovery of *The Sunday Mirror* sticking through the front door instead of *The Sunday Times*; after breakfast she rang the shop, knowing that they would be open till eleven, only to be told by a bewildered voice that surely that was what she had asked for, change it, you said on the 'phone, Thursday it was, for *The Sunday Mirror*, spicier, you said, good for a laugh. 'There's been some mistake,' said Muriel curtly. 'I don't know what you can be thinking of.' She slammed down the receiver and set about a massive cleaning of the house; it seemed the proper therapeutic thing to do.

After lunch she sat down at her desk to do some work; her article for *English Today* was coming along nicely. Soon it would be time to show a first draft to Paul. She took the lid off the typewriter and prepared to re-read the page she had left in on Friday.

Two minutes later, her heart thumping, she was ripping out the paper, crumpling it into a ball ... I never wrote such stuff, she thought, it's impossible, words like that, expressions like – I don't even *know* such expressions.

She sat in horror, staring into the basilisk eye of a thrush on her garden wall. There is something wrong, she thought, I am not myself, am I going mad?

She took a sleeping pill, but even so woke in the depths of the night (again, those muffled peals of laughter), too hot, the room heavy around her so that she had to get up and open the window further; the house creaked. There must be a fault in the heating system, she thought, I'll have to get the man round. She lay in discomfort, her head aching.

In the days that followed it seemed to her that she suffered from continuous headaches. Headaches, and a kind of lightheadedness that made her feel sometimes that she had only a tenuous grip on reality; in the house, after work, she heard noises, saw things. There was that laughter again, which must be from next door but when she enquired delicately of the milkman as to who her neighbours were (one didn't want actually to get involved with them) she learned that an elderly man lived there, alone, a retired doctor. And there were things that seemed hallucinatory, there was no other explanation; going to the cupboard where she had put the dummy, to have another go at that skirt, she had found the thing swathed not in her nice herring-bone tweed but a revolting purple chenille. She slammed the cupboard closed (again, the lurking shape of the dummy had startled her, although she had expected to see it), and sat down on the bed, her chest pounding. I am not well, she thought, I am doing things and then forgetting that I have done them, there is something seriously wrong.

And then there was the wallpaper. She had come into the sitting room, one bright sunny morning – her spruce, white sitting room – and, glancing at her Dufy prints, had seen suddenly the shadowy presence of the old, hideous wallpaper behind them, those entwined violets and roses that she and the decorator had so laboriously scraped away. Two walls, she now saw, were scarred all over, behind the new emulsion paint, with the shadowy presence of the old paper; how can we have missed them, she thought angrily – that decorator, I should have kept a sharper eye on him

– but surely, I *remember*, we did this room together, every bit was stripped, surely?

Her head spun.

She went to the doctor, unwillingly, disliking her list of neurotic symptoms, envying the bronchitic coughs and bandaged legs in the waiting room. Stiffly, she submitted to the questions, wanting to say: I am not this kind of person at all, I am balanced, well-adjusted, known for my good sense. With distaste, she listened to the diagnosis: yes, she wanted to say, impatiently, I have heard of menopausal problems but I am not the kind of woman to whom they happen, I keep things under better control than that, overwork is much more likely. She took his prescription and went away, feeling humiliated.

It was the examination season. She was faced, every evening, on returning home, with a stack of scripts and would sit up late marking, grateful for the distraction, though she was even more tired and prone to headaches. The tiredness was leading to confusion, also, she realised. On one occasion, giving a class, she had been aware of covert glances and giggles among her students, apparently prompted by her own appearance; later, in the staff cloakroom, she had looked in a mirror and been appalled to discover herself wearing a frightful low cut pink blouse with some kind of flower-pattern. It was vaguely familiar – I've seen it before, she thought, and realised it must be a relic of the rubbish in the house, left in the back of her cupboard and put on accidentally this morning, in her bleary awakening from a disturbed night. Condemned to wear it for the rest of the day, she felt taken over by its garishness, as though compelled to behave in character; she found herself joining a group of people at lunch-time with whom she would not normally have associated, the brash set among her colleagues, sharing jokes and a conversation that she found distasteful. In Paul's office, later, going over some application forms, she laid her hand on his sleeve, and felt him withdraw his arm; later, the memory of this made her shrivel. It was as though she had betrayed the delicacy of their relationship; never before had they made physical contact.

She decided to take a couple of days off from the college, and mark scripts at home.

The first day passed tranquilly enough; she worked throughout the morning and early afternoon. At around five she felt suddenly moved, against her better judgment, to telephone Paul with what she knew to be a trumped-up query about an exam problem. Talking to him, she was aware of her own voice, with a curious detachment; its tone surprised her, and the shrillness of her laugh. Do I always sound like that, she thought, have I always laughed in that way? It seemed to her that Paul was abrupt, that he deliberately ended the conversation.

She got up the next morning in a curious frame of mind. The scripts she had to mark filled her with irritation; not the irritation stemming from inadequacy in the candidates, but a petulant resentment of the whole thing. Sometimes, she did not seem able to follow the answers to questions. 'Don't get you,' she scribbled in the margin. 'What are you on about?' At the bottom of one script she scrawled a series of doodles: indeterminate flowers, a face wearing upswept spectacles, a buxom female figure. At last, with the pile of scripts barely eroded, she abandoned her desk and wandered restlessly around the house.

Somehow, it displeased her. It was too stark, too bare, an unlived-in place. I like a bit of life, she thought, a bit of colour, something to pep things up; rummaging in the scullery she found under the sink some gaily patterned curtaining that must have got overlooked when she cleared out those particular shelves. That's nice, she thought, nice and striking, I like that; as she hung it in place of the linen weave in the hall that now seemed so dowdy, it seemed to her that from somewhere in the house came a peal of laughter.

That day merged, somehow, into the next. She did not go to the college. Several times the telephone rang: mostly she ignored it. Once, answering, she heard the departmental secretary's voice, blathering on: 'Dr Rackham?' she kept saying, 'Dr Rackham? Professor Simons has been a bit worried, we wondered if . . .' Muriel laughed and hung up. The night, the intermediate night (or nights, it might have been, time was a bit confusing, not that it mattered at all) had been most extraordinary. She had had company of some kind; throughout the night, whenever she woke, she had been aware of a low murmuring. A voice. A voice of compulsive intimacy, coarse and insistent; it had repelled but at the same time fascinated her. She had lain there, silent and unresisting.

The house displeased her more and more. It's got no style, she thought, full of dreary old stuff. She took down the Dufy prints, and the Piper cathedral etchings, thinking: I don't like that kind of thing, I like a proper picture, where you can see what's what, don't know where I ever picked up these. She made a brief sortie to Boots round the corner and bought a couple of really nice things, not expensive either – a Chinese girl and a lovely painting of horses galloping by the sea. As she hung them in the sitting room, it seemed to her that someone clutched her arm, and for an instant she shuddered uncontrollably, but the sensation passed, though it left her feeling light-headed, a little hysterical.

Her own appearance dissatisfied her, too. She sat looking at herself in her bedroom mirror and thought: I've never made the best of myself, a woman's got to make use of what's she's got, hasn't she? Where's that nice blouse I found the other day, it's flattering – a bit of decolleté, I'm not past that kind of thing yet. She put it on, and felt pleased. Downstairs, the telephone was ringing again, but she could not be bothered to answer it. Don't want to see anyone, she thought, fed up with people, if it's Paul he can come and find me, can't he? Play hard to get, that's what you should do with men, string them along a bit.

Anyway, she was not alone. She could feel, again, that presence in the room, though when she swung round suddenly – with a resurgence of that chill sensation – there was nothing but the dressmaker's dummy, standing in the corner. She must have brought it from the cupboard, and forgotten.

She wandered about the house, muttering to herself; from time to time, a person walked with her, not someone you could see, just a presence, its arm slipped through Muriel's, whispering intimacies, suggestions. All those old books of yours, it said, you don't want those, ring the newsagent, have them send round some mags, a good read, that's what we want. Muriel nodded.

Once, people hammered on the door. She could hear their voices; colleagues from the department. 'Muriel?' they called, 'are you there, Muriel?' She went into the kitchen and shut herself in till they had gone. For a moment, sitting there, she felt clearer in her head, free of the confusion that had been dragging her down; something is happening, she thought wildly, something I cannot cope with, can't control . . .

And then there came again that presence, with its insistent voice, and this time the voice was quite real, and she knew, too, that she had heard it before, somewhere, quite recently, not long ago. Where, where?

. . . I thought what you said was quite interesting, and I'd like to tell you about this thing that happened to a friend of mine . . .

Muriel held the bannisters, to steady herself (she was on her way upstairs again, in her perpetual edgy drifting up and down the house): the Lit. and Phil., I remember now, that woman.

And it came to her too, with a horrid jolt, that she knew now, remembered suddenly, why, at the time, that evening, the face had been familiar, why she'd felt she'd seen it before.

It had been the face in a yellowed photograph that had tumbled from a tatty book when she had been clearing out the house; Violet Hanson, 1934, in faded ink on the back.

Sale by auction, by order of the Executors of Mrs Violet Hanson, deceased, No. 27 Clarendon Terrace, a four-bedroomed house with scope for . . .

Someone was laughing, peals of shrill laughter that rang through the house, and as she reached the top floor, and turned into her bedroom, she knew that it was herself. She went into her bedroom and sat down at her dressing-table and looked in the mirror. The face that looked back at her was haggard. I've got to do something about myself, she thought, I'm turning into an old frump. She groped on the table and found a pair of ear-rings, long, shiny ones that she had forgotten she had. She held them up against her face; yes, that's nice, stylish, and I'll dye my hair, have it cut short and dye it black, take years off me, that would . . .

There was laughter again, but she no longer knew if it was hers or someone else's.

Next term, we'll mash you

Inside the car it was quiet, the noise of the engine even and sub-dued, the air just the right temperature, the windows tight-fitting. The boy sat on the back seat, a box of chocolates, unopened, beside him, and a comic, folded. The trim Sussex landscape flowed past the windows: cows, white-fenced fields, highly-priced period houses. The sunlight was glassy, remote as a coloured photograph. The backs of the two heads in front of him swayed with the motion of the car.

His mother half-turned to speak to him. 'Nearly there now, darling.'

The father glanced downwards at his wife's wrist. 'Are we all right for time?'

'Just right. Nearly twelve.'

'I could do with a drink. Hope they lay something on.'

'I'm sure they will. The Wilcoxes say they're awfully nice people. Not really the schoolmaster-type at all, Sally says.'

The man said, 'He's an Oxford chap.'

'Is he? You didn't say.'

'Mmn.'

'Of course, the fees are that much higher than the Seaford place.'

'Fifty quid or so. We'll have to see.'

The car turned right, between white gates and high, dark, tight-clipped hedges. The whisper of the road under the tyres changed to the crunch of gravel. The child, staring sideways, read black lettering on a white board: 'St Edward's Preparatory School. Please Drive Slowly'. He shifted on the seat, and the leather sucked at the bare skin under his knees, stinging.

The mother said, 'It's a lovely place. Those must be the play-ing-fields. Look, darling, there are some of the boys'. She clicked open her handbag, and the sun caught her mirror and flashed in the child's eyes; the comb went through her hair and he saw the grooves it left, neat as distant ploughing.

'Come on, then, Charles, out you get.'

The building was red brick, early nineteenth century, spread-ing out long arms in which windows glittered blackly. Flowers, trapped in neat beds, were alternate red and white. They went up the steps, the man, the woman, and the child two paces behind.

The woman, the mother, smoothing down a skirt that would be ridged from sitting, thought: I like the way they've got the maid all done up properly. The little white apron and all that. She's foreign, I suppose. Au pair. Very nice. If he comes here there'll be Speech Days and that kind of thing. Sally Wilcox says it's quite dressy – she got that cream linen coat for coming down here. You can see why it costs a bomb. Great big grounds and only an hour and a half from London.

They went into a room looking out into a terrace. Beyond, dappled lawns, gently shifting trees, black and white cows graz-ing behind iron railings. Books, leather chairs, a table with maga-zines – *Country Life, The Field, The Economist*. 'Please, if you would wait here. The Headmaster won't be long.'

Alone, they sat, inspected. 'I like the atmosphere, don't you, John?'

'Very pleasant, yes.' Four hundred a term, near enough. You can tell it's a cut above the Seaford place, though, or the one at St Albans. Bob Wilcox says quite a few City people send their boys here. One or two of the merchant bankers, those kind of people. It's the sort of contact that would do no harm at all. You meet someone, get talking at a cricket match or what have you . . . Not at all a bad thing.

'All right, Charles? You didn't get sick in the car, did you?'

The child had black hair, slicked down smooth to his head. His ears, too large, jutted out, transparent in the light from the window, laced with tiny, delicate veins. His clothes had the shine and crease of newness. He looked at the books, the dark brown pictures, his parents, said nothing.

'Come here, let me tidy your hair.'

The door opened. The child hesitated, stood up, sat, then rose again with his father.

'Mr and Mrs Manders? How very nice to meet you – I'm Margaret Spokes, and will you please forgive my husband who is tied up with some wretch who broke the cricket pavilion window and will be just a few more minutes. We try to be organised but a schoolmaster's day is always just that bit unpredictable. Do please sit down and what will you have to revive you after that beastly drive? You live in Finchley, is that right?'

'Hampstead, really,' said the mother. 'Sherry would be lovely.' She worked over the headmaster's wife from shoes to hairstyle, pricing and assessing. Shoes old but expensive – Russell and Bromley. Good skirt. Blouse could be Marks and Sparks – not sure. Real pearls. Super Victorian ring. She's not gone to any particular trouble – that's just what she'd wear anyway. You can be confident, with a voice like that, of course. Sally Wilcox says she knows all sorts of people.

The headmaster's wife said, 'I don't know how much you know about us? Prospectuses don't tell you a thing, do they. We'll look round everything in a minute, when you've had a chat with my husband. I gather you're friends of the Wilcoxes, by the way. I'm awfully fond of Simon – he's down for Winchester, of course, but I expect you know that.'

The mother smiled over her sherry. Oh, I know that all right. Sally Wilcox doesn't let you forget that.

'And this is Charles? My dear, we've been forgetting all about you! In a minute I'm going to borrow Charles and take him off to meet some of the boys because after all you're choosing a school for him, aren't you, and not for you, so he ought to know what he might be letting himself in for and it shows we've got nothing to hide.'

The parents laughed. The father, sherry warming his guts, thought that this was an amusing woman. Not attractive, of course, a bit homespun, but impressive all the same. Partly the voice, of course; it takes a bloody expensive education to produce a voice like that. And other things, of course. Background and all that stuff.

'I think I can hear the thud of the Fourth Form coming in from games, which means my husband is on his way, and then I shall leave you with him while I take Charles off to the common room.'

For a moment the three adults centred on the child, looking, judging. The mother said, 'He looks so hideously pale, compared to those boys we saw outside.'

'My dear, that's London, isn't it? You just have to get them out, to get some colour into them. Ah, here's James. James – Mr and Mrs Manders. You remember, Bob Wilcox was mentioning at Sports Day . . .'

The headmaster reflected his wife's style, like paired cards in Happy Families. His clothes were mature rather than old, his skin well-scrubbed, his shoes clean, his geniality untainted by the least condescension. He was genuinely sorry to have kept them waiting, but in this business one lurches from one minor crisis to the next . . . And this is Charles? Hello, there, Charles. His large hand rested for a moment on the child's head, quite extinguishing the thin, dark hair. It was as though he had but to clench his fingers to crush the skull. But he took his hand away and moved the parents to the window, to observe the mutilated cricket pavilion, with indulgent laughter.

And the child is borne away by the headmaster's wife. She never touches him or tells him to come, but simply bears him away like some relentless tide, down corridors and through swinging glass doors, towing him like a frail craft, not bothering to look back to see if he is following, confident in the strength of magnetism, or obedience.

And delivers him to a room where boys are scattered among inky tables and rungless chairs and sprawled on a mangy carpet. There is a scampering, and a rising, and a silence falling, as she opens the door.

'Now this is the Lower Third, Charles, who you'd be with if you come to us in September. Boys, this is Charles Manders, and I want you to tell him all about things and answer any questions he wants to ask. You can believe about half of what they say, Charles, and they will tell you the most fearful lies about the food, which is excellent.'

The boys laugh and groan; amiable, exaggerated groans. They must like the headmaster's wife: there is licensed repartee. They look at her with bright eyes in open, eager faces. Someone leaps to hold the door for her, and close it behind her. She is gone.

The child stands in the centre of the room, and it draws in around him. The circle of children contracts, faces are only a yard or so from him, strange faces, looking, assessing.

Asking questions. They help themselves to his name, his age, his school. Over their heads he sees beyond the window an inaccessible world of shivering trees and high racing clouds and his voice which has floated like a feather in the dusty schoolroom air dies altogether and he becomes mute, and he stands in the middle of them with shoulders humped, staring down at feet: grubby plimsolls and kicked brown sandals. There is a noise in his ears like rushing water, a torrential din out of which voices boom, blotting each other out so that he cannot always hear the words. Do you? they say, and Have you? and What's your? and the faces, if he looks up, swing into one another in kaleidoscopic patterns and the floor under his feet is unsteady, lifting and falling.

And out of the noises comes one voice that is complete, that he can hear. 'Next term we'll mash you,' it says. 'We always mash new boys.'

And a bell goes, somewhere beyond doors and down corridors, and suddenly the children are all gone, clattering away and leaving him there with the heaving floor and the walls that shift and swing, and the headmaster's wife comes back and tows him away, and he is with his parents again, and they are getting into the car, and the high hedges skim past the car windows once more, in the other direction, and the gravel under the tyres changes to black tarmac.

115

'Well?'

'I liked it, didn't you?' The mother adjusted the car around her, closing windows, shrugging into her seat.

'Very pleasant, really. Nice chap.'

'I liked him. Not quite so sure about her.'

'It's pricey, of course.'

'All the same . . .'

'Money well spent, though. One way and another.'

'Shall we settle it, then?'

'I think so. I'll drop him a line.'

The mother pitched her voice a notch higher to speak to the child in the back of the car. 'Would you like to go there, Charles? Like Simon Wilcox. Did you see that lovely gym, and the swimming-pool? And did the other boys tell you all about it?'

The child does not answer. He looks straight ahead of him, at the road coiling beneath the bonnet of the car. His face is haggard with anticipation.

At the Pitt-Rivers

They've got this museum in Oxford, called the Pitt-Rivers; I spend a lot of time there. It's a weird place, really weird, stuff from all over the world crammed into glass cases like some kind of mad junk-shop – native things from New Guinea and Mexico and Sumatra and wherever you like to think of. Spears and stone axes and masks and a thousand different kinds of fish-hook. And bead jewellery and peculiar musical instruments. And a great totem from Canada. You can learn a lot there about what people get up to: it makes you think. Mostly it's pretty depressing – umpteen different nasty ways of killing each other.

I didn't start going there to learn anything; just because it was a nice quiet place to mooch around and be on my own, Saturdays, or after school. It got to be a kind of habit. There aren't often many people there – the odd art student, a few kids gawping at the shrunken heads, one or two serious-looking blokes wandering around. The porter's usually reading *The Sun* or having a snooze; there's not a lot of custom. The Natural History Museum is a bigger draw; you have to go through that to get into the Pitt-Rivers. You'll always get an audience for a dinosaur and a few nasty-looking jellyfish in formalin. Actually I'm partial to the Natural History Museum myself; that makes you think, too. All those fossils, and then in the end you and me. I had a go at reading *The Origin of Species* last term, not that I got very far. There's a room upstairs in the museum where Darwin's friend – Huxley –

117

had this great argument with that bishop and the rest of them. It says so on the door. I like that, it seems kind of respectful. Putting up a plaque to an argument, instead of just JOE SOAP WAS BORN HERE or whatever. It should be done more often.

It was in the Natural History Museum — underneath the central whale — that I first saw her, and since my mind was on natural selection I thought she wasn't all that good an example of it. I remember thinking that it was funny it doesn't seem to operate with girls, so you got them getting prettier and prettier, because good-looking girls have a better deal than bad-looking ones, you've only got to observe a bit to see that. I always notice girls, to see if they're pretty or not, and she wasn't. She wasn't specially ugly; just very ordinary — you wouldn't look at her twice. She was sitting on a bench, watching the entrance.

All the girls I know — at school or round where I live — are either attractive or they're not. If they're attractive they have lots of blokes after them and if they're not they don't. It's as simple as that. If they're attractive just looking at them makes you think of all sorts of things, imagine what it would be like and so forth, and if they're not then it doesn't really occur to you, except insofar as it occurs to you a good deal of the time, actually. This girl was definitely not attractive. In the first place she was in fact quite old, not far off thirty I should think, and in the second she hadn't got a nice figure; her legs were kind of dumpy and she didn't have pretty hair or anything like that. I gave her a look, just automatically, to check, and then didn't bother with her.

Until I came alongside, where I could see her face clearly, and then I looked again. And again. She still wasn't pretty, but she had the most beautiful expression I've ever seen in my life. She glowed; that's the only way I can put it. She sat there with her hands in her lap, watching the door, and radiating away so that in a peculiar fashion it makes you feel good just to look at her, a bit like you were joining in how she felt. Stupid, I daresay, but that's how it was.

And I thought to myself: oh ho . . . I mean, I've seen films and I've read books and I know a bit about things.

As a matter of fact I've been in love myself twice. The first time was with a girl in my class at school and I suppose it was a bit of a trial run, really, I mean I'm not altogether sure how much I was feeling it but it seemed quite important when it was going on. The second time was last year, when I was fifteen. She came to stay with her married sister who lives round the corner from us and though it's months and months ago now I still feel quite faint and weak when I go past the house.

Oh ho, I thought. I felt kindly – sort of benign – and a bit curious to see what the bloke would be like. I thought he couldn't be much because of her not being pretty. I mean, in films you can always tell who's going to fall for who because they'll be the two good-lookers and while I'm not saying real life's like that there is a way people match each other, isn't there, you've only got to look round at married people. Let me hasten to say that I'm not all that good-looking myself, only about B+. Not too bad, but not all that marvellous either.

But he didn't show up and I wanted to get on into the Pitt-Rivers, so I left her there, waiting. What I haven't said is that one of the things I go to the Pitt-Rivers for is to write poetry. I write quite a lot of poetry. I could do it at home – I often do – and it's not that I'm coy or anything, my parents know about it and they're quite interested, but I just like the idea of having a special place to go to. It's quiet there, and a bit odd like I've said, and nobody takes any notice of me.

Sometimes I feel I'm getting somewhere with this poetry, and other times it looks to me pretty awful. I showed a few poems to our English master and he was very helpful: he said what was good and pointed out where I'd used words badly, or not worked out what I was thinking very well, so that was quite encouraging. He's a nice bloke. I like his lessons. He's very good at explaining poetry. I mean, I think poetry's amazingly difficult: sometimes you read a thing again and again and you just can't see what the hell the person's getting at. He reads all sorts of poetry to us, our English master, and you really get the hang of it after a bit – hard stuff like Hopkins and the *Hound of Heaven*, and Donne. He read us some of those Donne poems about love the other day which are all very explicit and I must say first time round I hadn't quite got the point – 'Licence my roaving hands . . .' and so forth – but he wasn't embarrassed or anything, our English master, and when you realise that it's not geography he's talking about, the poet, then as a matter of fact I think that poem's lovely. I got a bit fed up with the way some of my mates were sniggering about it, being all knowing; truth to tell I doubt if they know any more than I do, it's all just show. And that's a beautiful poem: I mean, if anything makes it clear that there's nothing wrong about sex, that poem does, they ought to make it compulsory reading for some people.

Anyway, I went on into the Pitt-Rivers and I was up on the first floor, in a favourite corner of mine among the arrow-heads, when I saw her again, and I must say I got quite a shock. Because the man with her was an old bloke: he was older than my father, fiftyish and more, he must have been at least twenty years older than her. So I reckoned I must have made a mistake. Not that at all.

They were talking, though I couldn't hear what they were saying because they were on the far side of the gallery. They stopped in front of a case and I could see their faces quite clearly. They stood there looking at each other, not talking any more, and I realised I hadn't made a mistake after all. Absolutely not. They didn't touch each other, they just stood and looked: it seemed like ages. I don't imagine they knew I was there.

And that time I was shocked. Really shocked. I don't mind telling you, I thought it was disgusting. He was an ordinary-looking person – he might have been a schoolmaster or something, he wore those kind of clothes, old trousers and sweater, and he had greyish hair, a bit long. And there was she, and as I've said she wasn't pretty, not at all, but she had this marvellous look about her, and she was years and years younger.

It was because of him, I realised, that she had that look.

I didn't like it at all. I got up, from where I was sitting, with quite a clatter to make sure they heard me and I went stumping off out of the museum. I wasn't going to write any more poetry that day, I could see. I went off home and truth to tell I didn't really think much more about them, that man and the girl, mainly because of being rather disgusted, like I said.

A couple of weeks later they were there again. They were on the ground floor, at the back, by the rush matting and ceremonial gear for with-it tribesmen, leaning up against a glass case that they weren't looking into, and talking. At least he was talking, quiet and serious, and she was listening, and nodding from time to time. I was busy with some thinking I wanted to do, and I tried not to take any notice of them; I mean, they were neither here nor there as far as I was concerned, none of my business, though I still thought it was a bit creepy. I couldn't see *why*, frankly. You fancy people your own age, and that's all there is to it, is what I thought. What I'd always thought.

So I ignored them, except that I couldn't quite. I kept sneaking a look, every now and then, and the more I did the more I felt kind of friendly towards them; I liked them. Which was a bit weird considering they didn't know I even existed – they certainly weren't interested in *me* – so it was a pretty one-sided kind of relationship. I thought he seemed like a nice bloke, whatever you thought about him and her and all that. It was something about the way he smiled, and the way he told her things (not that I ever heard a word they said, I wasn't eavesdropping, not ever, let's be quite clear about that) that made her look interested and say things back and so on. I thought it was obvious they liked talking to each other, quite apart from anything else. I thought that was nice.

I only took out that girl I mentioned – the one who came to stay with her sister – once, and as a matter of fact we couldn't find much to talk about. I was still in love with her – no doubt about that – but it was a bit sticky, I don't mind admitting. In fact I was quite glad when it was time to take her back to her sister's. In many ways the best part was just thinking about her.

Every time I looked at the girl – the Pitt-Rivers one, that is – I found myself imagining what it must be like being able to feel that you've made someone look like that. Radiant, like she was. Which is what that bloke must have been able to feel. I found myself putting myself in his place, as it were, and wondering. I've done a lot of wondering about things like that – everybody does,

I suppose – but mostly it's been more kind of basic. Now, I began to think I didn't really know anything. Looking at those two – watching them, if you like – was a bit like seeing something go on behind a thick glass window, so it was half removed from you. You could see but not hear, hear but not touch, or whatever. I could see, but I didn't know.

I suppose you could say I was envious, in a funny kind of way. I don't mean jealous in that I fancied the girl, or anything like that. As I've said already, she wasn't pretty, or even attractive. And I wasn't envious like you might be envious of someone for being happier than you are, because I'm not specially unhappy, as it happens. I think I was envious of them for being what they were – as though one fossil creature might be envious of a more evolved kind of fossil creature, which of course is a stupid idea.

When I was in the Pitt-Rivers again I looked for them, quite deliberately, but they weren't there. I was disappointed, though I pretended to myself it really didn't matter. I wondered about why they went there in the first place; I mean, people have to meet each other somewhere but why *there*? It doesn't exactly spring to mind as a romantic spot. I supposed there were reasons they didn't want to meet somewhere obvious and public: maybe he was married, I thought, or maybe she was, even. I wondered if that was the only place they met, or did they have others. Once, walking through the botanical gardens, I found myself looking for them in the big glasshouses there.

I know the inside of the Pitt-Rivers pretty well by now. Considering it's not anthropology or ethnology or whatever I went there for in the first place, it's quite surprising what a lot I could tell you about the things people believe and do. Primitive people, that is – what the Pitt-Rivers calls primitive people. And I think it's all very sad, actually: sad because it's like children, not understanding how things work and getting it all wrong, and carving each other up because of it a lot of the time. It does actually make you feel things get better – wars and bombs and everything notwithstanding. Nobody wants to go on being a child all their lives.

I was thinking about this – looking at a case full of particularly loony stuff to do with witchcraft – when I saw them again. At least I saw her first, standing by the totem with her hands in her coat pockets, and I didn't have to look at the door to know he'd arrived: her face told you that. He came up to her and gave her a kind of hug – arm round her shoulders and then quickly off again – and they wandered away up the stairs, heads together, talking.

I didn't follow them; it had been nice to see them again, and know they were there, and that was it. I was busy on a poem I'd been writing and unpicking and re-writing for some time. It was a poem about an old man sitting on a bench in a park and getting into conversation with a boy – someone around my age – and they swap opinions and observations (it's all dialogue, this poem, like a long conversation) and it's not till the end you realise they're the same person. It sounds either corny, or pretentious, I know; and what I could never decide was whether to have it as though the old man's looking back, or the boy's kind of projecting forwards – imagining himself, as it were. So I went on fiddling about with this, and didn't really think much about the man and the girl, until I saw it was lateish and there was no one else in the museum except me and some feet on the wooden floor of the gallery overhead, walking round and round, round and round. Two pairs of feet. They'd been doing that for ages, I realised; I'd been hearing them without registering.

I saw them go past – just their heads, above the glass cases – and something wasn't right. They weren't talking. She had her arm through his, and she was looking straight in front of her, and when I saw her face I had a nasty kind of twinge in my stomach. Because she was miserable. Once, she looked at him, and they both managed a bleak sort of smile. And then they walked on, round the gallery again, and next time past they still weren't talking, just holding on to each other like that, like people who're ill, or very old. And then the attendant rang the bell, and I heard them come down the stairs, and they came past me and went out into the Natural History Museum.

I went after them. I saw them stop – under the central whale, just where I first saw her – and then they did say something to each other. I couldn't see her face; she had her back to me. He went off then, on his own, out through the main entrance, quickly, and she sat down on a bench. For a moment or two she just sat staring at that wretched whale, and then she felt in her bag and got out a comb and did her hair, as though that might help. And then she dropped the comb and didn't seem to have noticed, even, because she just sat; she didn't bother to pick it up or anything. I could see her face then, and I hope I don't ever see anyone look so unhappy again. I truly hope that.

I don't know what had happened. I never will. Somehow, I don't think they were ever going to see each other again, but why . . . well, that's their concern, just like the rest of it was, except that in this peculiar way I'd come to feel it was mine too. I didn't think there was anything disgusting about them any more, or creepy — I hadn't for a long time. I suppose you could say I'd learned something else in the Pitt-Rivers, by accident. I never did go on with that poem. I tore it up, as far as it had got; I wasn't so sure any more about that conversation, that there could even be one, or not like I'd been imagining, anyway.

Nice people

James Winton, in faded drill trousers and flowered shirt, his bathing towel and trunks in a roll under his arm, a large, battered
straw hat on his head, walked slowly up the path from the beach.
He took it easily, in stages, a fifty yard leg at a time, and then a
pause to look back at the sea, which glittered in the late afternoon
light, quilted by the wind, roving through all the blues from pale
turquoise to the darkest midnight. He sat, breathing a little heavily, on a slab of rock, and saw that he was accompanied by the
children and the goats. They moved up the hillside parallel to
him, not using the path, flitting through the scrub, the prickly
pears and small thorny bushes and striped green and yellow cacti
that furnished the island's landscape.

The children came down to the beach every day at this time, as
he did. He was never clear why. While he swam and sunbathed,
they squatted at the back of the beach, in the scruffy hinterland of
rusty tins, seaweed and snatches of torn plastic – chattering,
throwing stones, and occasionally chivvying the goats. They
paid no attention to James. Once, they had watched and commented, giggling behind their small brown hands, fleeing in
simulated panic if he approached them. They would never
respond much to his attempts at conversation, refusing to be
drawn on the subject of names and ages, glancing shyly at each
other and shaking their heads though he guessed that they knew
quite enough English to understand. But nowadays they hardly
seemed to notice him; the goats swarmed up the hillside, sharply

black and brown, surprisingly clean, their udders huge and swinging, and the children swarmed with them, calling to each other, ignoring the more slowly moving James. This pleased him: he felt accepted.

Though, heaven knows, one should be accepted now. Two years it would be, this summer. He sat in the sun, relishing the heat, the rasp of grasshoppers around him, the whiff of some aromatic plant, the sight of his own body, burnt as dark as the children. One had made absolutely the right decision, no question about it, the island was (except for a few small things) an earthly paradise, hot, cheap, the people so nice, and oneself quite amazingly fit for one's age.

A plane flew low overhead (packed with holiday people, their fortnight done, bound for Heathrow, poor things) – the six o'clock one presumably, which reminded him that he must pick up a bottle of gin at Mary Vella's on the way home, so he got up and set off again, his heart thumping a little uncomfortably. The hill was steep, of course, which accounted for that, but it might be wise all the same to lose a bit of weight.

He reached the car, and sat for a moment to rest before starting the engine. Heat quivered off the seats, although he had left all the windows open (quite all right to do that here, not like Spain or Italy, the islanders were quite staggeringly honest). The children were all around, foraging in the litter that accumulated everywhere (their honesty, unfortunately, was not matched by tidiness). James watched them for a moment, thinking that some were undoubtedly old Mary's progeny, Lucia's brothers and sisters. He searched for a family likeness, but truth to tell they all looked much the same, thin and dark with boot-button black eyes. 'Lucia?' he said encouragingly, 'Lucia Vella?', and they scattered with smiling, backward glances, clambering over the stone walls that divided the neatly terraced fields. The sight of their bodies, their graceful brown limbs, never failed to give him a sense of well-being; they were most attractive in youth, the islanders, less so, alas, as adults. That boy in particular – the thin, very dark lad perched on the wall now, looking back – sad to think that he would mature into someone like old Joe Vella in the

126

bar. Starting the car, James waved a friendly hand, but the boy, staring, did not wave back.

He drove to the village, noticing with distaste that a great ugly board on the outskirts heralded yet another burst of new building. There was always the nagging fear that this place might be spoiled within a few years, like the Spanish coast after the war, like some of the Greek islands. Of course, there was no airport, nor any possibility of one, people would always have to come by ferry from the main island, which was a help, but even so, the danger was there. Oh, he thought, it'll last my time, with any luck.

They were obviously going to be hideous, too, the new houses, from the garish illustration on the agent's board: cheap, vulgar little boxes. That, of course, was what was a pity about the island, that almost everything – except, of course its natural assets of sun and sea and rock – was aesthetically unpleasing. The islanders, somehow, had never been blessed with that lightness of touch of most Mediterranean peoples; they had, one was bound to admit, unswervingly bad taste. Their houses were ugly, plonked down without regard for the natural contours of the landscape, uncompromisingly squat and dumpy – a little like the people themselves, who were also without the physical grace of Greeks, Italians, Spaniards, stout and temperamentally a little dour. A bit, James sometimes felt in irritation, like displaced English. That was one of the minor snags tempering the island's paradisial quality: it was always slightly mortifying to see one's visitors' expressions as they surveyed, on their first day, the scene, noting the banal villages, the unappetising little bars plastered with Coke and beer advertisements (no gay pavement cafés), the ubiquitous photographs of the Queen and the Duke of Edinburgh. He had then to point out the older farmhouses, like his own, with their pleasantly pink-washed walls and more graceful arched windows, stress the quality of the light (which one's painter friends, of course, were always quick to appreciate), the variety of vegetation and amusing local quirks like the ripening pumpkins that decorated the rooftops, the roadside shrines (garish, but fun) the marvellously pagan and atavistic bull-horns above the doors.

And, of course, the cheapness of everything: wine, cigarettes, labour.

The restoration of the farmhouse had cost considerably less than he had expected; it was always pleasing to detect the gleam of incredulous envy as he detailed the cost of the new flooring, electricity, plumbing, pretty wrought-iron balconies, terrace overlooking the valley, construction and paving of the garden. Really, James? they would say, but it's amazing, in England you'd have paid three times as much. I know, he'd say, I know, the thing is you see that they are quite unspoilt, as yet, these people, they are *not* grasping, not ambitious, they are simple people leading simple lives and satisfied with what they have. The great thing, he would say, is that they should stay like that, not be spoiled, I do so pray this place doesn't go the way of so much of the Med. They are such nice people. And his visitors, watching Lucia wash the chequered black and white stone floor or potter in the kitchen, would say yes, they do seem to be, I must say I envy you, James.

Lucia was Mary Vella's daughter. James, crossing the village square towards the Union Jack Bar outside which Mary sat, her enormous bottom quite engulfing the three-legged stool, reflected that she could not be much more than forty. She looked sixty. They aged so young, the island women. A brief slim girlhood, then fifteen years of child-bearing, and a precipitate middle-age. The Church, James thought severely, has a lot to answer for.

Mary was conducting a conversation at the shout with a neighbour on the other side of the square. What the islanders lacked in Latin gaiety they fully made up for in stridency of voice; the women screamed to one another all day long. James had had to be firm with Lucia about that, right at the beginning. No bawling to the neighbours or passers-by, and when you have something you want to ask me, Lucia, you come to me and say it quietly, do you see, not shout from the other side of the house. And Lucia, in the first flush of submission and anxiety to please, had nodded and smiled and remembered for at least two days.

It was not that they were stupid; child-like, more. Not child-ish, but child-like — which was what, of course, made them so attractive, in many ways. If somewhat exasperating. You had to tell them everything two, three times. The training of Lucia had been a long, laborious affair of many recessions, many defeats. Now, at last, one was beginning to reap the fruits.

Mary Vella, had seen him, and was heaving herself to her feet, yelling to Joe her husband back in the dark gorge of the bar that Mr Winton was here, and where are the crates? and get a beer from the fridge, Mr Winton is tired, will want a drink.

'Not now, Mary' he said — Tom Harley was coming in for supper, and the Pierces — 'I haven't time. Just the crates, please, and a bottle of gin'.

She bustled about him as they went together through the bead curtains and into the stuffy gloom of the bar, children attendant at her heels. 'Lucia is good, yes, you are pleased? She do her work well?'

Lucia, of course, was the eldest. 'Yes, fine, fine' said James ab-stractedly. He was trying to remember if he had some whisky for Tom Harley, or not. 'And a bottle of Scotch, Mary, and twenty Embassy. Perhaps I will have a beer after all, while Joe puts the stuff in the car.'

He sat outside, on Mary's stool; that, of course, was one of the pleasant little things about the island, people being so willing and helpful, Joe taking the stuff to the car, not those wretched imper-sonal supermarkets that were everywhere in England now. Mary was standing beside him — at a level with his eyes, the varicose veins coiled like vines around her legs, poor old dear, now the Health Service is something they really *could* do with out here — wanting to know about groceries for next week: the bar's func-tion extended beyond that of an English pub, dealing in food-stuffs as well as drink. He remembered the time Mary had brought Lucia for interview, toiling up the hill to the house with Father Grech in tow, like, he had thought in amusement, some kind of chaperone. As though one might pounce on one or the other of them, though heaven knows the choice was not really to one's taste, either way . . .

It would have been a relief to her – and a local scoop – to get a daughter placed in a secure, well-paid job. The island was over-populated; there was widespread unemployment; the young left for Italy, Australia, England. The airport on the main island teemed, day and night, with excited, distraught relatives, entire families seeing off departing members, welcoming returning ones home on a visit. Mary Vella, standing foursquare in the middle of the terrace, Lucia at her elbow, Father Grech lurking in the background, had depicted Lucia as the domestic paragon of all time (not, of course, that one had been in the least taken in, having observed the islanders' home habits), in ferocious pursuit of a job that scores of local girls would jump at. And the deal had been struck, the priest nodding approvingly, assuring James of the wisdom of his choice. ('Very nice people, Mr Winton, a very good family, good mother, a good girl, she will work hard'.) James had been quite firm and sensible, not offering more money than was proper, the girl must not be spoilt – 'Five pounds a week to start with, and in a year's time, when she's learned what to do, we'll think about it again'.

And he would, he thought, put it up to six, in all probability. She had turned out well. She cleaned assiduously, washed and ironed exquisitely, cooked – well, cooking was the main stum-bling-block (their own cuisine, of course, was non-existent) but even that, with constant guidance and instruction, she was pick-ing up. You had to keep on at her all the time, but she could do a few dishes quite passably now, salads and pizzas could be left to her, her cold soups were not bad at all.

Oh yes, she was worth six pounds a week, well worth it.

Six? – friends from England would say – Nan Chalmers, Roger Bates. *Six*, James, you must be joking. Goodness, you are pampered out here.

He finished his beer and drove home. Things seemed to be under control. Lucia was laying the table – on occasions when people were coming in for supper she had a few hours off in the afternoon and came in for the evening instead – and appeared not to have made too much of a hash of it. She was wearing one of the striped cotton frocks he had got Roger to bring out from Marks and Spencer for her and looked reasonably neat. Her appearance had been a problem, at the beginning. She had arrived in her own tawdry 'best' clothes, which were of distressing vulgarity – shrill and cheap of texture and design. He had toyed with the idea of putting her into a simple little uniform, but had thought that might seem a bit affected. Finally he had solved the problem with plain, inoffensive cotton frocks from England. Lucia, he knew, did not like them; she thought them dowdy, and changed into her own clothes to go home. She was not a pretty girl, but there was a certain attractive oddity to her face, something to do with an unevenness about her large dark eyes. Lopsided, Roger had said, she looks like a Picasso, charming – and for a while they had called her La Demoiselle d'Avignon. How is La Demoiselle? Roger would say, in his letters, still trying to polish the silver with Windolene? It was Roger who had set what had become the accepted tone of visitors towards Lucia – quietly teasing, making a bit of fuss of her, even, sometimes, James feared, spoiling her rather with little presents. One would have to watch that; Lucia, of course loved it. Her eyes would light up at the sight of air-mail envelopes – 'Mr Bates, he is coming to stay, yes? Mrs Fletcher – here is a letter from Mrs Fletcher, perhaps she is saying she will come back soon . . .'

There was a letter from Roger now, and one from Nan Chalmers. He sat on the terrace reading them, while Lucia hovered, anxious to share the contents. 'What? Yes, I'll get the wine out in a minute, see that there are glasses at every place, the green ones, not the plain. No, Mr Bates didn't send any message and no, he isn't coming for his holidays.'

Good luck to him, James thought, with a spurt of malice, with his film friend who has this villa on Spetsae, and yes of course I understand, only too well as it happens. He put Roger's letter aside and turned to Nan Chalmers', perking up as he read that Nan would adore to come out in June, for a good fortnight if he could bear her for that long, she couldn't wait to see the house and . . .

One did feel just a tiny bit cut off, sometimes, on the island. Of course, with everything being so cheap it was possible to be extravagant with subscriptions to papers and periodicals, so that really one had all the advantages of London life – of English life – without having to live there. No, it was just that when the summer visitors had gone, the island could seem just a bit restricted, despite all its advantages. But things were bound to improve; the English community was growing all the time, with one or two live wires who were really getting things off the ground a bit – a Dramatic Society that might be rather fun, and a literary group with visiting speakers from time to time, and so on. And the mechanics of life were looking up, too, the little things that had seemed, initially, part of the island's appeal – the bad roads and uncertain services – but which had begun to pall after a few months. Most of the roads were being surfaced now, and the telephone exchange no longer remained incommunicado for half the day, which had been so infuriating when one was trying to arrange a little dinner or something.

So Nan would be here in June. And then in July there would be the Fletchers. Restored, in pleasant anticipation of the evening, the next few weeks, he set about the necessary briefing of Lucia. 'And you hand the dishes from the left, remember, Lucia, the left side of people – which is the left? Oh, Lucia, how many times have I told you. The side they wear their watch, the side ladies have their wedding ring.'

Mary Vella sat outside the bar and continued the shouted conversation with her neighbour; the conversation distracted her in no way from her own anxieties, which were several, or the pain in her legs, which was habitual. She was pregnant, though she did not count that among her anxieties, and indeed had hardly registered the fact; fertility was something to be proud of, especially a fertility as proven as hers. The anxieties were matters of money, spiritual offences, a discrepancy between the number of crates of Double Diamond there ought to be in the store and the number there actually were (and the part that her husband Joe might have played in this), and her daughter Lucia.

Lucia would be twenty-two next birthday. Mary herself had

been married and a mother by that age. Lucia was no prettier than the next girl – indeed rather less so; there were fewer marriageable men on the island every year. A Lucia with a small nest-egg accumulated by the judicious saving of several years' wages, or the best part of them, on the other hand, was a marketable proposition. Mary Vella, totting up figures in her head, shifting her weight from one ham to the other, screaming tit-bits of information across the dust and the parked cars and the playing children, considered all this and balanced it against the risks, the imponderables, the unknown quantities.

She did not like Mr Winton. She did not like his clothes (shabby, for a man so evidently rich, and more suitable for a woman, often, and a young woman at that, flowered shirts, bright colours . . .) or his way of talking or, most particularly, his friends. It was his friends who worried her where Lucia was concerned. There were young men whose winning smiles and over-friendliness made her uncomfortable; one, once, had brought Lucia home in Mr Winton's car, late at night, after she had helped at a party. Appalled, Mary had screamed at the girl for half the next day; a Lucia whose morals were open to doubt would not be a marriageable prospect at all. And there were women as distasteful as the men – women as old as herself and older who would stroll into the bar with blouses unbuttoned over bathing-costumes, with bare legs, with skirts as short as a child. One of them, once had given Lucia a discarded dress; it was indecent and Mary had thrown it angrily into the dustbin.

But it was a good job, well-paid. And almost certainly less risky, less imponderable, than a job in one of the hotels or bars on the main island, even had such a job been obtainable. Mary Vella calculated and assessed and worried, discussed the price of a plastic-covered kitchen table, cuffed a straying child, beamed and bobbed at Father Grech, performing his evening tour of the parish.

James made careful plans for Nan's visit. One wanted her to get the best possible impression of the place; she had been just a bit derogatory (as had one or two other friends) when he had announced his intentions. 'There, James? But isn't it awfully English – why not Greece or Italy? Yes, I daresay prices are lower . . .' Nan, of course, had been a great traveller all her life; whatever obscure French village you mentioned, whatever remote Greek island, she had been there, probably years ago, before it got so spoilt, when it was really lovely and untouched. It could be irritating, even in as old and dear a friend as Nan. The house, he knew, could not fail to impress – to inspire envy (pretty as one had to concede was Nan's Georgian Cheltenham house) – it was the island's shortcomings that were a nuisance. But there was nothing to be done about it except make a joke of the worst eyesores and exploit all that was most exploitable – sea, climate, the abundance and cheapness of all those fruits and vegetables that would be most expensive and unavailable in England.

And Nan was gratifyingly appreciative. She arrived wan and tired (the winter had been appalling, life not easy with everything so dear now, what a wise decision you did make, James . . .) and unfurled within the first week, becoming tanned and gay, her old amusing self. She must be pushing sixty now, one would hardly believe it. She had a great way with people, of course, Nan. Within days she was much in demand, socially – invitations galore for them both. And she had nice things to say about the quality of the social life the island offered, such interesting people, people who painted and wrote and that kind of thing, really, it wouldn't be hard to settle down here, you'd hardly miss London theatres and exhibitions at all. They swam and sunned themselves, ate and drank, explored and talked.

She was sweet to Lucia (and very good with Mary Vella, whenever they were in the bar, a graceful mixture of jokiness and charm). She gave Lucia some bits and pieces (but nothing too lavish – just a simple little blouse, oddments of junk jewellery), taught her how to make a really delicious gazpacho, was able, with amazing tact, to achieve what James had never managed and persuade the girl to use a deodorant.

All in all, it was a most agreeable fortnight. Nan was a pleasant and stimulating companion (if, occasionally, just a tiny bit inclined to go on about plays one hadn't seen, or books one hadn't come across) – always eager and interested, sympathetic and understanding about things like the way people let you down – Roger, the French boy. Nan, of course, was a very intelligent and sensitive person; broad-minded, perceptive. James, in an appreciative mood, told her so. Nan laid a hand on his arm in graceful acknowledgement of the compliment.

'I do think, you know,' she said, 'I do think that honestly our generation had the best of things' – an elegant return, this, Nan must be ten or twelve years younger than he was. 'It was so much easier to get about in our day, travel, see something of what life is like for other people. And I do believe,' she went on, 'I really do believe, James that that has done so much for us. I mean, we mustn't be smug, and I know it's a cliché, but travel *does* broaden the mind, we *don't* have quite the same outlook on things as if we'd just lived in one little pond, but now, of course, it's so difficult for people, the young, how can they move around?' She sighed, leaning back in the new cane garden chair that looked so well on the terrace, against the background of vine and pergola. 'What an eye-opener it's all been. I am just so thankful that we had the opportunity.'

James nodded. Peacefully, gratefully, they watched the sun set over the island while in the background Lucia hummed pop songs in the kitchen, pattered out from time to time to replenish glasses, fill the ice-bucket.

He would have been pleased enough for Nan to extend her fortnight, but at the end of it she seemed quite eager to get back to Cheltenham – incomprehensibly so, James felt. Oh well yes, I know, she said, no doubt it'll be pouring with rain and one blanches at the thought of all that grind of housework and shopping again – it has been the most wonderful break, James – but there are things coming up, the Festival and then all the London things, so one way and another, and it's sweet of you to suggest it, I think I'll get back.

He felt a bit flat, after she had gone. There would be the Fletchers next month, and in the meantime Tom Harley had some very amusing people in television staying, making a documentary about the island for the BBC, so that there were diversions, and others to look forward to, but even so a bleakness crept over him from time to time. He was wheezing a bit, for no apparent reason, and toyed with the idea of going over to the main island to see one of the English doctors at the hospital (the local man was quite all right for run-of-the-mill things but for a proper check-up he wouldn't really do, of course). It could no doubt be left for a month or two, though. And in the meantime he could cheer himself up by deciding to have a new car in the autumn (and that was something he could never have afforded in England), and getting Lucia's second cousin to re-decorate the bathroom a very successful terra cotta colour at a quite ridiculously low price.

When the blow fell he could hardly believe what he was hearing, at first. He had to make the girl repeat what she had said before he could be quite clear what it was she was on about. Lucia was incoherent to begin with, and then truculent, defensive even, in the face of James's indignation. Finally he ordered her out of the house. It took a good stiff drink to restore him sufficiently to get onto the telephone and relieve his feelings slightly by telling the whole story to Tom Harley and the Pierces, who, he reflected bitterly, were among those who had been most taken with Nan and her little ways.

To think that they must have worked all this out behind his back, the pair of them. All those little chats in the kitchen; so this was what they had been about. No wonder Lucia had seemed moody and restless since Nan's departure.

'Your friend say if I like to come to England she give me good job, and at first I say no, because of my family, you see, and then after she go I think and think about it and I think maybe yes. I would much like to see London . . .'

'She doesn't live in London,' said James savagely, 'and how precisely do you imagine you're going to pay for the air fare?'

Lucia delved in her pocket. Out of an air-mail envelope she produced a single BEA ticket to London, and a lot of instructions in Nan's neat handwriting.

'When she go she say all right, my dear, you think it over and let me know. So when I have think, I write where she tell me, and she send these.' Lucia folded the documents with care, and returned them to her pocket. Not a word of regret, of apology; the ingratitude was unbelievable, absolutely unbelievable, the lack of any sense of obligation.

'Get out,' said James, near to tears.

Mary Vella had not much idea where London was; she knew only that it was further away than Rome, since the aeroplane reputedly took longer to get there, but nearer than Australia. That was neither here nor there; Rome would have been preferable, in any case. She sat outside the bar, not, for once, talking to anyone, and her head churned and ached. She had a sense of things slipping from her grasp, of an erosion – by incalculable forces – of her matriarchal position. Lucia had been a good girl, always – docile, biddable, reasonably industrious. What had happened was as though some dependable aspect of the physical world had revealed itself to be quite otherwise – as though a stone had talked. And stones do not talk without provocation. Bitterly, Mary Vella's thoughts centred on James Winton. She cobbled, with large, inept stitches, a child's shirt, muttered to herself, wept a little, schemed, and knew that what had happened could not be undone by any scheming, that it was part of the order of things, part of that lurking retribution for sins and inadequacies, part of the wilful world that could be manipulated only so far. She could not picture London, nor England, and did not wish to do so. What she could picture was the reduction of her daughter – or rather her daughter's familiar presence – to a series of blue, red and white air-mail envelopes. She fretted, and sewed, and sought, presently, the dark, cool, reassuring womb of the church. There, on her knees, she recited her anxieties, for herself, for Lucia, for Lucia's immortal soul, for Lucia's prospects of marriage and maternity.

James got a girl through Paul at the garage and set about the wearisome task of training her. She was worse than Lucia had been. Irritably, he instructed and instructed again and chivvied and snapped when patience had been exhausted and nothing else would do. There was little prospect of Carmen knowing what was what by the time the Fletchers came out, that was clear enough.

He did not feel all that good, either. The business had brought back his headaches; he got tired easily; some days it seemed almost too much of an effort to go down to the beach. He slopped about the house and garden through the long, hot days. The heat did not worry him at all, he had always liked it – that, after all was what one was here for. But he felt oppressed, all the same, and the island's landscape, encircling his garden – the cluttered little fields and squat villages and dry scrubby vegetation – seemed alien in a way they never had before. He would lie on the terrace with his eyes closed, between the hard blue sky and the hot dry earth that rasped all day long with grasshoppers, and experience a sense of displacement, of unease. It annoyed him. One was, after all, a person accustomed to moving around – had lived, at one time or another, in four different countries, had never really been settled anywhere in particular, called nowhere home, was not bound by restrictions of place or culture. He tried to divert himself by re-planning the garden, and planted roses ('Iceberg', for coolness and sparkle) all along the pergola, but the plants withered and sulked, water them as he might.

Mary Vella came up with Father Grech.

'Oh, so she went, did she?' snapped James. 'Well, I really don't know what it's got to do with me now. It wasn't any of my doing, you know.'

It was Father Grech who did the talking this time, with Mary standing a few yards back, silent but omnipresent, for all the world like the black governessy I-told-you-so figure in a Greek chorus.

He launched forth, Father Grech, into a long, faintly accusatory monologue, about how worried the girl's mother was, and in his own doubts about the girl's welfare, and so forth and so on, to which James listened with mounting exasperation. Good heavens, with a brood like that you'd think the old girl would be glad enough to get one of them off her hands, anyone would think she'd been whipped off into the brothels of Soho or somewhere. Neither of them, clearly, had given a moment's thought to him, left in the lurch like this. He felt like pointing out that it was entirely thanks to his efforts that Lucia was now a desirable commodity as a servant. She hadn't known a thing, when she came to him in the first place.

'What?' he said crossly. 'No, I really can't imagine how she'll get the fare home again if she's not happy, she should have thought of that in the first place, shouldn't she? She'll have to save up for it, presumably. Teach her not to be so silly.' My God, they weren't surely going to have the nerve to suggest that one stump up for the price of an air ticket? 'And no, I don't know if there's a Catholic church there. I should think Cheltenham's jolly Protestant, as a matter of fact.' His temples throbbed; there was a filthy headache coming on.

Finally they went. James, standing on the terrace with thumping head, watched them walk slowly down the dusty road, a few yards apart, as though they had nothing left to say to each other. Mary had been sullen and remarkably silent, standing there with her eyes fixed on James and a kind of blaze to them that had been disconcerting; he had wondered if possibly the woman had gone a bit funny in the head. In any case, he thought, turning to go into the house, it is all quite ridiculous, they are making an absurd fuss about nothing, what on earth do they think can happen to the girl in Cheltenham, of all places? It's not exactly a den of iniquity. Come to that, it might do her good to get away from that family for a bit. They're smothered in family, these people. Family and priests.

He spent a week or so quietly at the house, hardly going out at all, and felt considerably better by the end of it. The nasty little pains in his chest seemed to have gone away, and he was not getting so breathless. He went for one or two short walks in the evenings, and was none the worse. He was longing for a swim, and decided to risk a trip to the beach.

The children were down there, the children and the goats. The sight of them was a tonic; he felt quite a rejuvenating little rush of something as he sat down on the sand, stripping off shirt and trousers, and stretched himself out in his bathing-trunks, lying on his stomach so that he could watch them – the boys' neat brown bodies and their lovely agility as they played football with a tin can picked from the rubbish at the water's edge. When he had swum, and dried himself, he walked up to them and tried, yet again, to make contact. One of the boys, he saw now, was older than he had thought – fifteen or sixteen at least. James stood there for a few minutes, fastening his trousers, rubbing the towel across his salted, sticky skin, and chatted encouragingly. Name? School? Interests? But the boy shook his head and shuffled, his eyes darting to James's trouser pocket: money, cigarettes, was that what he was after? No, thought James severely, one is not going to corrupt these people, and when all his chat had fallen upon stony ground, and the boy was retreating, edging backwards to join the others, he went back to sit for a while and rest before the upward climb to the car.

It was early evening, and hot still, though he had tried to time his bathe so that it would be cooler for his walk up the hill. There was a slight breeze; small waves frilled up the beach, leaving the sand laced with white foam. The sea was marbled with different blues; far out on the horizon there was a wispy layer of cloud. Not, of course, that that indicated anything but the inevitable sunshine tomorrow; one could be absolutely confident of the weather, that was one thing. Oh, he thought, really everything is quite all right, this little upset over Lucia is over and done with now, no point in harping on it. As for Nan Chalmers . . . Bitterness and resentment welled up, clouding the perfection of the evening. For the umpteenth time he went over the scathing, unanswerable, things that should (but never would, for Nan would take good care to see there was no opportunity) be said to her, and gained some little satisfaction. The emotion, though, made his heart race, and at last, with a deliberate effort, he forced himself to clear his head, lie in the sun, and relax.

He must have dozed off for a while. When he came to he could not for a moment think where he was; it was like one of those times of perplexity and faint panic when one wakes in a strange bedroom and cannot think, for a few seconds, where or why . . . He sat bolt upright, staring round, and he was quite alone on the golden crescent of the beach, quite quite alone, with nothing but the noise of the sea, and a long way away someone shouting. And he had the horrid sensation of having been left behind, abandoned, by who or what he could not say. He scrambled to his feet, awkwardly, stumbling and panting, and then all of a sudden things fell into place, he knew where he was, on the familiar beach, on the island, the car not far away, out of sight at the top of the hill.

The children had gone (that, perhaps, accounted for the sense of abandonment, of loneliness). He gathered up his things and set off up the path, and as he climbed he saw them not far ahead, picking a leisurely way over the stones and through the bushes, twittering like a flock of migrating birds. He took the hill very slowly – it was hotter than he had anticipated, and the breeze had dropped – but even so it was an effort and seemed steeper, longer, than ever it had before. He trudged on, and there was a nagging pain in his chest, and a mistiness before his eyes; I am not well, he thought, I am really not too well, it was rash to come down here, I must get back and take things easy, have an early night.

He climbed, and paused for a while, and then climbed again because he felt unaccountably exposed here, unsafe – the place had lost, for the moment, its appeal and seemed hostile, alien, unfamiliar. He tripped on a stone and almost fell, and the slight shock set his heart pounding, and that pain came again, hard, a sickening jolt to the chest.

Just ahead, the children's voices were shrill; it came to him, as it had never done before, that he could not understand a word they were saying.

And then something strange began to happen. His whole body was going numb, and everything had become blurred and distant. He had fallen, he realised, though he had hardly felt himself hit the ground. He was lying there, and knew that things were not right, not right at all, that he must get help. He tried to shout, and some sound must have come out, because he was aware of the children drawing near out of the darkness, the almost total darkness, at the periphery of his vision. And then the darkness swallowed him, and it had all gone – the island, the children, everything.

The children stood a few yards off and looked at the old man. They chattered excitedly. They asked each other if he was dead. Presently one of the older girls, Maria, crept closer to make an inspection. The boys, the two big boys, had gone on ahead, missing this drama, and she was now the eldest present so that on her devolved the responsibility of action, if action was to be taken.

She squatted down in the dust beside him, and stared. She thought that he was breathing still. His face, though, was a very strange colour. Her uncle Tony, she remembered, had looked like that when he was so ill last winter, and the doctor had come, quickly, in the middle of the night, and they had taken him away to the hospital in an ambulance, there had been much commotion and haste and rushing about in the dark. It seemed to her that there was the same urgency needed here. She discussed this with the other children (one of them, a very young one, poked James's inert leg, gingerly, and then skittered back into the bushes in panic) and then they all scampered away up the hillside, taking the goats with them.

The village was a mile and a half away. When they came to the road, Maria hurried on ahead; the younger ones were already forgetting about the old man and had reverted to their usual dawdling, scavenging pace, comfortably in step with the goats. She walked and ran, walked and ran, and arrived at the bar quite breathless, so that she had to stop and swing on the bead curtains, panting, for a moment or two, before she could explain to her mother what had happened.

Mary Vella listened. She went on counting the crates of 7-UP empties, and occasionally interrupted with a question. She was not as excited or interested as might have been expected, though this did not altogether surprise Maria; her mother had been excited and interested by very little since Lucia had gone away.

Maria concluded her account of what had happened and asked if she should go to Father Grech and get him to telephone for the doctor.

Mary Vella wrote down the total of the empties on the slate. She did not answer for a moment or two, staring out through the bead curtains, as though her mind were on something entirely different. Finally, she said, 'No. It may not be necessary; you should not waste the time of doctors. I will go myself and see if Mr Winton is all right now'.

Maria was a little taken aback by this; she pointed out that Mr Winton had not seemed, in her opinion, likely to be all right; she referred to her uncle; she reminded her mother of the distance, on foot, to the beach path. Mary Vella, in response to this, produced some of her old vigour and authority; she gave her daughter a shake, and demanded to know who decided how things were to be done, around here? Then she instructed another child to mind the bar until she came back, put a shawl around her shoulders, and set off through the square, at her usual deliberate pace, with Maria pattering along in attendance, sometimes behind, sometimes a yard or two ahead.

It took them nearly three quarters of an hour to get to the spot. The old man was still lying there; nothing had changed, except one thing, which Maria, who, in her short life, had seen death several times, recognised at once. They stood, the woman and the child, at either side of him, and crossed themselves. An ant was crawling on James's bare stomach which Maria, with a quick apologetic gesture, flicked aside. Mary muttered a prayer, and crossed herself again. She took James's towel, and with a business-like movement, spread it across his face. Then she turned and began to walk up the hillside, Maria once more trotting behind.

At the road, she stopped for a moment, and said to the child, 'Father Grech's telephone does not always work, and in any case Mr Winton was very bad, it would not have made any difference'. Maria nodded sagely, and as the sun sank behind the island, and the heat was tempered with the freshness of evening, they set off back to the village, to arrange, now, for whatever should be done.

A World of her Own

My sister Lisa is an artist: she is not like other people.

Lisa is two years younger than I am, and we knew quite early
on that she was artistic, partly because she could always draw so
nicely, but also because of the way she behaved. She lives in a
world of her own, our mother used to say. She was always the difficult one, always having tempers and tantrums and getting
upset about one thing and another, but once mother realised
about her being artistic she made allowances. We all did. She's
got real talent, the art master at school said, you'll have to take
care of that, Mrs Harris, she's going to need all the help she can
get. And mother was thrilled to bits, she's always admired creative people, she'd have loved to be able to write or paint herself
but having Lisa turn out that way was the next best thing, or
better, even, perhaps. When Lisa was fifteen mother went to
work at Luigi's, behind the counter, to save up so there'd be a bit
extra in hand for Lisa, when she went to art school. Father had
died three years before. It worried me rather, mother going out
to work like that; she's had asthma on and off for years now, and
besides she felt awkward, serving in a shop. But the trouble is,
she's not qualified at anything, and in any case, as she said, a deli-
catessen isn't quite like an ordinary grocer or a supermarket.

I was at college, by then, doing my teaching diploma. Lisa
went to one of the London art schools, and came back at the end
of her first term looking as weird as anything, you'd hardly have
known her, her hair dyed red and wearing black clothes with

pop art cut-outs stuck on and I don't know what. It was just as well mother *had* saved up, because it all turned out much more expensive than we'd thought, even with Lisa's grant. There was so much she had to do, like going to plays and things, and of course she needed smarter clothes, down there, and more of them, and then the next year she had to travel on the continent all the summer, to see great paintings and architecture. She was away for months, we hardly saw anything of her, and when she came back she'd changed completely all over again – her hair was blonde and frizzed out, and she was wearing a lot of leather things, very expensive, boots up to her thighs and long suede coats. She came home for Christmas and sometimes she was gay and chatty and made everybody laugh and other times she was bad-tempered and moody, but as mother said, she'd always been like that, from a little girl, and of course you had to expect it, with her temperament.

Mother had left Luigi's by then, some time before, because of her leg (she got this trouble with her veins, which meant she mustn't stand much) but she started doing a bit of work at home, for pin-money, making cushions and curtains for people: she's always been good at needlework, she sometimes says she wonders if possibly that's where Lisa's creativity came from, if maybe there's something in the family . . .

It missed me out, if there is. Still, I got my diploma (I did rather well, as it happens, one of the best in my year) and started teaching and not long after that I married Jim, who I'd known at college, and we had the children quite soon, because I thought I'd go back to work later, when they were at school.

Lisa finished at her art college, and got whatever it is they get, and then she couldn't find a job. At least she didn't want any of the jobs she could have got, like window-dressing or jobs on magazines or for publishers or that kind of thing. And can you blame her, said mother, I mean, what a waste of her talents, it's ridiculous, all that time she's spent developing herself, and then they expect her to be tied down to some nine-to-five job like anyone else!

Lisa was fed up. She had to come and live at home. Mother

turned out of her bedroom and had the builders put a skylight in and made it into a studio for Lisa, really very nice, with a bare polished floor and a big new easel mother got by selling that silver tea-set that was a wedding present (she says she never really liked it anyway). But then it turned out Lisa didn't do that kind of painting, but funny things to do with bits of material all sort of glued together, and coloured paper cut out and stuck onto other sheets of paper. And when she did paint or draw it would be squatting on the floor, or lying on her stomach on the sofa.

I can't make head nor tail of the kind of art Lisa does. I mean, I just don't *know*, if it's any good or not. But then, I wouldn't, would I? Nor Jim, nor mother, nor any of us. We're not experienced in things like that; it's not up to us to say.

Lisa mooched about at home for months. She said she wouldn't have minded a job designing materials for some good firm — Liberty's or something like that — provided there was just her doing it because she's got this very individual style and it wouldn't mix with other people's, or maybe she might arrange the exhibitions at the Victoria and Albert or the Tate or somewhere. She never seemed to get jobs like that, though, and anyway mother felt it would be unwise for her to commit herself because what she really ought to be doing was her own work, that's all any artist should do, it's as simple as that.

Actually Lisa did less and less painting, which mother said was tragic, her getting so disillusioned and discouraged, such a waste of talent. Mother would explain to people who asked what Lisa was doing nowadays about how disgraceful it was that the government didn't see that people like her were given the opportunities and encouragement they need. Goodness knows, she'd say with a sigh, it's rare enough — creative ability — and Mrs Watkins next door, or the vicar, or whoever it was, would nod doubtfully and say yes, they supposed so.

And then Bella Sims arrived and opened up this new gallery in the town. The Art Centre. Before, there'd only been the Craft Shop, which does have some quite odd looking pictures but goes in for glass animals and corn dollies and all that too; Lisa was vicious about the Craft Shop. But Bella Sims' place was real art, you could see that at once – lots of bare floor and pictures hung very far apart and pottery vases and bowls so expensive they didn't even have a price on them. And Lisa took along some of her things one day and believe it or not Bella Sims said she liked them, and she'd put three of them in her next exhibition which was specially for local artists. Mother was so thrilled she cried when Lisa first told her.

Lisa was a bit off-hand about it all; she seemed to take the attitude that it was only to be expected. She got very thick with Bella Sims.

Bella Sims was fiftyish, one of those people with a loud, posh voice and hair that's just been done at the hairdresser and lots of clunky expensive-looking jewellery. She scared the wits out of me, and mother too, actually, though mother kept saying what a marvellous person she was, and what an asset for the town. I didn't enjoy the preview party for the exhibition, and nor did Jim; I was expecting Judy then, and Clive was eighteen months, so I was a bit done in and nobody talked to us much. But Lisa was having a good time, you could see; she was wearing all peasanty things then, and had her hair very long and shiny, she did look really very attractive. She met Melvyn at that party.

Melvyn was Bella's son. He taught design at the Poly. That meant he was sort of creative too, though of course not a real artist like Lisa. He fell for her, heavily, and who could blame him I suppose, and they started going round together, and then quite soon they said they were getting married. We were all pleased, because Melvyn's nice – you'd never know he was Bella's son – and we didn't realise till later that it was because of Francesca being on the way. Mother was rather upset about that, and felt she might have been a bit to blame, maybe she should have talked to Lisa about things more, but frankly I don't think that would have made any difference. Actually she worried more about Lisa not being able to paint once the baby was born. She was pleased, of course, about Francesca, but she did feel it might be a pity for Lisa to tie herself down so soon.

Actually it didn't work out that way. Lisa got into a habit almost at once of leaving Francesca with mother or with me whenever she wanted some time to herself – she was having to go up and down to London quite a lot by then to keep in touch with her old friends from college, and to try to find openings for her work. I had my two, of course, so as she said, an extra one didn't make much difference. It did get a bit more of a strain, though, the next year, after she'd had Jason and there was him too. Four children is quite a lot to keep an eye on, but of course mother helped out a lot, whenever her leg wasn't too bad. Bella Sims, I need hardly say, didn't go much for the granny bit.

Lisa had Alex the year after that. I've never understood, I must say, why Lisa has babies so much; I mean, she must *know*. Of course, she is vague and casual, but all the same . . . I've had my two, and that's that, barring accidents, and I'm planning to go back to work when I can, eventually. I daresay Lisa would think that all very cold and calculating, but that's the way I am. Lisa says she doesn't believe in planning life, you just let things happen to you, you see what comes next.

Alex had this funny Chinese look from a tiny baby and it took us all ages to cotton on, in fact I suppose he was eleven months or so before the penny finally dropped and we realised that, to put it frankly, Melvyn wasn't the father.

It came as a bit of a blow, especially to poor mother. She went all quiet for days, and I must admit she's never really liked Alex ever since, not like she dotes on the others.

The father was someone Lisa knew in London. He was from Thailand, not Chinese, actually. But in fact it was all over apparently sometime before Alex was born and she didn't see him again.

Melvyn took it very well. I suppose he must have known before we did. In fact, Melvyn has been very good to Lisa from the start, nothing of what's happened has been his fault in any way. Not many men would have coped with the children like he has, right from the beginning, which he had to because of Lisa being away quite a bit, or involved in her own things. Truth to tell, he was better with them, too. It's not that Lisa's a bad mother – I mean she doesn't get cross or impatient, specially, she just doesn't bother about them much. She says the worst thing you can do is to be over-protective; she says mother was a bit over-protective with her.

Bella Sims had some fairly nasty things to say; but then soon after that she sold the gallery and moved back to London and we never saw any more of her. This was the wrong kind of provincial town, apparently; art was never going to be a viable proposition.

Things got worse after Alex was born. Lisa went off more and more. Sometimes I'd find we had the children for days on end, or Melvyn would come round, pretty well at the end of his tether, saying could we lend a hand, Lisa was down in London seeing about some gallery who might show her stuff, or she'd gone off to Wales to see a woman who was doing the most fantastic ceramics.

It was after the time Francesca wandered off and got lost for a whole day, and the police found her in the end and then it turned out Lisa had been somewhere with Ravi, this Indian friend of hers, that things rather came to a head. Lisa and Melvyn had a row and Lisa brought all the children round to me, late one night, in their pyjamas, and said she was so upset about everything she'd have to go off on her own for a few days to try to think things over. Jim had 'flu and I'd just got over it myself so I was a bit sharp with her: I said couldn't Melvyn have them, and she said no, Melvyn had to teach all next day, which was probably true enough. And anyway, she said, they're my children, I'm responsible for them, I've got to work out what to do. She was wearing a long red and blue thing of some hand-blocked stuff, and lots of silver bracelets, and she looked exhausted and very dashing both at the same time, somehow; the children were all crying.

So I took them, of course, and she was gone for a week or so. We talked things over while she was gone. Jim and I talked, and Jim said (which he never had before) that he thought Lisa ought to pull herself together a bit, and I had to agree. It was easier with her not being there; somehow when Lisa's with you, you always end up feeling that she really can't be expected to do what other people do, I actually feel bad if I see Lisa washing a floor or doing nappies or any of the things I do myself every day. It does seem different for her, somehow.

And mother talked to Melvyn, who'd been round to find out where the children were. Mother was very sympathetic; she knows what living with Lisa is like; we all do. She said to Melvyn that of course Lisa had been silly and irresponsible, nobody could deny that. She told Melvyn, with a little laugh to try to cheer things up a bit, that there'd been occasions when Lisa was a small girl and was being particularly wilful and tiresome that she'd been on the verge of giving her a good smack. And then, she said, one used to remember just in time that there is a point beyond which she – people like her – simply cannot help themselves. One just can't expect the same things you can from other people.

I don't know what Melvyn thought about that; he didn't say. After the divorce came through he married Sylvie Fletcher who works in the library; I was at school with her and she's very nice but quite ordinary. Mother always says it must seem such a come down after Lisa. They've got a little boy now, and Melvyn takes a lot of trouble to see Francesca and Jason (and Alex too, in fact) as much as he can – and it *is* trouble because he has to trail down to London and try to find where Lisa's moved to now, unless it's one of the times Jim and I are having the children, or mother.

Mother and I had a talk, too. I'd gone round there and found her up in Lisa's old studio, just standing looking at a great thing Lisa had done that was partly oil paint slapped on very thick and partly bits of material stuck on and then painted over; in the top corner there was a picture of the Duke of Edinburgh from a magazine, sideways on and varnished over. I think it must have been meant to be funny, or sarcastic or something. We both stood in front of it for a bit and mother said, 'Of course, it is very good, isn't it?'

I said I honestly didn't know.

We both felt a bit awkward in there; Lisa has always been very fussy about her privacy. She says the one thing people absolutely have no right to do is push themselves into other people's lives; she is very strong for people being independent and having individual rights. So mother and I just had a quick tidy because the dust was bothering mother, and then we went downstairs and drank a cup of tea and chatted. Mother talked about this book she'd been reading about Augustus John; she's very interested in biographies of famous poets and artists and people like that. She was saying what a fascinating person he must have been but of course he did behave very badly to people, his wife and all those other women, but all the same it must have been terribly exhilarating, life with someone like that. You could see she was half thinking of Lisa. I was feeling snappish, the children were getting me down rather, and I said Lisa wasn't Augustus John, was she? We don't really know, do we – if she's any good or not.

There was a silence. We looked at each other. And then mother looked away and said, 'No. I know we don't. But she just might be, mightn't she? And it would be so awful if she was and nobody had been understanding and helpful'.

Lisa came back for the children once she'd found a flat. She'd had her hair cut off and what was left was like a little boy's, all smoothed into the back of her neck; it made her look about sixteen. Lisa is very small and thin, I should say; people always offer to carry suitcases for her, if you see her doing anything involving effort you automatically find yourself offering to do it for her because you feel she won't be able to manage and anyway it makes you feel guilty watching her.

She said the hair was symbolic; she was making a fresh start and getting rid of the atmosphere that had been holding her back (I suppose she meant poor Melvyn) and actually everything was going to be good because Ravi's father who was an Indian businessman and quite rich was going to buy a little gallery in Islington that Ravi was going to run and she was frantically busy getting enough stuff together for an exhibition.

The gallery didn't last long because it kept losing money and after a bit Ravi's father, who turned out to be quite an ordinary businessman after all and not as sensitive and interested in art as Lisa had thought, said he was cutting his losses and selling up. In fact Ravi and Lisa weren't living together by then anyway because Lisa had realised that the reason her work wasn't really right was that she'd always been in cities and in fact what she needed to fulfil herself properly was to get away somewhere remote and live a very simple, hard-working life. Actually, she thought, pottery was the right medium for her, once she could scrape up enough for a wheel and everything.

Mother helped out with that, financially, and Lisa took the children down to this place in Somerset where a man she knew, someone quite rich, had this big old house that was a sort of commune for artists, and for parties of young people to come and study nature and the environment. We went down there, once, when Lisa wanted us to take Alex for a bit, because he'd not been well and she was finding it a bit of a strain coping with him. There was certainly a lot of environment there, it was miles from anywhere, except the village, and there wasn't much of that, so that there seemed to be more artists than ordinary village people. It was a hot summer and Lisa and the rest were going round with just about no clothes on, more like the south of France than west Somerset and I rather got the impression that some of the older village people didn't like it all that much, and there was an outdoor pop festival one weekend that went on to all hours, and this man who owned the place had made the church into an exhibition room for the artists. It was one of those little grey stone churches with old carvings and so on and it looked queer, all done out inside with huge violent-coloured paintings and peculiar sculptures. Lisa said actually it was frightfully good for these people, to be exposed to a today kind of life, they were so cut off down there, and to be given the sort of visual shock that might get them really looking and thinking.

Eventually Lisa began to feel a bit cut off herself, and there'd been some trouble with the County child care people which Lisa said was a lot of ridiculous fuss, it was just that Francesca had got this funny habit of wandering off sometimes and actually it was good that she felt so free and uninhibited, most people *stifle* their children so. Francesca was six by then, and Jason five. Jason had this bad stammer; he still has, sometimes he can't seem to get a word out for hours.

Lisa came home to mother's for a bit then, because rents in London were sky-high and it would have meant her getting a job, which of course was out of the question, if she was going to

153

keep up her potting, and the weaving she had got very keen on now. And at mother's she had the studio, so it might work out quite well, she thought, provided she kept in touch with people and didn't feel too much out on a limb.

Jim and I had Alex more or less permanently by then; we are very fond of him, he seems almost like ours now which is just as well I suppose. It is just as well too that Jim is the kind of person he is; Lisa thinks he is dull, I know, but that is just her opinion, and as I have got older I have got less and less certain that she gets things right. In fact, around this time I did have a kind of outburst, with mother, which I suppose was about Lisa, indirectly. She had gone down to London to keep in touch with people, and there had been a business with Francesca at school (sometimes she steals things, it is very awkward, they are going to have the educational psychologist people look at her) and I had had to see to it all. I was feeling a bit fed up too because what with Alex, and having so much to do, I'd realised it wasn't going to be any good trying to go back to work at the end of the year as I'd planned. Maybe you should be like Lisa, and not plan. Anyway, mother was telling me about this biography of Dylan Thomas she'd been reading, and what an extraordinary eccentric person he was and how fascinating to know. Actually I'd read the book too and personally I don't see why you shouldn't write just as good poetry without borrowing money off people all the time and telling lies.

Once, when I was at college, one of the tutors got this well-known poet to come and give a talk to the second year English. He had glasses with thick rims and a rather old-fashioned looking suit and frankly he might have been somebody's father, or your bank manager. He was very friendly and he talked to us in the common room afterwards and he wasn't rude to anyone. I told mother about it, later, and she said she wondered if he was all that good – as a poet, that is.

And I suddenly blew up when she was going on like this about Dylan Thomas. I said – shouted – 'T. S. Eliot worked in an office. Gustav Holst was a bloody school-teacher'.

Mother looked startled. She said, 'Who?' She's less interested in musicians.

I said crossly, 'Oh, never mind. Just there's more than one way of going about things'. And then the children started squabbling and we were distracted and the subject never came up again, not quite like that.

Lisa got a part-share of a flat in London with a friend; she had to be down there because there was this person who was talking of setting up a craft workshop for potters and weavers and that, a fantastic new scheme, and she needed to be on the spot for when it came off. It was difficult for her to have the children there, so Francesca stayed with mother and the two little ones with us. Francesca settled down well at school and began to behave a lot better, and Jason's stammer was improving, and then all of a sudden Lisa turned up, as brown as a conker, with her hair long again, and henna-dyed now, and said she'd met these incredible Americans in Morocco, who had this atelier, and she was going to work there and learn this amazing new enamelling technique. That was what she ought to have been doing all along, she said, if only she'd realised, not messing about with pots and fabrics. She was taking the children with her, she said, because growing up in an English provincial town was so stultifying for them, and it was nice and cheap out there.

She took Alex too, but after six months she suddenly sent him back again with a peculiar German friend of hers; we had to collect him at Heathrow. He kept wetting the bed apparently and although Lisa isn't particularly fussy about that kind of thing she said she had the feeling he wasn't very adaptable.

And so it goes on. She came back from Morocco after a couple of years, and there was a spell in London when a rather well-off Dutch person that we thought she was going to marry bought her a house in Fulham. For six months Francesca went to a very expensive school where all the teaching was done in French, and then the Dutch person went off and Lisa found the house was rented, not paid for like she'd thought, so she came home again for a bit to sort things out, and Francesca went to the comprehensive.

And then there was Wales with the Polish sculptor, and then the Dordogne with the tapestry people, and London again, and back here for a bit, and the cottage in Sussex that someone lent her . . .

The last time she was here she had a curious creased look about her, like a dress that has been put away in a drawer and not properly hung out, and I suddenly realised that she is nearly forty now, Lisa. It doesn't seem right; she is a person that things have always been in front of, somehow, not behind.

Mother and I cleaned out her old studio, the other day. Mother has this feeling that Francesca may be talented in which case she will need to use it. We dusted and polished and sorted out the cupboard with Lisa's old paintings and collages and whatnot. They all looked rather shabby, and somehow withered – not quite as large or bright as one had remembered. Mother said doubtfully, 'I wonder if she would like any of these sent down to London?' And then, 'Of course it is a pity she has had such an unsettled sort of life'.

That 'had' did not strike either of us for a moment or two. After a bit mother began to put the things away in the cupboard again, very carefully; mother is past seventy now and the stooping was awkward for her. I persuaded her to sit down and I finished off. There was one portfolio of things Lisa did at school, really nice drawings of flowers and leaves and a pencil portrait of another girl whose name neither mother nor I could remember. Mother put these aside; she thought she might have them framed and hang them in the hall. Holding them, she said, 'Though with her temperament I suppose you could not expect that she would settle and at least she has always been free to express herself, which is the important thing'. When I did not answer she said, 'Isn't it, dear?', and I said 'Yes. Yes, I think so, mother'.

Presents of Fish and Game

'Well,' said the Fellow in Philosophy and Senior Tutor, 'this is a sad task. And an impossible one, too, as I see it.' He looked round at the other members of the Committee to appoint a Fellow and Tutor in Modern History. 'We won't find a man of Bob's standing, and that's for sure.'

The Fellow in French said plaintively, 'I must say he has rather left us in the lurch, taking up this appointment for January. Can we get someone else by then? Of course it's a tragedy he's leaving us'.

'Quite,' said the Bursar. He added, after a moment 'How much does Berkeley pay?'

A figure was suggested.

The Bursar whistled.

'Wouldn't we all?' said the Fellow in Politics.

'Personally,' said the Senior Tutor, a little stiffly 'I would find the attractions resistible. However, to our muttons . . .'

Muttons, thought the Fellow in Economics, who was twenty-four, and impressionable in several ways. Muttons. Hams. Thighs. He thought lovingly of a girl he knew, and addressed himself sternly to the problem of the appointment of a new Fellow in Modern History. He listened with attention to the Senior Tutor, an older and wiser man.

'We have to go all out for the best chap we can get,' the Senior Tutor was saying. 'And no two ways about it. Put out feelers of our own – see if we can't attract some applications the advertisement may not pull in. Sound people out – you never know who may be ripe for a move.'

The Fellow in Politics said, 'I must say myself I'd like to see if John Herbert would be interested'.

'Hasn't he got a Chair somewhere?' said the Bursar sharply.

'Yes, of course.'

'He'd want a stipend a bit over and above what Bob was getting, then.'

'Oh come,' said the Senior Tutor with a laugh, 'we're not counting pennies – we're trying – insofar as it's possible – to replace one of the most distinguished scholars the College has.'

The Fellow in Economics, who believed profoundly in the sanctity of scholarship, nodded with vehemence.

'Quite,' said the Bursar, 'we're all with you there.' He was scanning some sheets of figures. 'Anyway, I'm not absolutely clear that even *with* economies we could give ourselves a rise this year – or possibly next either. Or get the new squash courts off the drawing-board.'

There was a brief silence. The Fellow in Politics looked reflective, 'I doubt if John Herbert would want to move, in fact, when it came to the point'.

'I thought,' said the Tutor in French plaintively, 'there was no question about an increase in October. I must say it would be awfully inconvenient if . . .'

The Senior Tutor cleared his throat. 'So the usual advertisement, of course. But we look around, too. I don't think there's any doubt that we want an older man – someone with plenty of teaching experience, quite apart from the academic distinction we're looking for. The Governing Body has been getting younger over the last few years, very nice too' – with a benign glance at the Fellow in Economics – 'but in this instance I do feel that in replacing Bob, we must have a person of his seniority.'

'Definitely,' said the Fellow in Economics, who was sometimes taken for an undergraduate, which un-nerved him.

'Of course', said the Bursar thoughtfully, 'wage for age . . .' He did not complete the sentence, appearing distracted by some figures he was totting up.

Today I am twenty-four, thought the Fellow in Economics, and this time last year I was twenty-three, and this time next year I shall be twenty-five and when I am thirty-five I shall get six thousand a year, or is it seven? and my F.S.S.U. contributions will be of incalculable value to the widow I do not at the moment have. He thought again of the girl he knew; the thought threatened to become improper so he pushed it firmly aside, since he was a serious young man who believed in a time and a place for everything, and this was the time and place for the administration of a distinguished academic institution. He said, with diffidence, 'Are we going for a social historian again? Or should we possibly be thinking more of someone in the political field, since George Templer's interests . . .'

'Of course the University will want to stick their oar in', said the Bursar with a yawn.

'The University, I'm sure, will accept our recommendation', said the Senior Tutor.

The Fellow in Politics sighed, 'It's a pity George is on sabbatical – we could do with his advice. You know the thought does cross my mind that given we can't *replace* Bob, as Peter so rightly says, then I wonder if we *are* right in setting our sights on a very senior chap – academic distinction, yes, of course, that goes without saying, but I wonder if age is necessarily . . .'

'I never really see the need for all this stress on publications,' said the Fellow in French, who had none to his name.

The Fellow in Economics, who knew himself to be undistinguished but promising, looked out of the window and observed the Bursar's secretary, who had nice legs, crossing the quad. He resolved to work very hard and write a great many books in order never to become like the Fellow in French. There were times, he had sadly to admit, when academic life was a disappointment to him. The cut and thrust of intellectual debate was not all it was held to be; some of his colleagues could spend an entire meal discussing the merits of a particular make of car. He sighed, and looked hopefully at the Senior Tutor, in whom he had faith.

The Senior Tutor was attending to his pipe. He frowned.

'Y – es . . . Possibly. Of course you don't want to feel you're getting someone whose important work is behind them, as it were.'

'Quite', said the Fellow in French, for whom this was not a problem.

The Fellow in Politics held his hand out across the table to the Bursar. 'Could I just have a look at those stipend scales.'

The Fellow in Economics said, 'From a teaching point of view, I do think the greatest need is for someone whose interests are on the political side, then he could help out with the . . .'

'We want someone who'll teach the whole range', said the Fellow in French. 'Bob used to farm out no end of people. Cost the College a lot. I can't understand this passion for specialisation' he added disapprovingly, having none himself.

'Good Lord', said the Fellow in Politics, in reflective tones. 'As much as that . . .' He was doing sums on the back of the agenda.

The Bursar leaned forward and murmured, 'And you've got to take the housing allowance into consideration, Tony, it works out rather more like this . . .' More figures were scribbled.

The Fellow in Economics, despite his trade, had been surprised to discover how much of academic life was a matter of house-keeping. He said, a little anxiously, 'Surely there's no question – I mean, Peter's absolutely right, we've got to get someone as good as Bob and . . .'

The Fellow in Politics sat back in his chair looking meditative. 'We could save, at my estimate, around three or four thousand, which in terms of a capital sum . . .'

'Would that mean . . ?' said the Fellow in French, to the Bursar.

'Should be O.K.' said the Bursar.

The Senior Tutor said, 'That's interesting, Tony, not of course that it's a consideration that would sway us in any way. What's really at issue is, what does the College most need – an established figure, or someone on the way up who possibly . . .'

'I must say I think there's a lot to be said for a younger man', said the Fellow in French.

'Under thirty', said the Bursar, 'would keep us below the fifth increment on the . . .'

'Yes', said the Senior Tutor hastily, with a quick glance at the Fellow in Economics, whose face perhaps betrayed a sudden wild surmise about the circumstances of his own appointment. 'And it's not as though the College hasn't a fine reputation in History as it is, with George, and the goodwill, as it were, of Bob's fifteen years here. It's not exactly that we *need* a big name, in fact . . .'

'In fact', put in the Fellow in Politics, 'there is a sense in which it might be held to be incumbent on us to offer a helping hand, as it were . . .'

'To a chap on the way up', said the Bursar. 'Under thirty.'

'Quite', said the Senior Tutor, avoiding the eye of the Fellow in Economics. 'Or, another thought occurs, which is that perhaps' – he frowned at the Fellow in French, who was asking the Bursar if by any chance he had that latest tender for the squash court handy – 'perhaps we might consider the idea of a lectureship, and not appoint to a Fellowship at all.'

'Ah', said the Fellow in Politics thoughtfully. 'That's an interesting idea, Peter. Or course it's perfectly true that if George agreed to increase his teaching load a little – which I'm sure in the interests of the College he'd be happy to do – and we sent out the second year people, and possibly some of the prelim. lot, then . . .'

'Bob was always off on sabbaticals or leave of absence anyway', the Fellow in French remarked. 'Hardly ever seemed to be here.'

'A scholar of his standing . . .' said the Senior Tutor severely. 'Naturally he was much in demand. But it's true that possibly from the point of view of run-of-the-mill teaching . . .'

'No point in being overstaffed', said the Bursar.

'Quite', the Senior Tutor went on. 'Not of course that there would be any question of cutting back, merely that we ought to look carefully at the . . .'

The Fellow in Economics, who was given to reading outside his subject, said with a slightly frantic laugh, 'Oh come, this is beginning to sound like an exercise in self-deception. We shall end up with some presents of fish and game'.

'What?' snapped the Fellow in French. 'I don't take your point, Nick.'

The Senior Tutor said in tones of gentle reproof, 'Not really, Nick – it's just that we need to review the situation in terms of the College as a whole, rather than the immediate demands of the subject, of the teaching situation. Tragic as Bob's loss is, it does give us the chance to look carefully, to think about . . .'

'A Research Fellowship?' offered the Fellow in Politics. 'Two years. Non-renewable.'

'Without dining rights' said the Bursar.

'They always manage to hang on after their time's up, Research Fellows', said the Fellow in French. 'Why bring someone in specially?'

There was a moment's silence, tampered with only by the Fellow in Economics, who seemed to be having difficulty with something he would have liked to say. The Senior Tutor, who knew him to be a bright young man, but diffident and perhaps a little inexperienced, gave him an avuncular smile and said, 'Why bring someone in? Now that's an angle I hadn't thought of'.

'There's Ken Lambert', suggested the Fellow in Politics.

'Lambert?' said the Fellow in French.

'Research student', said the Bursar.

'Ah', said the Senior Tutor thoughtfully.

'He'd be glad of a bit of teaching', the Fellow in Politics went on. 'Good practice for him.'

'Cheaper than sending them out', said the Bursar.

'If he needs teaching practice', said the Fellow in French 'I should have thought he'd be grateful enough for the chance without us feeling we need . . .'

'Well, that's something we can look into another time.' The Senior Tutor spoke firmly, gathering up his papers. 'There are bound to be a few loose ends to tie up, but I think we've had a very useful session, and a valuable discussion of the broader aims of College policy. Perhaps, Tim' – to the Bursar – 'I could look in this afternoon and run through some figures with you?'

The Committee to appoint a Fellow and Tutor in Modern History broke up. The Senior Tutor laid a friendly hand on the arm of the Fellow in Economics, thinking that the lad was looking a trifly peaky, and suggested a glass of sherry before lunch.

A Clean Death

The train windows were still painted midnight blue for the black-out. Here and there, people had scraped at the paint, making channels and circles of bare glass behind which fled the darkening landscape. They had left King's Cross at four, in twilight, would be home, Aunt Frances said, by seven at the latest. Do, she had announced at the ticket office, assembling her welter of Christmas shopping – parcels and boxes from Harrods, Fortnums, Marshall and Snelgrove – do call me Frances, just, I don't really like aunt, and Clive would like to be Clive, I'm sure. And Carol, smiling sideways, not looking at her, had known she could not, would have to say 'you' now, for always, be for ever picking her way round the problem. She huddled into her school coat, stiff with cold, her knees raw red between the top of her socks and hem of her skirt, and fingered again the ticket in her pocket, checked the brown suitcase in the rack, in which were her holiday clothes, her good tweed skirt and her two jerseys and the tartan wool dress bought today by Aunt Frances – Frances – with money sent by her father from India. The money had meant complicated arrangements of cheques and deposit accounts and Frances irritated, queueing at the bank, glancing at her watch. Money from the bank in Calcutta, hot and crowded, rupees not pounds and shillings. Don't think of it, she told herself, the tears pressing again behind her eyelids, don't think of India. But it came, as it never ceased to do, clamorous with smells and sounds and what-used-to-be, and she sat, miserable with longing, watching the lights of Suffolk villages twinkle through the tattered black-out paint.

Frances, in her corner, was wedged beside a young soldier with hair so short his head seemed almost shaven, and battledress that smelled of damp and sweat; she had flinched away from him, Carol could see, turning to the window, reading her London Library book. She looked up, caught Carol's eye, and said 'Ipswich in another few minutes now – lovely thought!'

I've put you in the spare room, she had said earlier, not in with Marian, I thought you might rather be on your own, and Carol, who had feared to be classified with her cousins, as child, had been relieved. She did not know how to be with children, what to say, they made her feel awkward, inadequate. But I don't know how to be with grown-ups either, she thought, there is no one I talk to, I am quite by myself, it is as though I was some kind of thing there is only one of. At school she was not unpopular, but had no friends; she never walked with her arm round someone else's waist, or gathered over the tepid radiator in the form room, warming her hands and whispering. The other girls alarmed her; they were so worldly-wise, so cushioned by their confidence in how things were done, how to talk and act and respond. The school bewildered her, with the jungle of its customs and taboos. She remained uninitiated, an outsider, doing her best to use the right language, show the right interests, have the right emotions. She collected, as the others did, photographs of the royal family cut from newspapers; she stared at the battered fashion magazines passed from hand to hand, exhaustively discussed and analysed. At night, she lay silent in bed, hearing their whispers of cinemas and London musicals, and India created and re-created itself in the darkness, and she could hardly bear it. It set her apart from them, she knew; it was not quite the thing, to have been born in another country. It was not good to be different. She knew it, and felt inadequate; there was nothing she could do about it, nothing could make her one of them. Sometimes, not often, they asked her about India, but their curiosity was brief, it would evaporate within minutes. She would be talking – of the house, the garden, the heat, the people – and they would be gone, their attention switched, back with their own concerns. The other thing they never mentioned. The girl who had shown her round, her first day – one of the prefects – had said, 'Bad luck about your mother, Carol,' and she had known that it was unmentionable, death you did not talk about, like God, or love.

She had learned how she ought to be, what was expected, and was quietly pleased that she had learned so much. She made fewer mistakes now, was more acceptable. She was managing.

The train slid to a stop. Frances opened the door, and steam oozed up between carriage and platform, cold air gushing in, and country voices, voices all related to one another, Carol could hear. Accents. There was a girl at school who had an accent; that was not good either, she too was apart. Her parents did not pay, it was said, she had the Scholarship. Listening, in streets, on buses, Carol felt dizzied, sometimes, by voices: different, the same, connected. Like the babel of tongues in an Indian bazaar. You have to know who you are, she thought, who other people are, or it is impossible, you do everything wrong. Often I do not know who I am.

They got out, festooned with parcels. If you could take the children's stocking presents, Frances said, and Nigel's train-set, I can manage the Fortnum's bag and the curtain stuff. And Clive will get the cases, no hope of a porter of course, not these days.

Clive had come up almost at once, out of the darkness, and Carol thought wildly: do I kiss him or not, I can't remember, is it all relations, or not men ones? But he solved the problem himself by holding out a hand, and they shook awkwardly, and yes, she said, I had a good term, and yes, it is lovely to think it's nearly Christmas.

In the car, bumping through the East Anglian night, Frances recounted the day. London was awful, she said, I can't tell you, the shops so crowded, such a struggle on the buses, but I got everything, nearly everything, there was a problem with John's school things, they hadn't the games socks in yet . . . She sounded tired, but triumphant, like a huntsman at the end of the day, the job done. The road shone wet black in the car headlights and the fields that slid by were ribbed with snow; it was bitterly cold. A frost tonight, Clive said, Marian's cold seems a bit better – oh, and Mrs Binns left a pie in the oven for supper, she said give it another half hour or so, after you get back.

They were close, easy, in their concerns, the running of their lives. Once or twice, remembering, they passed questions to her, or comments, over the back of their seats. Is it this summer you do School Cert., Carol, or next? This village is called Kersey, the church is so pretty, you'll have to walk over one day and have a look.

They arrived, and the house seemed to burst, spilling out into the night like a ripe fruit; light, voices, the small shapes of children running and leaping beside the car. Dogs barking. Wireless music. The country night lay black and still and freezing all around, and here was this confident, unassailable place, waiting. The children bounced and shrieked. Did you find the balloons? they cried, and have you got my ribbon, and are there any sweets? Mummy! they shrieked, Mummy! And Frances was hugging and recounting and saying, oh, and here's Carol, say hello to Carol.

Hello, they said, and then their voices were back on that note of excitement and demand, and everyone was going into the house, shutting out the darkness – the endless snowy fields, the black roads.

She woke early in the morning, perished with cold. She had got up in the night to put on her underclothes beneath her pyjamas, and then her jersey on top, and still had lain frozen in the bed, curled knees to chest, the rest of the bed an icy pond. She listened to the noises of the house expand around her: the children's scampering feet, their voices crooning to cats or dogs, the rattle of a boiler being filled, Frances and Clive talking in the bedroom. It was an old, wooden house; it rang and echoed. Presently she got up and went to the bathroom that Frances had said she should share with the children. It smelled of flannels and damp and toothpaste; there was a full pottie in the corner. She stripped to the waist, as you had to do at school, and washed under her arms, up her neck, over the growing breasts that she felt must be so obvious, that slopped and bounced under her jerseys.

She dressed and went downstairs. On the bottom step there was a dog, a great golden lion-headed thing, lying right across it. She stood there, not knowing what to do, and it did not move, but looked at her and away again. And then one of the children – Nigel, the youngest – came from some room and saw her and said, 'Are you frightened of her?' And before she could answer he had gone running into the kitchen and she could hear him shout, 'Daddy! She's frightened of Tosca – Carol's frightened of Tosca'.

She could hear them laughing. Frances said 'I expect she's not used to dogs, darling'. She came out and tugged at the dog's collar, still laughing, saying what a stupid, soft old thing she was, wouldn't hurt a fly, you mustn't mind her. And Carol could think of no reply: she was not afraid of dogs, liked them, but in India a dog may be rabid, you do not go near a strange dog, never. It was instinctive, now, the hesitation, a conditioned response, just as at night, always, she thought, for the rest of her life, she would feel unsafe without the shrouding security of a mosquito net.

Clive was in the kitchen, nursing a cat. He stroked and tickled it, talking baby-language to it so that Carol was both embarrassed and fascinated. There was something wrong, apparently, it was ill. 'Poor Mr Patch,' crooned Clive. 'Poor pussy. Poor patchums', and the children gathered round, soft with sympathy, offering it tit-bits. 'We are a terrible animal family, I'm afraid, Carol' said Frances, frying bacon. 'Everybody is mad about animals. The children will show you the pony after breakfast.'

She trailed with the children, in a wind that cut through her mack, clutched her bare knees, was shown the garden and its secret places, the hens, the rabbit hutches, the pony, the orchard. And then they became involved in some game of their own and she came back into the house alone and stood at a loss in the kitchen, where Frances mixed things and talked to a woman washing up at the sink.

'This is Carol, Mrs Binns' she said. 'My niece, you know.' And Carol felt herself appraised, not unkindly, not critically, just with the shrewdness of a person who liked to see what was what, how things were.

'You'll be much of an age with my Tom, I should imagine,' said Mrs Binns. 'Fourteen he was, in October. We'll have to get you together. He's at a loose end, in the holidays, Tom, there's no one much his age, not nearer than the village.'

At school there were girls who had, or who were rumoured to have, boyfriends. The reputation gave them an aura, of daring but also of distinction; they too were set apart, but in a desirable way. They had moved on a little, on and up. Carol knew no boys, had not, she thought, spoken to one since long ago, since nursery days on another continent. She stared at Mrs Binns in alarm.

'Mmmn,' said Frances. 'What a good idea,' and Carol, puzzled now, saw that for some reason it was not. But Mrs Binns, saying 'Well, you must look in at the cottage, dear, your auntie'll tell you where it is,' had turned now to the table and taken up the pink and pimpled carcase of a chicken. 'I'll do this for you, Mrs Seaton, shall I?'

Frances looked at the chicken with distaste. 'Yes, please, if you would. A beastly job. I'd be sunk without you, I really would.'

Mrs Binns laughed. She stood at the sink, rummaging with deft, knowledgeable hands in the chicken's insides. 'It's a matter of what you're used to. I did my first bird when I was – oh, younger than Carol here.' Appalling things slid from within the chicken and lay on the draining-board. Frances, Carol saw, had turned firmly away, busy with her pie-dish. Carol said, 'In India you buy chickens live. They hang them up by their feet in the bazaar, in bunches'.

'How absolutely horrid!' Frances exclaimed; her voice was tense with emotion. Mrs Binns, halted in her work, looked up. Frances went on, vehemently, 'That is what is so awful about those places – they are so foul to animals. One really cannot stand it. I remember going to Morocco, before the war, and it simply spoiled the holiday, the way they treat the donkeys and things. You had to walk about trying not to notice – it was wretched, we were so glad to come home'.

Mrs Binns said in neutral tones, 'It's not nice to see, cruelty to animals.' She swilled the chicken out under the tap and put it on a plate. 'His dad give Tom a gun for his birthday, for rabbitting, but he told him he's to use it properly, no maiming things, he's to see there's a clean death.'

Frances's face was set in disapproval. 'Mmmn. Isn't fourteen a bit young for a gun?'

Mrs Binns was packing the chicken with stuffing now. Crumbs of it fell from her fingers and lay on the table, smelling of herbs, of summer. 'Rabbits are terrible round us now – had all my cabbage. He's the makings of a good steady hand, Bob says – Tom has. Three he got, last week.'

'Mmmn' said Frances again. She got up, putting away flour and fat. 'Could you do the bedrooms next, Mrs Binns, and then I think the dining room windows need a going over.'

At lunch, Frances and Clive talked of Mrs Binns. Clive said that she was a card, quite a character, and tales were recounted, remarks that Mrs Binns had made, her opinions, her responses. They were told with affection, with indulgence – much, Carol noted, as the children were spoken of in their absence. 'But', said Frances, 'I cannot approve of that boy being given a gun. They *will* start them off slaughtering things so early, people like that, I hate it.'

Marian said in stricken tones, 'Does he kill rabbits, Tom? Oh, *poor* rabbits . . . Mummy can't you tell him not to?'

'No, I can't, darling, it's not up to me. There, don't think about it – I don't expect he does it much. Finish up your sausage and then you can get down.'

One girl at school got letters from her boyfriend. It was known, and envied. She took them away and read them alone, in the cloakroom, and later could be seen, pink-faced and giggling, poring over selected passages with her best friend. Carol said, staring at the bowl of frost-nipped chrysanthemums in the middle of the table, 'Mrs Binns said I could go over to her cottage sometime'.

There was a silence. Clive picked up the cat and blew softly into its fur, murmuring to it. 'Poor Mr Patch,' he mumbled. 'How are your insides today – how's your poor tummy?'

'Yes'. said Frances. 'Well, just as you like, Carol.' She began to clear the table. 'I think a walk this afternoon, to the village and back, I need some things from the Post Office, anyway.'

The landscape was black and white under huge white skies — black ploughlands striped with white runnels of snow, criss-crossed with the dark lines of hedges, trimmed with the stiff shapes of trees. They walked along a road bordered by fawn-coloured rushes and grasses, each one starred and bearded with frost; icy wind poured through the skeletal hedges; there was a chain of crisp puddles along the uneven surface. The children skittered ahead, sliding on the ice, darting off into the fields on brief excursions. Clive and Frances walked arm in arm, Carol a few paces behind. Their talk and occasional laughter came back to her in irrelevant, incomprehensible snatches. I am so cold, she thought, colder than I have ever been, colder even than I am at school, will I ever be warm, how do people get warm, ever, in their lives? In India, in childhood, she had been too hot; always, one was sticky with sweat, looking for a place out of the sun. I cannot remember that now, she thought, I have no idea, really, how it was, it is like something in a book, something that happened to someone else. The gap had lengthened between her and the others; Frances, looking back over her shoulder, called 'Not far now — we shall have to get you used to walking, Carol'.

At the house, in Frances's sitting room, on the desk, there was a photograph of her and her brother, Carol's father, in youth. Around seventeen or eighteen. It was a bad photograph, muzzy, and Carol had not at first recognized the faces. Then, her father's familiar features had somehow emerged, but displaced and distorted; the boy in the photograph was him, and yet not him. She thought of this, and of herself; her hands, thrust into the pockets of her school coat, were rigid with cold; it was three o'clock in the afternoon, there was no reason, it seemed to her, why this day should not go on for ever. She stumped behind Frances and Clive, through the sphere of that silent, suspended landscape; it is so lovely here in summer, Frances had said, quite perfect, you must come in August, in the holidays.

At nights, at school, the other girls planned and recalled; the long thin room in which she slept with eight others was filled with disembodied voices, whispering in the dark of holidays past and holidays to come, of what they had done and what they would do. The limbo of the term was put away; they roamed into other times, other places. And Carol lay silent; to roam, for her, had too many dangers. Recollection must be checked; that way lay disaster. And the other way? She had nothing there, either, to offer; no plans nor expectations.

The children came running from a field, solemn-faced and important, with a dead bird they had found, a lapwing, bright-plumaged and uncorrupt, its eyes closed by filmy lids. Marian was on the brink of tears. Her father took the bird and they huddled round him, quiet and comforted, as he dug a grave, lined it with leaves, buried the body, marked the place with a ring of berries collected from the hedges. 'I don't expect it *felt* anything, Mummy, did it?' begged Marian. 'It didn't *hurt* it, did it?'. And Frances said 'No, darling, it would be just like going to sleep, it would hardly know anything about it'.

In the village, Frances bought things in the warm, cluttered Post Office that smelled of soap, matches and bacon; the children fingered and fidgeted, their voices shrill and confident. 'This is my niece Carol,' Frances explained, 'who is here for the Christmas holidays.' And the shop lady, petting the children, giving them each a toffee from a personal store behind the till, hesitated, the open tin in her hand, as also did Carol hesitate; we neither of us know, she thought in despair, what I am, if I am a child or not. The shop lady reached a decision, good or bad, and put the tin back on its shelf, unproffered.

On the way back, Marian pointed suddenly over the fields and said to Carol, 'That's Mrs Binns' cottage, down that track: they've got chickens, and a dog called Toby'.

Carol stared over a grass field, patched with unmelted snow; smoke filtered from a chimney, barely darker than the sky; washing hung limp on a line in stiff geometric shapes of sheets, towels, shirts with outstretched arms.

On Christmas morning she lay in bed hearing the children open their stockings in their parents' room across the corridor;

their high-pitched voices alternated with their parents' deeper ones like a series of musical responses, statement and commentary. She heard their feet pattering on the bare boards, the dogs barking in excitement; the animals too had Christmas presents – bones wrapped in scarlet crêpe paper, beribboned rubber mice. The day proceeded through a series of ceremonies and rituals: after breakfast we have presents under the tree, before church we telephone grandmother, in the afternoon we walk to Clee Hill. Frances said, 'I forgot to tell you, Carol – tomorrow our old friends the Laidlaws are coming. Mark is fifteen so he will be someone for you, I thought – it is dull for you, being always with the younger ones'.

The children did not like her, she knew. At first they had been shy, the small boys arch, trying to appeal as they would appeal to a grown-up. But they saw her now for what she was, neither fish nor fowl, not exempt like them from adult obligations, but without adult privileges either. Sharp-eyed, they noted her position as a classless person, without position, and exploited their own the more; if she would not join in their games when they wanted her to they complained to Frances, and Carol felt her aunt's resentment, unstated but nonetheless evident. I have a hundred things to do, her silent back said, the least you could do is help to amuse them for a while. They danced around Carol, more agile in every way; they made her feel lumpish of mind and in body.

The prospect of Mark filled her with apprehension. He is at Marlborough, said Frances, he is awfully clever, he has such nice manners, we have always liked him so much.

They came, the Laidlaws; there were kisses and hand-shakes and the house was filled with talk, with people at ease with one another. Mark, Carol furtively noted, had longish hair that flopped over one eye and was dressed as a man – tweed jacket, grey flannels, grown-up tie. He sat next to Frances at lunch and talked with what Carol saw to be charming attention, listening when listening should be done, taking the initiative when that was appropriate. After lunch he played with the children – an absurd game of crawling on the floor, romping, and he was in no way diminished by it, it made him seem more grown-up, not less

174

so. And Frances beamed upon him.

He had said to Carol, 'Where do you go to school?' She had replied to this. He had asked her how many School Cert. subjects she was doing and she had replied to that too. And then there had been a silence, she had searched wildly for something to fill it, and seen that he wanted to get away from her, to get back to the others, that she did not interest him. 'It must have been awfully exciting, growing up in India,' he said. 'What was it like?', and India swirled in her head, a kaleidoscope of sights and sounds and responses, and there was nothing she could say. 'Yes,' she stammered. 'It was . . . I mean . . . Yes, I . . .', and felt Frances's gaze upon her, observing, regretting. 'Have you ever seen Gandhi?' he asked, and she shook her head.

Later, in the evening, Frances said, 'The Laidlaws are having a small party for Mark, at the New Year, but of course you will be gone by then, Carol — they were so sorry'.

It snowed in the night. She drew her curtains and saw the landscape powdered over, not deeply, but shrouded as it were, in a state of suspension once again, motionless. The children, outside, were rushing about trying to scoop up enough for snowballs or snowmen; they came in wet and querulous, their hands scarlet with cold. Their exhilaration disintegrated into tears and fretfulness; Frances was irritable. Later, she had letters to write, and the children wanted to go to the village, to buy sweets. Carol can take us, they cried, and Frances, relieved, said yes, of course, Carol can take you — wrap up well; don't let them run on the road, Carol.

They met him on the way back. She was walking behind the children, who were quiet now, amiable, tamed by chocolate. He came down the track from the cottage, the gun crooked over his arm, and they arrived together precisely at the gate. Marian said 'Hello, Tom'.

He nodded, 'Hello'. And then he looked at Carol and smiled, and quite easily, without her eyes sliding away to left or right, without a problem, she smiled back. He said, 'Mum told me you were stopping with your auntie'.

The children wanted to see the gun. But their curiosity was

tinged, even at this remove, with Frances's disapproval. In silence they watched him demonstrate its workings; his thin fingers clicked this and pressed that, ran over the sleek metal, caressed the polished butt. He was immensely proud of it; in his light voice, not yet broken, a boy's voice, but with its sudden odd lurches into manhood, he described the make and model. It was not a toy, it was real, serious, it marked him. It told him what he was. 'My dad gave it me for my birthday. My fourteenth. He reckoned you can learn to use a gun, then, when you're fourteen, it's time.'

The children were restive, moving away. Come on, they said, let's go, it's cold, let's go home.

Tom turned to Carol, 'I'll be going out tomorrow morning, shooting. Early, when it's getting light. Sevenish. You could come if you like'.

She said 'Yes, please', before she could stop to think. 'Right', he said. 'Come by the cottage then, and we'll go.'

She walked back to the house amazed; things like this did not happen, it was astonishing, she could hardly believe it.

It was in the cold, wakeful reaches of the night that it struck her she should have told Frances, asked Frances. But now it was too late. Frances was asleep: at seven – before seven – she would not be about. And suppose she said no, or even just implied no? I have to go, Carol thought, I must go, it is the only thing that has ever happened to me.

She woke again long before dawn and lay looking at her watch every few minutes. When it said half-past six she got up, making as little noise as possible, and dressed in all her warmest things. But she was warm already, for the first time in days, weeks, it seemed, and when she crept down the stairs, and opened the back door the air outside was tinged with mildness, she thought. The wind that met her face was not so keen, and the snow, in the drive, had melted. Only in the lee of the hedges it lay still in thickish drifts.

It was almost dark. The sky was streaked with light in the east; dark clouds lay like great fish along the horizon. She walked down the road and there was no one else in the world, except her;

she was alone, and it was quite all right, she felt confident, at ease
with things, she walked briskly with her hands in her pockets and
there was beauty in the landscape that wheeled around her, she
could see that. It was still and quiet, clenched in its winter state,
but there was a flush of reddish brown on the plough, where the
snow had melted, and the bare shapes of the trees on the skyline
were of amazing delicacy, they held the suggestion of other
times, the ripeness to come, summer.

She hesitated outside the cottage door; there was an easy murmuring of voices from inside, and the chink of crockery, and
smells of toast and something frying. And then a man came out, at
that moment, in old jacket and muffler, his trousers clipped ready
for a bicycle – Tom's father, presumably – and told her to go on
in, Tom wouldn't be a moment.

Mrs Binns gave her a cup of tea, but she could not eat the food
offered; she felt in her stomach all the instability of before a
journey, before an event. But it was good, it was the best thing
she had known, beyond things which must not be remembered,
things from other times. Tom said little; he attended to the gun
with oil and a rag and a stick, and when he had done he got up
and said, 'We'll be off now, Mum,' and Carol rose too, in a state
still of amazement. She felt quite comfortable, quite in place. I
have a friend, she thought, and could hardly believe it.

He led her over the fields, up a shallow hillside. Out of the cottage, he became talkative. He told her about the ways of rabbits,
and how you must go after them downwind, towards their burrows, towards the slope where he knew they would come out to
graze around now. He had shot two, he said, the week before,
and Carol said, no, three your mother said, and he corrected her,
carefully – two it was, one I missed, I told Mum, she got it
wrong. I'm not good with sighting, he said, seriously, not yet,
and I've got a shake in my wrist, I'll have to work on that, and she
nodded, intent, and stared at his wrists. They were bony wrists,
white-knobbed, sticking out from the frayed sleeve of his too-
short jersey. His hair was cut short, almost cropped, like the soldier in the London train. He spoke with the accent of the place,
this place to which he belonged, where he had been born, where

his parents had been born; sometimes she could not quite follow what he said. She thought confusedly of this, as they climbed the hill, the ground wet and springy under their feet: of her own speech, which was quite different, and of the place where she had been born, none of whose many tongues she spoke. Once, climbing a gate, he gave her the gun to hold for a moment; she felt the sting of the cold metal on her hands, and cradled it gingerly, with reverence.

They reached the side of the field where, he said, the rabbits would come. It ran downhill from a small copse, and she could see the brown markings of burrows at the top. He edged cautiously along the ditch until he came to a place in long grass where they could lie and wait. 'They might have heard us,' he said. 'We'll have to sit tight a bit, and they'll come out again.'

They lay flank to flank on the wet grass. She could feel its damp and cold creep through to her skin, and the faint warmth of his body beside hers. Their breath steamed. Occasionally they whispered a little; it was better, though, he said, to stay quiet. He seemed to expect nothing of her; if she had not complied, if she had infringed the rules in any way, he did not let her know. He let her hold the gun again, and she peered down the long barrel into the field and saw, suspended cinematically beyond it, the cropped turf with its dark enigmatic holes and scrapings of rich earth and pockets of snow. He said, 'They're a long time about it, usually they come out quicker than this, once you've sat quiet a bit,' and she could feel the tension in him; the rabbits mattered, they were the most important thing in his life just now. She said suddenly, amazed at her own temerity, 'What is it like, killing something, do you like it?' And turning to look at him, saw with shock that a slow tide of colour had crept up his face.

'I don't like them dying' he said, mumbling with his head to the ground, so that she could hardly hear. 'I hate that. The first time I came out with my Dad, I felt sick, I didn't want to do it. I couldn't say, not to him. He gave me the gun, see, for my own. Now it's all right. They die quick, it's over just like that.' He looked at her, his face still red. 'It's not for the killing, it's not for that.'

She nodded. There wasn't anything to say. And then suddenly he touched her arm, pressed his fingers down on her coat, and she looked out towards the field and there was movement on the turf, something brown shifting against the green – two, three of them. One sat up, nosing the wind, and she saw its pricked ears, and, as it turned, the white scut.

He lifted the gun, aimed; she was clenched in excitement, breathless. And then he pressed the trigger, and the noise was startling, louder than ever she had imagined, but in the second before, in a fraction of a second, something had happened out there and the rabbits had bolted, homed back on their burrows, gone. The field was empty.

She said '*Oh* . . .' He sat up, breaking the gun apart angrily, unloading. 'Won't they come out again?'

He shook his head. 'Not for hours, maybe. That's done it, that has. Something scared them.' His hands were shaking, she could see that, they had been shaking earlier too, when he lay still on the grass, aiming. Now he seemed almost relieved. 'Come on,' he said. 'Have to get back. Mum'll be wondering.'

They ran down the field; there was no longer any need to be quiet. At the gate he showed her how he could vault over it, and she, who was unathletic, who lumbered hopelessly around the games pitch at school, found that she could do it also; there was no end, it seemed, to the surprises this day held. There are bits of me I knew nothing about, she thought, I am not so clumsy after all, I can talk to people, I can feel part of something. The sky was crossed and re-crossed by ragged flights of birds. 'What are they?' she asked. 'What kind of bird is that?', and he told her that those were rooks, and these on the plough, in the field, were lapwings, surprised at her ignorance but uncritical. 'Mum said you grew up somewhere else', he said, 'somewhere foreign,' and she talked about India; she brought heat and dust and the sound of the place onto this wintry Suffolk field and it was painless, or almost so.

At the corner of the track to the cottage he asked her if she would like to come out again the next morning; she had half-expected this and yet not dared to hope. Such coincidence, in the normal way of things, of what you would like and what was available, did not happen. She said 'Yes please,' and thought it sounded childish, and blushed.

Back at the house, she was amazed to find it past breakfast-time, Frances clearing the table, the children staring as she came in at the kitchen door, Clive reading a letter. Frances sounded annoyed. '*There* you are, Carol, we were beginning to wonder, where have you been?'

She had prepared nothing, given no thought to this moment. She stood, silent with confusion, and then one of the children said, 'She's been shooting rabbits with Mrs Binns' Tom. We heard him ask her yesterday'.

Frances swept things off the table onto a tray. 'Oh, really. I can't imagine why you should want to, Carol, I must say.'

'Did he kill any rabbits?' said Marian.

Carol muttered 'No'. She could feel her face scarlet; the day, and all that it had held, died on Frances's kitchen floor; she felt dirty.

'Goody' said Marian. 'Can I go out now?'

Clive had not spoken; he had put down his letter and was play-ing with the dog, gently pulling its ears, mumbling to it; Carol, catching his eye by accident, saw it go cold, excluding her. 'Well,' he said to the dog, 'Walkies, is it? Walkies for a good girl?' The dog beamed and fawned and swished its feathered tail.

All that day was sourly flavoured with Frances's disapproval; nothing was said, but it hung in the air at lunchtime, in the after-noon, over tea. Mrs Binns did not come for which Carol was grateful; there would have been references, Tom would have been mentioned, and that she could not endure.

In the afternoon there was a letter from her father, enclosed in one to Frances. She read it by the drawing room fire, and it seemed to come not from another country but from another time; his familiar handwriting, speaking of the house, the garden, neighbours, referred to things that no longer were, they had perished long ago. 'Poor Tim' said Frances, reading her own letter. 'He is so anxious to get home, pack things up out there. It must be trying for him, but it is not long now, he has booked his passage.' Carol read that the bulbuls had nested again in the bush outside the laundry, that the cannas were a lovely show this year, that the rains had come early; it was as though he were frozen in another age, her father, in an imagined world. She asked, in sudden panic, 'Will he really be here this summer, here in England?' And Frances, preoccupied now with the demands of the children, of the hour, said that of course he would, he was bound to, the house was sold, the furniture to be packed and shipped. If you are writing to him, she went on, you had better put it in with mine, and save the stamp.

Lying awake, after everyone else had gone to bed, Carol knew that she would go with Tom in the morning. She had thought about it, on and off, all day; she felt grubby, condemned by Clive's cold eye, by the children's indignation. '*Poor* rabbits' Marian said once. 'I think it's beastly. Horrid Tom', and she had answered nothing, being without defence. Now, staring at the dim square of the window, she knew that she would go, had to go, whatever they thought, whatever happened. Guilt clutched her; she lay sleepless for most of the night.

He was waiting for her at the bottom of the track. 'Hello,' he said, 'I thought you weren't coming', and his innocence compounded her guilt. She carried now the burden not only of what she was doing, but of the fact that he did not know what they were doing, did not know that what they did was wrong, despised by decent people.

They climbed the hill again. It was raining; the wind blew wet sheets into their faces and they walked with heads down, not talking much. At the gate Tom did not vault but climbed over; Carol noticed how thin his legs were, childishly thin, like his bony wrists. Walking behind him, she observed that his hair made a ducktail at the nape and that the cleft had the softness, the look of vulnerability that the back of a small boy's neck has. She saw, for a moment, the ghost of the child that he had recently been; Mark Laidlaw's stocky frame had suggested the man from whom he stood at one remove. She thought of her own body, which seemed always to scream out in conflict – the alien, uncontrollable breasts, the pudgy hands and face, the scar on her

181

knee that remembered a fall when she was ten. Her body held her back; at the same time it dragged her inexorably onwards.

At the place where they had waited before, he gestured her down into the grass. They lay again side by side, staring through rain-studded greenery at the point in the field where something might happen. The time passed slowly; it stopped raining and a weak sun shone opalescent behind the clouds. Occasionally, they murmured to each other. 'Taking their time again,' he said. 'Hope I'll have better luck today.' And she nodded and murmured yes, hope so, and ssh! look, isn't that one? no, it's just a thistle, sorry. Something had lifted, things had eased once more, guilt had been put to flight; Frances, Clive and the children no longer hovered behind her shoulder. The crystal globes of water on the grass blades shivered with a thousand colours; the dried head of a summer flower held between delicate stalks a miniature of the landscape beyond – skyline trees, clouds; the sun on the back of her hand was a breath, a promise, of warmth.

And then, together, they saw it on the grass beside the burrow; a moment ago it had not been there and now suddenly there it was, quietly munching grass, bobbing away a yard or so, sitting up to snuff the wind.

He raised the gun, hesitated for what seemed far too long, fired.

The rabbit bucked into the air. Bucked, and at the same time screamed. The sound was hideous; it rang over the field, obscene in the quietness of the morning. She cried, 'You got it! You hit it!', and they jumped up together and ran across the grass.

And saw, together, at the same moment, that the rabbit was not dead. It lay threshing and writhing and as they came near it screamed again, humanly, like a hurt child, and they pulled up short and stood there in horror, a few yards off, staring. Blood welled from its ear; it writhed and twitched.

Tom was shaking. His voice was high-pitched, out of control, 'I got to do something. You got to kill them, when that happens, you got to finish them off'.

She said 'Oh, I don't want to see!', and turned away, her hands over her eyes, but then turned back, moments later, and he was standing above the rabbit, white-faced, and the rabbit bleated again, and arched its back, and kicked. He said, 'I don't know what to do. I've seen my Dad do it — you have to break their necks. I don't know how to do it'. He was distraught.

She covered her eyes again.

When she looked back he had the rabbit in his hands, and the rabbit was limp. Blood dripped from it. He put it on the ground and it lay still. He was shaking violently. He moved away a few paces and sat on the grass, turned from her, and she could see his whole body tremble. She felt sorry for him, and yet at the same time exasperated. She could not help him; they were quite separate now, it was as though they did not know each other; the whole fragile structure of confidence, the sense of being at ease with the world, had been destroyed with the rabbit. She saw Tom, wretched, and could think only: I am wretched, too, I hate myself, and what we have done, and what people must think of us for it.

He got up, without a word, and began to walk away down the field, and wordlessly she followed him. He carried the gun all anyhow, not with pride, cradled over his arm; it looked, now, disproportionately large, as though it had grown and he had shrunk.

At the road he turned to her. 'Don't say anything about what happened — not to my Mum.'

She shook her head.

'Cheerio, then.'

'Good-bye.'

It was raining once more. She trudged towards the house; she was shrivelled with guilt. They did not know what had happened, could not know, but she felt that the very look of her announced the incident; she carried still, in her head, the rabbit's scream.

They were having breakfast. As she came into the kitchen silence fell and the children looked expectantly towards Frances.

Frances said, 'You'd better have something to eat, Carol'; her voice was not friendly. When Carol was sitting at the table she went on, 'It would have been a good idea, you know, to mention that you were going out with Tom Binns again. Clive and I are responsible for you, while you are here'.

Carol stared at the table. 'I'm sorry' she said.

Clive had not looked once at her. He kept his back half-turned. Now, he busied himself giving milk to the cat. He poured the creamy top from a bottle into a saucer and put it by the stove. 'There, Mr Patch,' he murmured. 'There. Come on then, puss.' The kitchen was filled with well loved, well tended animals.

'Did Tom kill a rabbit?' said Marian in her small, clear voice.

Scarlet-faced, Carol noted the bordered table-cloth: red flower, cluster of leaves, spray of berries, red flower again. 'Yes' she muttered.

'Children' said Frances, 'you can get down now and go up and do your teeth. Oh, and tidy your bedroom, please, Marian darling.'

They went. Clive said he thought he would just go now and do the hens and the pony before he went into Ipswich. He went.

Frances began to clear the table. The room was charged with feeling; once, she dropped a cup, and swore. Carol sat, the rabbit's scream still in her ears, behind and above the sounds of the children upstairs, of Frances running water at the sink, of the cat lapping milk.

Frances slapped plates onto the draining-board and spoke again, her voice assured and tinged with indignation, 'What I cannot understand – what Clive and I cannot understand – is why you should *want* to. I daresay it has been a bit dull here for you given that the children are a good deal younger and I am frightfully busy what with little or no help these days, not like it was for people before the war, but we've tried to find things for you to do and had Mark Laidlaw over who I thought would be just right for you, so I simply cannot understand why . . .'

The room spun; Frances's voice roared. Carol wrung the table-cloth between her shaking fingers and burst out, 'He didn't mean to. Tom didn't mean to – he meant to do it like his father said, a clean death, not hurting it, and something went wrong, it wasn't. He felt awful about it. I don't think he'll go shooting again. *I* don't want to, not ever. I hated it. It was beastly, the rabbit being

184

hurt like that'. She fought back tears.

Frances turned from the sink; she was staring now, in surprise, across the kitchen table. She said, 'What rabbit? What do you mean? I'm not talking about shooting rabbits, Carol, which is really neither here nor there, lots of people round here shoot rabbits and of course one wishes they wouldn't but there it is. I'm talking about why you should want to go off doing things with someone like Tom Binns, as though he were a friend or something, when surely you must realise that it really won't do. I don't know what Mrs Binns was thinking of, suggesting it, she is normally such a sensible woman'. She paused, and then went on, 'I know it has made things difficult for you, growing up out there in India, sometimes it is a bit confusing for you here, I daresay, but surely you must see that a boy like Tom Binns . . . well, it really doesn't do, you should know that, Carol'.

The rabbit's scream died away; in its place there came, all innocent and unaware, Tom's voice of yesterday, explaining the workings of the gun. She stared at her aunt in bewilderment and thought: I don't know what you are talking about, I knew I had done one thing and now you are saying I have done another. It came to her suddenly that there was no way, ever, that she could oblige everyone, could do both what was expected of her, and what her own discoveries of what she was would drive her to do; she would have to learn to endure the conflict, as her body endured the conflict of what she had been and what she was bound to be, like it or not.

Party

She gets out of the taxi, Ellen Greaves, the grandmother, and
pays with the change that she has assembled, carefully, on the
way from Paddington. Then she picks up her suitcase once more
and climbs the short flight of steps to the front door of the house,
her daughter's house. It is a tall, thin terrace house, nineteenth
century, in the middle of a street of similar houses. Aircraft
lumber overhead. She rings the bell.

The door is opened, by an adolescent she does not recognise,
who explains that they are all in the kitchen. From down below,
in the basement, her daughter's voice calls up 'Hallooo . . .
Mum? Down here . . . It's a shambles – be warned'. And Ellen
dumps her case in the hall and goes with caution down the steep
stairs to the basement kitchen which is full of people and certainly
most untidy. There are bottles everywhere, and food, both
cooked and uncooked, and many loaves of bread. She kisses, and
is kissed. Her grandchildren are there: Toby who is seventeen
and Sophie who is eighteen and Paul, the little one, who is only
eleven. And there are others, a dark girl and two boys and yet
another she does not at first see, who is apparently mending the
back of the fridge. They smile and greet; they have nice manners.
Ellen smiles and greets too, and notes their appearance: all are
shabbily, not to say scruffily, dressed, but their voices suggest a
reasonable prosperity. Ellen finds this interesting.

Her daughter, Louise (who has got very thin again – indeed
everyone is thin, they all have a lean and hungry look, despite the

187

plenitude of things to eat) is furiously applied to something at the stove. She chops and stirs and flies to cupboards and despatches someone to the freezer and explains that *she* is doing the food for *their* party, for the grown-up dinner, and *they* are coping absolutely on their own with *their* stuff (and indeed, as Ellen now sees, Sophie is also chopping and stirring, though with what seems to be a less refined approach). The two parties, Louise explains, will coexist but there will be no mixing, in all probability – we shall be upstairs and they will do their own thing down here, and nobody will get in anyone else's hair that way. But, she adds, doing it like this means that we are here to keep an eye, Michael and I, there will be no hanky-panky, no nonsense. And she casts a look at the young, who grin.

Ellen sits down at the kitchen table and wonders if, amid all this, there will be a cup of tea going. She decides (rightly, as it turns out) that there probably will not. Someone goes out and comes back in with a crate of bottles which is put on the dresser; Louise shrieks no, no! not there, for heaven's sake! The crate is removed to the floor beside the fridge. There is a brief, whispered consultation among the young, two of whom leave; they move with a slouching purposefulness. Louise, on the other hand, darts from point to point. Her mother observes her thoughtfully.

We, Louise explains, are having a salmon trout and a rather lavish pud that I haven't tried before. They – and there are to be absolutely no more than thirty, do you hear, as agreed, no last minute additions (Sophie and Toby nod emphatically) – are having plonk and some goo that Sophie is fixing.

Chilli con carne, murmurs Sophie, stirring. She peers through her hair into the saucepan; the kitchen is very hot and close. Ellen looks at the window and at the same moment Louise dashes to it, throws up the sash, and returns to her chopping-board.

Ellen, who is really here for her annual visit to the dentist, says that she hopes she won't be in the way. If she had known, she says, she could quite easily have made it another day . . . But before she can finish Louise is saying that there is absolutely no question of her being in the way, her usual room is empty because no one is staying the night, that's for sure (another sharp look at the young), and this is an absolutely inter-generational night so in fact it is very appropriate that she should be here. Louise, in mid-chop and mid-stir, pauses to smile fondly at her mother. Not everyone's mum, she says, would fit in, as it happens, but you will be all right, I can count on you, I know, and actually you may rather like some of the people who are coming. There is Tony Hatch who . . . But Tony Hatch remains undeveloped, because at this moment the two departed young return bearing cardboard boxes full of glasses and there is an altercation over the disposal of these, which must not be put there, nor there, nor above all on the dresser . . . Indeed, the kitchen is silting up rapidly, there is not an uncluttered surface nor much uncluttered floor. Louise and the rest dart and shuffle amid the confusion, with remarkable adroitness; Ellen decides that she is safest where she is. She sits there at the table, and looks at Paul, who is perched on a stool, intent on some map or plan he is studying; he seems quite impervious to what is going on around. Once, he says 'Mum, have you got any glue, my tube's almost used up?' and Louise says 'What?' and goes to the stairs to deal with Toby, who, with a friend, is trying to bring a table-tennis table down; there are accusations and denials concerning scraped paint. Louise comes back into the kitchen scowling (she is also sweating profusely, her mother observes, which is odd for someone so thin); Paul sighs, slithers from the stool, and goes out.

Ellen surreptitiously re-washes some crockery stacked on the draining-board, having noted its condition with disquiet.

Louise says 'Oh, Christ, the man never came about the stereo', and rushes out. She can be heard upstairs, vehemently telephoning.

Ellen, who has been able to do some prospecting from her seat at the table, and has established the whereabouts of cups, tea, sugar etc., makes herself a cup of tea. She sits drinking it and listens to the conversation of two people at her feet. They are not so much exchanging observations or opinions as making statements, separate and unrelated. The girl says that she simply cannot stand anything fried nowadays, she doesn't know why, she thinks perhaps it is psychological, and the boy says there is this master at school, this bloke who has really got it in for him, it's a hassle. They are joined by another girl, who is concerned about the state of her finger-nails. She sits peering at them and saying there are these little white spots, look, I'm worried, what should I do; then for a few moments these assorted themes come together in a united objection to honey (however did they get onto that?) before each is off again on a saga of personal revelation. Ellen, one of whose feet is being sat on, shifts, as unobtrusively as possible, and pours herself another cup of tea.

Louise returns, followed by Paul, who says again, 'Is there any glue anywhere, mum?' Louise says 'Why?' and darts with exclamations of dismay to her saucepan. Paul begins 'Because I haven't . . .', but now Louise remembers that no one has counted and allocated cutlery, so the group under the kitchen table are jolted into action, or rather into a state of gentle drift.

It is five o'clock.

At six o'clock Louise has the most ghastly headache. Further, she is seized with some compulsion that sends her on frequent brief and furtive excursions into the large room next to the kitchen, Toby's room, in which the youthful party is to take place. She seems to be hunting for something. During these hunts the young, in the kitchen, exchange glances and roll their eyes. Once or twice, Ellen cannot help hearing whispered snatches on the stairs, unspecified threats about what Louise will do if there is the slightest suspicion of, if anyone is so damn stupid as to bring, if anything other than absolutely straightforward . . . During one of these fraught exchanges, Paul reappears, sliding past his mother and siblings without paying them any attention. He delves in the bread-bin, helps himself to bread, butter and jam, and sits once more upon the stool, lost in perusal of yet another printed sheet. Ellen says 'What is that, dear?'

It is, Paul explains, the instructions for the assembly of the model aircraft on which he is currently working. He is stuck, he says, because he has run out of glue, almost, but also because there is a bit that he simply cannot get the hang of. It doesn't, he says, seem to make sense. The aeroplane is a De Havilland Mosquito, he explains, and the problem is that . . .

190

Ellen asks if she can have a look. She reads, frowns, puts her glasses on and reads again. After a few moments everything falls into place; the problem, as it turns out, is a semantic one. The model aircraft kit has been made in Japan, and the translation of the instructions, while for the most part admirable, has fallen down just at the end here, where in fact 'right' should read 'left', and 'front', 'back'. Paul is gravely grateful, and goes off again.

Michael arrives home. He kisses his mother-in-law, and immediately busies himself stowing bottles in the fridge, placing others by the stove; he says it is amazingly brave of Ellen to let herself in for all this, and Ellen, who is now repairing the zip on Toby's jeans (they have not been washed for some time, which makes the job a mite disagreeable), says not at all, a bit of gaiety will be a nice change, she leads a quiet enough life in the normal way of things. Louise, whose voice has become peculiarly shrill, interrupts to point out that the table needs laying; Sophie comes in and has an argument with Toby about some gramophone records; the telephone rings. Michael and Louise exchange clipped words about some gin, of which, it seems, there is not enough. Subdued accusations are made about responsibility.

Ellen goes up to her room, which is on the top floor. On the way, she passes the open door of Sophie's room. Sophie, within, can be seen seated at a dressing-table with tears pouring down her cheeks, a staggering sight, the incarnation of tragedy. Her grandmother, disturbed, ventures to ask if there is anything she can do, to be told, in tones of choked stoicism, that there is nothing, nothing, no one can help, it would be impossible to explain to anyone, it is to do with her friend, or rather ex-friend, Mike, and furthermore there is this dress she was to wear which is stained all down the front, ruined . . . Her grandmother nods understandingly and withdraws.

In her own room, Ellen unpacks her overnight case, hangs up a dress, and goes to the bathroom for a wash. She pats the hot water tank in exploratory fashion; a hot water-bottle, she suspects, might be a comfort later on, but the water is not very hot. She will have to see about a kettle.

Downstairs, there are sudden bursts of loud music, as from a fairground. Louise is to be heard, also.

Ellen changes into her tidy dress and does her hair. Then she sits for a while on the edge of her bed, apparently looking out of the window over the ranges of grey London roof-tops. She was sixty-three last birthday, a small, neat person, a little fatter than in youth, her hands brown-mottled, her teeth not all her own. She sits so still, is so relaxed, that to an observer the room might appear to be empty. She watches the slow progress of an aeroplane along the line of a roof and thinks, in utter tranquillity, of her husband, ten years dead. She tells him, as is her habit, what has been happening to her today, and with the telling there is a faint, fragrant gust of sexual memory. Come now, she tells herself, this won't do, I am not here to be unsociable, and she gathers herself to go downstairs.

The house is strung up now, like a bow, any minute something might snap. As Ellen progresses downwards, people slip past her, dash from room to room, drop things. Louise comes from her bedroom, in a long dress, screwing on ear-rings, and says oh, there you are, mum, I say you do look smart, come down and Michael will find you a glass of sherry, would you believe it, the fridge has decided to play up again, now of all times. And she is gone down the stairs at a gallop, her skirt looped over her arm, her neat muscular calves visible beneath. Her mother remembers that at school she was good at games. It is not wise to mention this, though; for some reason that recollection is ill-received nowadays. Louise has a partnership in a small art gallery.

At eight, the guests begin to arrive. They arrive simultaneously on both floors — the young presenting themselves at the basement door, in twos and threes, furtive of manner, being admitted in silence, without greeting; Louise and Michael's friends climbing the steps to the front door, shedding coats in the hall, loud in greeting and comment. They are presented to Ellen: this tall thin man who is a psychiatrist, Tony Hatch, and his dark, shrieking wife; the small round unattached man who works at Sotheby's; two more couples whose allegiances she cannot for a while get straight, since they all arrive together and treat one another with indiscriminate familiarity. We are all such *old* friends tonight, declares Louise, flying from drinks cupboard to guests, it is lovely, everyone knows everyone else, I don't have to do any of that tiresome sorting people out. Except of course you, mum, she adds – and you are such a splendid adaptable lady, aren't you? She beams upon her mother and the other guests smile kindly. Ellen, who is not deaf, though it is apparently expected of her, has already heard Louise in the hall explaining that her mum is here for the night which actually is not the snag you'd think because she is really marvellous for that generation, nothing bothers her, she is amazingly well-adjusted, you'll love her.

Drinks are drunk. Ellen sits on the sofa beside the psychiatrist who tells her with boyish candour that he and Josie are recently married, just this year. He is in his early forties, and wears jeans and a jacket that reminds Ellen of her husband's old tropical bush-shirt. He is a little stout for the jeans and during the course of the evening the zip of the fly is to descend, which worries Ellen, not for herself but because embarrassment in others distresses her. As it turns out, though, there is no cause for distress; he is never aware of his plight. He talks to Ellen with nostalgia of his first wife, his divorced wife, who was the most super person; across the room, the new wife bites her finger-nails and occasionally shouts out some personal comment; the niceties of social intercourse do not seem to interest her.

The volume of noise from the basement is increasing; several times Louise, or Michael, go to the stairs and remonstrate.

Dinner is had in the dining room, which glows agreeably with candlelight and furniture polish and silver. Louise and Michael have some nice things. Ellen sits between the man from Sotheby's and one of the other husbands (she has sorted out now who is attached to whom, for what that is worth). The man from Sotheby's turns to her and says (in pursuit of the tail-end of a subject that had been bandied around earlier, upstairs) what does she think about the Mentmore sale, and does she feel that the government should or shouldn't have stepped in earlier, but while she is giving proper consideration to what she thinks (and she does, in fact, have a number of thoughts on the matter) it turns out that what he really intended was to tell her what he thinks, which he proceeds to do. Ellen listens with attention; he is telling her, in fact, a great deal more than he realises. I . . . he says . . . my opinion is that . . . personally, I feel . . . consulted me earlier . . . Ellen nods thoughtfully. Down at the other end of the table, the second wife of the psychiatrist screams that Tony is getting a bald pate, just look at him, look at his pate! Everybody laughs; the psychiatrist blows his wife a kiss; the husband on Ellen's right says that Josie is a riot, she is such a direct person, she says just what comes into her head.

By now, everybody has had a good deal to drink, except Ellen, for whom a glass of sherry has always been quite enough.

There is a muffled crash, from below; Louise, who is listening to an anecdote told by the psychiatrist, leaves the room, sharply, a frozen smile on her lips. She returns and serves the salmon trout with what seems an unnecessary amount of clatter. Everybody says what a lovely treat.

Ellen, who has got up to help Louise pass the vegetables, asks if Paul has had something earlier, or what, and is told that he is absolutely fine, he is up in his room with a plate of bangers and beans, of course he is rather out on a limb tonight, poor love, neither one thing nor t'other. Michael, who is circulating more wine, says it is a tiresome time for him, poor chap, he longs to be out in the great wide world like the others.

The psychiatrist has finished his anecdote, and the man from Sotheby's is now having his turn; people are very given to interruption, Ellen notes, they do not so much listen as interject. She watches the young woman opposite her, who has been trying for the past hour to make various points about herself, without success, chiefly because she has to compete, at that end of the table, with Louise and the psychiatrist's wife, both of whom have louder voices. The psychiatrist's wife, at this moment, bawls to Michael that Tony gets awfully randy in hot weather, it's a real sweat. Ellen, interested, is trying to define her origins (Ellen likes to know where she is about people). She thinks she can detect, beneath that stridency, a residual hint of the west country, and would like to know if she is right – in a momentary lull she leans forward and asks the girl where her home is, but she is busy now picking her teeth with a finger-nail and does not hear, or does not care to.

Downstairs, there is a steady thump of music, with intermittent louder bursts; Louise occasionally frowns, but her reactions are becoming slower. A sound of splintering glass escapes her altogether, engaged as she is in banter with the man from Sotheby's. She forgets to pass the biscuits with the pudding; Ellen rescues them from the sideboard and puts them on the table.

They move back to the sitting room, for coffee. Ellen, following Louise down to the kitchen to give a hand, peeks through the half-open door of Toby's room at a scene of semi-darkness, peopled with murky, shifting presences like an aquarium. Louise, juggling a trifle unsteadily with hot water, coffee and a strainer, is muttering darkly about having a good mind to go in there and just have a thorough check . . . Sophie comes in, hand in hand with a boy, wreathed in smiles; she says 'Hello, gran' warmly, and her grandmother says 'Good, so everything's all right now'; Sophie beams uncomprehendingly.

They take the coffee upstairs. In the sitting room, there is an impression of dishevelment, as though everyone had slumped a notch or two, in every sense. Michael has been handing out brandy; the psychiatrist's wife has her shoes off and is sprawled over the arm of the sofa; the man from Sotheby's is reading a book; there is talk, a little incoherent, Ellen thinks. She picks up, without anyone noticing, a couple of glasses that are threatened by people's feet.

Coffee is dispensed. Ellen takes the opportunity to go upstairs to the bathroom for a minute; on the way, she looks in at Paul's room. He sits cross-legged on the floor, in a dressing-gown, the dismembered De Havilland Mosquito around him. He says, 'You were quite right, gran – I've got the tail on now, all but'. Together they examine his achievement; he points out a further technical hitch; Ellen, who is steady-fingered, is able to complete a tricky matter of inserting a door. Regretfully, she goes downstairs again.

The telephone rings. The neighbours, it appears, are less than happy about the noise emanating from the basement. Louise makes soothing remarks and assurances of action; putting the receiver down she says that really it is a bit thick, I mean, it's only once in a blue moon. She goes to the stairs and bawls, 'Turn that thing *down*, do you hear, Toby . . .' The noise is reduced by a decibel or two.

Ellen goes down to see if there is any more coffee; she has been inspecting one of the male guests, unobtrusively, and thinks it would be a good idea if he had some, at least if he is intending to drive home. She glances again into Toby's room; there are many more than thirty people there, it seems to her. She makes coffee, humming to herself; she straightens a picture that has gone awry; she peeks into the freezer and is surprised by the orderly array of bags and parcels within, labelled and classified. 'For Xmas dinner' she reads, '6 helps'. A boy, unfamiliar to her, slinks into the room, takes something from the fridge and slinks out again, with deprecating smile.

Upstairs, there is further deterioration. The man from Sotheby's talks, but no one listens. Michael, on the sofa, has his arm round one of the girls. Louise, on the floor, talks intently to the psychiatrist. Someone else says something about Dorchester; the psychiatrist's wife looks up suddenly and shouts, 'Dorchester? I know Dorchester – Tony and I first copulated at Dorchester, in the back of a car'.

Ellen thinks, you poor dear, what a time you do have. She pours coffee for the man she feels could do with it; he is effusively grateful, but forgets to drink it.

The neighbours complain again.

At midnight, Ellen gets up and goes quietly from the room. To those who register her departure, she says a polite goodnight.

The light is still on in Paul's room. She goes in. They get to work. The De Havilland Mosquito is almost finished. A quarter of an hour later, it is complete. They contemplate it with pleasure. Almost casually, Paul produces the box containing the Heinkel 447 which he has not yet opened. They look at it; it presents, they agree, an interesting challenge. After a minute or two they open the box. They spread the pieces out and study the instructions. They look at one another: it is half past twelve.

Conspiratorially, Ellen says that if they are going to do it a cup of cocoa might be nice; also, she would like to get into something comfortable.

She goes up to her room and puts on her housecoat and a pair of slippers. On her way down again she is joined by Paul and the two of them pad down the stairs. They pass the sitting room, from which, now, there is the sound of music (quieter, though, and different in style from the music below). Ellen remembers her glasses, which are on the mantelpiece; she slips in to get them, with a murmur of apology, but in fact no one pays her any attention. The psychiatrist's wife would seem to be weeping; someone else is asleep; there is a kind of heaving on the sofa which Ellen does not stop to investigate.

In the hall, they are passed by Louise, who is saying something sourly about someone being stoned out of their minds. She must be talking to herself, though, for the sight of her mother and younger son does nothing for her, in any sense. She lurches back into the sitting room.

It is a good deal quieter now, in Toby's room. The door is closed.

Ellen and Paul make a large jug of cocoa, which they load onto a tray, along with mugs, and a plate of cheese and biscuits. They open up the freezer, because Paul fancies there is probably an ice-cream; others appear to have been here first, though — there is a certain dishevelment, and depletion of the bags and parcels. 'For Xmas dinner' has gone, Ellen notices, and so, to Paul's annoyance, has the ice-cream. He stands for a moment in the middle of the kitchen, hitching his dressing-gown (which has lost its cord) around him; he sighs; he says, with a toss of the head that includes both the room next door and the sitting room above, 'They are all being a bit silly tonight, aren't they?' After a moment he adds, 'I suppose they can't help it'.

Ellen says she doesn't think they can, poor dears. She suggests a mousse that she has found in the fridge as an alternative to ice-cream.

They take the tray upstairs, comfortable with anticipation. There are fifty-three people in the house now. Ellen and Paul alone are in a state of unsullied consciousness.

At ten past two in the morning they are well into the Heinkel, but they have quite run out of glue, as feared. Separately, they scour the house. Paul goes through the drawers of his mother's desk (which involves shifting the man from Sotheby's, who is asleep in front of it, no mean feat for an eleven year old). Louise does not seem to be around, nor yet the psychiatrist; nor, indeed, Michael, or the psychiatrist's wife. Paul draws a blank, so far as the desk is concerned, and turns to the drawers of the sofa table; he ignores the goings-on on the sofa, which do not interest him.

Downstairs, Ellen is systematically searching the kitchen. She comes across a girl, deeply asleep (or something) between the dresser and the sink, and covers her with a rug that she fetches from the cloakroom; the child is inadequately clad as it is. She rummages in drawers, and on the shelves of the dresser, and at last, in triumph, turns up a nearly full tube of something that will certainly do. She sets off up the stairs, and then becomes aware that the gramophone in Toby's room is most irritatingly stuck; no one seems to be doing anything about it. She goes into the darkened room, and gropes her way across, to where in the muted light of a table-lamp, the record is hiccupping away; on the way she stumbles several times on recumbent forms. 'Sorry, dear' she says. 'Excuse me just a minute . . .' She adjusts the instrument, and goes out again.

She meets Paul on the stairs and they go up together.

At three-thirty a policeman, who has been tipped off by a disgruntled would-be gatecrasher, knocks on the front door. He has reason to believe that there is consumption of . . . But when the door is opened to him by an elderly woman, wearing her dressing-gown and holding, for some reason, the superstructure of a model aeroplane, he loses his nerve, apologises, and says there has probably been a mistake.

As the dawn seeps upwards into the sky, extinguishing the street lights and re-defining the London roof-tops, they finish the Heinkel. It has gone almost without a hitch; it is a triumph. They sit back, weary but aglow with satisfaction, and contemplate their craftsmanship. The house is quite quiet now; they must be the only ones still capable of celebration. Paul goes down to the kitchen and fetches a bottle of cider, the sole survivor of the night. He pours them a helping each, in tooth-mugs, and in silence and in mutual appreciation they drink to one another.